# BLOOD AND SORCERY

## HISTORICAL PARANORMAL ROMANCE — WITH A STEAMPUNK EDGE

## ANN GIMPEL

Edited by

ANGELA KELLY

CONTENTS

# BOOK DESCRIPTION: BLOOD AND SORCERY

Joshua committed his life to fighting Black Magick. Not sure who he hates worse, dark sorcerers or the clerics who tortured and mutilated his family, he lives on the road with his horse and his magic, working as a Coven enforcer. Breana Giraud is the only woman he's ever loved, and until very recently she was married to someone else.

Breana's husband, Don, sold his soul to the devil, embracing dark practices. Along the way, he corrupted their daughter. While Breana could've turned him in to Coven justice without a second thought, she couldn't bring herself to implicate her child. Still reeling from her daughter's death at the hands of evil, and grateful her husband met the vicious end he deserved, she feels broken, damaged. The last thing on her mind is falling in love.

Joshua tries to hold back, give Breana room to mourn her losses, but if he has his way, she'll become his wife. With Don dead, and the path to his heart's true love finally clear, he'll do anything he can to make her his. Even if it means fighting his way past the dark mages' leader, who wants her for his own.

# CHAPTER 1

*S*alt Lake City, Utah Territory

Breana Giraud bolted upright in her bed, the darkness around her shattering into fire-tinged motes of black. Heart thudding hard against her chest, throat constricted with fear, she reached for power, intent on shrouding herself in a protective spell. Goddamn her husband. He was at it again. It was like him to wait until she was sleeping—and she had to sleep sometime.

Once upon a time, she'd cared about Don—a witch with power to match her own. But he'd been seduced by the dark and become deeply entrenched in Black Magick. Shielding herself against him drained her, but she didn't have any choice. Sucking air around the narrow place that used to be her throat, she sent magic spiraling outward. She didn't sense him near, but the enchantment that just dragged her from a sound sleep had Don's name—and sliminess—stamped all over it.

Her eyes snapped open. Don was dead.

*Dead.*

What the hell was happening to her?

He couldn't harm her anymore, so why was his stench all over the room? It wasn't even the bedroom they'd shared. She'd moved to the far end of the hall to escape the horrible memories that swamped her every time she thought about him.

*Guess that didn't work very well.*

She pressed her tongue hard against her teeth and reached for her magic again. Surely she could summon a mage light. Simplest of spells, it required almost nothing in the way of power. Finally, after she was shaking and sweating with effort, a wavery blue light formed, casting the bedroom in eerie shadows. Breana urged her light to burn hotter, brighter. Her teeth were chattering, and she felt as if she'd never be warm again. Icy sweat dripped down her sides.

She tugged the heavy, wool blanket around her shuddering form, but it didn't help so she dragged air hard into lungs that had nearly forgotten how to cooperate. And then did it again. And again, until she was able to clamp her jaws in a harsh, desperate line.

Her light flickered and brightened, and the ball of fear making it hard to breathe eased the slightest bit. Falling back asleep was laughable, so she dug her way out from under the covers and pulled a robe woven from soft, cream-colored wool over her linen nightdress. Sheepskin slippers came next.

At least the godawful chill that had permeated the air was dissipating, and the reek of evil along with it. Brimstone held a sulfur taint that burned the back of her throat and made her skin prickle with a million points of discomfort.

She blinked back tears as she made her way downstairs, her mage light bouncing over one shoulder. The dark had taken both her husband and her daughter, and robbed her of what had once been a warm and comfortable marriage. She hated Black Magick with a passion. Hated what it had almost done to her as she walked a tightrope between her husband's demands and her responsibility to the Coven.

"Yeah, and I did a shitty job all the way round," she muttered as she poured a cup of tepid coffee into a mug. It was bitter as all get out from sitting on the back of the woodstove since early the previous morning, but she gulped it down anyway, wanting the quick stimulation.

Too keyed up to sit, she wandered to a window and looked to the east. Dawn wasn't far off, but the horizon was still dark. Days were growing longer, but it was still winter, and it might not get light until seven. She'd sent a meticulous letter to Coven headquarters in New York. Within it, she detailed her sins in not turning her husband and daughter over to Coven justice—once she fully understood their allegiance had shifted to dark power.

That letter had certainly arrived by now.

What would they do to her?

A snort of derision curled her mouth into a bitter smile. She knew what she'd do to someone in her position. Banish them from the Coven for starters. After that, it would be anyone's guess, but the Coven wouldn't be out of line demanding her life as punishment for shielding her family from what they deserved.

Not much she could do. About any of it. No. She needed to keep going, day by day, and let the wheel spin as it would. She'd find out soon enough. Certainly by this coming summer when most—if not all—of the Coven had relocated to Utah Territory. At least she'd given Luke and Abigail a good start by marrying them. Memories of that day—and their joy—kept her going through the hardest spots.

She plodded back to the stove and poured the last of the coffee into her cup before she opened the woodstove door and sent a jot of magic to stir the embers. Once they crackled merrily, she added chunks of wood and refilled the kettle on the back of the stove with water from the pump next to the sink. The chores were automatic, and they settled her nerves enough to dissect what had driven her awake.

Coven enforcers, a group of hard-bodied, sharp-eyed men, who kept witches on the straight and narrow, had seen to it that both Don and her daughter, Carolyn, met their end in mage fire, purging their souls of darkness. And they'd killed Alistair MacDuff, head of the Alchemical Council. She and Abigail had seen to the death of Alistair's henchman before he, too, was dumped in the purification of mage fire.

"Guess we didn't get them all," she muttered as she ground coffee beans with a mortar and pestle.

"If *them* refers to who I think it does," Joshua drawled from the kitchen doorway, "of course they're not all dead. That fresh coffee I smell?"

Breana curved her mouth into a soft smile. "You know damn good and well it is. I drank the dregs from yesterday morning. Hang on till the water boils, and I'll brew a fresh pot."

"Don't rush. I got time." Joshua moved closer to the stove, extending his hands toward its warmth. Tight-fitting, buff-colored leathers, similar to what most Coven enforcers wore, hugged him like a second skin. Flame red hair hung loose to the middle of his back.

Breana turned to face him squarely and crossed her arms beneath her breasts. "Looks as if you got up in a hurry. Your hair's not braided."

"Hell, it's not even brushed," he countered. "Reckon whatever dragged you out of bed before the sun was likely the same disturbance that woke me."

"What about Chris?" She asked about the other enforcer living in the barn with Joshua. Both men had been part of a contingent that had shown up after her daughter died. While

Sam and Luke had left, these two stayed on to help her run the ranch.

"Oh, he's up too, and ready if I say the word, but we didn't figure there was much call for both of us to charge on in here until we knew what was going on."

His words hung in the air between them, heavy with unspoken questions, and he impaled her with his shrewd hazel eyes as he straightened.

Breana uncrossed her arms and held her hands palms upward. "I have no idea what happened a little bit ago. I was deeply asleep, so far gone that at first I pulled magic to shield myself from Don. I'd forgotten he was dead." She closed her teeth over her lower lip. "Damn if it didn't feel like him though. That same rotten, Black Magick stink. The one that smells like dead things left in the sun too long."

"Did you notice anything else?" Joshua narrowed his eyes.

"Cold. Freezing cold. It took maybe half an hour for my teeth to quit chattering."

He set his mouth in a thin, hard line. "Not good. Means whatever it is can't be far away."

"Damn! You didn't recognize it, either." Fear shrilled her voice, and the fragile equanimity she'd established in her familiar kitchen frittered away.

"What Chris and I felt was nowhere near as strong as your encounter." He clamped his jaws together.

"So?" She made come along motions with both hands. "It means I'm the one they want, right?"

"Maybe. Although I can't imagine the Alchemical Council not wanting revenge against us all. We not only killed their leader. We purified his black, black heart and robbed the Dark Angel of Alistair's immortal soul. Come to think of it—" Joshua drew his red brows together "—we might have trouble from way higher up than the Alchemical leaders."

"Isn't that just peachy." Breana moved to the stove and poured hot water over the freshly ground coffee beans. "Nowhere we can hide from something that powerful, huh? I hadn't even considered the Dark Angel, but I should've."

"Hiding's never been my style. Yours, either, which is why I suspect it was hell to conceal what your husband turned into." A corner of his mouth twisted downward.

Breana ignored his comment. There wasn't any way to answer it. Not really. "How soon do you think the rest of the Coven might show up?"

"Not soon enough if you're hoping for help from that quarter. We have to solve this one on our own. Wagon trains move slow. I'm not thinking we'll see anyone for at least a month, at the earliest."

"Mmph. Not that they'd knock themselves out to help me anyway."

Joshua kept his unreadable gaze locked on her, but held silence.

Breana busied herself sprinkling cold water over the coffee mixture to settle the grounds. After a few minutes, she poured a cup for Joshua and refilled her own. When she spoke, she picked her words carefully. "It's been kind of you and Chris to stay and watch over me, but I don't expect you to put your lives on hold until the rest of the Coven shows up. Besides—" she looked away from his direct gaze "—like as not they'll either banish me or kill me when they do come. No reason to wait around for that."

"Hold up there." Joshua set his cup down and moved right in front of her, settling his hands on her shoulders. "Look at me, Breana," he commanded, and a compulsion spell eddied around her.

"Stop that." She writhed to break loose from his grip, but he held tight.

"How're you going to know what I say is true if you're staring at your slippers?" he demanded.

"Fine." She squared her shoulders and latched onto his unsettling gaze, trying not to think about how close he was—how male—and how long it had been since anyone had touched her with anything even close to tenderness.

His eyes, more gold than green in the first rays of dawn creeping through the windows, softened, but he didn't let go of her. "Better. Me and Chris—Luke and Sam too—we didn't save you to walk away now. No matter what you say, we're staying until that Coven wagon train shows up. And we'll speak for you. I got letters from Sam and Luke before they left. So you'll have the word of four Coven enforcers saying you're a good woman, and the Coven should let you get on with your life—even if you're no longer part of our leadership."

Tears pricked, hot and bitter, just behind her lids. "You didn't have to do that, and you don't have to stay here, either."

"I know that. So does Chris. We secured permission to remain with you for as long as we think you need us."

"That's only because the Coven didn't know about me then."

He scrunched his stark features into a frown. "You'd be surprised what they knew and didn't know. I shouldn't tell you this, but you and Don were the topic of many a conversation." She opened her mouth, but he shook his head. "Keep listening—for now. Do you honestly think no one noticed when you stopped showing up at the New York headquarters, except on rare occasions? Or when Don's energy changed?"

Anger flashed through her, bright and brittle. "If other witches knew, why didn't anyone reach out to me? Or to

Carolyn?" The tears that had threatened fell thickly, too many to blink away, but Joshua still didn't let go of her.

"Keep talking. You have a lot of pain bottled up inside." His touch gentled, and he caressed her shoulder blades.

Words choked her, clotting in her throat. "My baby. She was my only baby. Maybe, if someone had given a good goddamn—" Breana couldn't talk anymore. She was crying too hard.

Joshua drew her against him and stroked her hair. "Hush. Ssht. None of us knew about your daughter. Children never come to any Coven functions until they're of age, and she hadn't begun to bleed yet."

Breana slumped against his warm solidity as the fury bled out of her, washed away by her tears and weariness. Joshua held her, murmuring in Gaelic, until her emotional storm blew itself out.

"You haven't done much grieving for Carolyn," he said quietly and led her to a chair near the fire.

She sank into it and closed her hands around her coffee cup. It had felt good in Joshua's arms. Too good. He was a decent man, and magic ran strong in him. He deserved a woman who hadn't been tainted by evil and soured by loss. Better to not encourage so much as a sexual fling.

*Better for him, not necessarily for me.*

He shot an appraising look her way before settling across from her with his own mug. She was afraid he'd been inside her head. All enforcers were competent mind readers.

Rather than saying anything about her inner turmoil over him, he murmured, "You need to find a way to keep living in a world without your daughter in it."

"It shouldn't be this hard."

"Why not? You tell me why losing a child should ever be easy."

"Because I bid my daughter farewell after Don seduced her with evil."

"Maybe so." He nodded sagely. "But you never gave up hope you could figure out a way to save her."

"You're sounding like a parent, but you don't have children."

"Don't have to. I had a mother, and I fully understand she'd have done murder to protect me and my brothers and sisters. Pa too."

"Of course. I wasn't thinking." Breana closed her teeth over her lower lip and bit until she tasted blood. "The truth of it is I knew my daughter was lost forever when Don let that Salem witch have access to her body. If I'd played host to Sarah, I'd have had a hell of a time getting to the far side of it with my sanity intact—and Carolyn was only a child. Wickedness is seductive, alluring. The ones on that side, they don't have to spend the years we do learning to summon and control power. Black Magick flows through them like wildfire, impossible to resist."

"Abigail came close to succumbing when Sarah Osborne hitched a ride inside her," Joshua said, his voice grim.

"She told me. Scared the bejesus out of her too, and she's a seasoned witch. Strong as any we have in the Coven. Carolyn had no chance once Sarah possessed her. None at all. I still can't believe her own father offered her up like some sort of vestal virgin sacrifice."

"For all you know, that was part of his plans." Joshua's nostrils flared with disgust. "The dark like to take them young, and Sarah enjoyed her men. I still remember the unnatural heat from that bitch before we lured her out of Abigail and torched her with mage fire."

Breana laced her fingers together, pressing until the knuckles turned white. "Maybe that's part of why I haven't thought too long or too hard about any of this. I have no idea what my baby went through. Or if she suffered at all until the very end when she finally understood Sarah had no use for her."

"Sorry if I was too blunt, but no point pussyfooting around about evil. We need every ace in the deck, and for that we can't underestimate what the other side is capable of. You didn't hear Alistair bargaining for his life with Sam. His exact words were: 'Want to switch sides, buddy? We have better pay, much better hours. All the women you can fuck. Young ones too. Untouched. The finest food—'"

"I get it. You can stop now." Breana squared her shoulders.

"I can, but they never will. I want to make certain you don't forget that. We've been targeted, and before the day's out, we need to come up with a better defensive perimeter around this house than what we've got now."

Breana tossed back half her coffee. "I'll help every way I can with that."

"Anytime you want to talk about…well, about any of it. Don. Carolyn. Your fears about Coven justice. Find me. There's nothing so bad it doesn't go down a little easier when it's shared." He pushed to his feet. "I'm going to let Chris know we need to do some scouting. If The Dark Angel is about—or some of his henchmen—we're far from ready."

"I'll get something going for breakfast," she called after his departing back. "Come back in an hour."

"Thanks. See you then."

The kitchen felt empty without Joshua in it, but she didn't dwell on that. Instead, she trotted upstairs and dressed, trading her robe and nightgown for a simple homespun skirt, dark-colored blouse, and a green sweater that had always been one of her favorites. Next she laced up a pair of stout boots and headed out to the henhouse to gather eggs. Her second stop was the goat pen where she filled a pail with milk and used magic to soothe the goats who wanted her to stay and visit.

Breakfast came together quickly. Cornmeal mush made with leftover cornbread from the previous night, milk and eggs with a few greens, and some sliced pork from a hog the men had slaughtered and salted a few weeks back.

Her head was full enough, she was grateful to have something else to focus on. One thing was certain. She needed to stop feeling sorry for herself. Breaking down and spilling her soul to Joshua was an indulgence. If evil had her in its gunsights, she'd damn well better keep her guard up, which meant sleeping shrouded in protection spells.

Or not sleeping at all.

Witches could get by with very little sleep, but only for short periods.

One of the worst parts of dealing with her husband once the dark got its claws into him, was he slithered away from direct confrontation. She didn't do well with enemies she couldn't face off against, and the stealth attack that had jolted her from sleep didn't sit well.

"Better rein it in." She spoke to the empty kitchen. "The quickest way to get what you want is to ask for it. And I'm not ready for a full on fight. Not yet."

Joshua's observation had been deucedly accurate. She had to get to the far side of the hell she'd lived through. To do that, she needed to think about it. Talk about it. Open herself to the slashing emotional storm she'd held at bay. Until she could do those things, she'd be a shadow, a shell, and not strong enough to help the men mount a defense against whatever faced them.

At least she had a direction—finally. It might flay her raw, but she'd take the hard road until the demons that dogged her gave up and went home. Breana surveyed the pot bubbling on the cook stove. It was done enough, so she snapped up her wool cloak and went out to roust the men, determined to keep right on talking about both Don and Carolyn over breakfast. Talk was the first step. Once she could do that, accepting their choices—and their deaths—would be at least possible. Not easier, but within her grasp.

# CHAPTER 2

Joshua Kingman made his way out of the kitchen. It took discipline to leave Breana's side. He'd been attracted to her for years—actually, far more than attracted. Smitten came closer to the mark, but she was another man's wife. Or she had been when they first met. Granted Don was dead, but she needed to grieve her losses. And move past the horror of what her husband and child had turned into. For him to court her before she had time to do that would be a mistake.

For one thing, it would divert her from the work she needed to do right now, squaring things with her conscience. He wanted Breana Giraud, but he wanted her to come to him on her own, because she wanted him for himself. Having her fall into his arms as a hedge against her guilt and grief might feel good in the moment, but eventually it would blow up in both their faces.

He raked his hands through his hair, wincing when they caught on snarls. She'd been absolutely correct about him being in a hurry to get inside the house. When the blast of evil rousted him from sleep, she was his main concern, and he'd even chafed at the delay dragging his leathers on.

Shouldering the barn door open, he found Chris dressing. The other enforcer glanced his way. "Couldn't have been that bad, bro, or you'd have called me."

The door banged shut behind Joshua, and he bent to his saddlebags, extracted a hairbrush, and set about braiding his hair for the day. "It's bad enough," he gritted out. "Just not immediate. Evil came calling all right, but whatever it was left after giving Breana a good scare."

Chris dropped his butt onto a hay bale and narrowed his brown eyes in thought. Curly brown hair fell to his shoulders, and he wore the same style leathers as Joshua, snug garments with lace closures. "Doesn't make a lick of sense," he said and went to work securing his boots.

"Unless they weren't strong enough to do more than they did," Joshua countered. He'd gotten his hair unsnarled and quickly sectioned and braided it, fastening the ends with bits of leather tied into knots.

"Why tip us off they're here, though?" Chris asked.

"Because they're stupid."

"Still doesn't make sense," Chris persisted. "They've got power to burn. Fuckers are rolling in it. They just let us know they're close, but why?"

"Don't have the answer to that one, but let's walk the perimeter. See what we can sense out there."

"Good idea." Chris stood. "'Sides, we should see to the horses. Haven't been down to that far paddock for a couple days."

Joshua draped a leather vest over his shoulders, followed by his gun belts and bandoliers. He eyed Chris and his lack of weaponry. "You going out there naked?"

"Guess not." The other enforcer made a noise between a grunt and a snort. "Can't take the peer pressure." He hefted his revolvers and drove them into twin holsters on his belt. "What's your ammo situation looking like?"

"Iron and silver mixed in, like always. Yours?"

"Same, but I'm running low. Need to make more pretty damn soon."

"Good project for tonight after supper. Ready?" Joshua furled his brows.

"Lead out. Speaking of food, I hope Breana's making something for breakfast."

"She is." Joshua kept his tone curt. He had no idea if anyone knew how he felt about Breana, and he wanted to keep his hopes about her becoming his wife private. It was entirely possible the Coven would toss him out on his ear if he hooked up with her, but if they did that to him, they'd have to kick Luke out too since he'd married Abigail after her flirtation with evil.

Somehow, Joshua didn't believe the Coven would be up for losing two of their best enforcers.

Chris headed for the eastern fence line. "You got a plan for this?" he inquired. "After we check on the horses."

"Not really. Mostly just being out here with our power deployed to see if we can tell what direction those bastards' poison came from. If we get really lucky, maybe we'll figure out what they were."

Chris settled into an easy, loping trot, headed for the lower paddock. Grass grew thickly by the creek, even in the dead of winter, and it was as close to grazing as the animals got.

A frenzied whinny, followed by high, thin neighs, reached them, and Joshua sprinted for the corral with Chris hard on his heels. Because of rolling tableland, he couldn't see anything until they got closer, but the unmistakable taint of evil rolled over him, tightening his gut into a knot of fury. He yanked both his revolvers free, ready for damn near anything, and tried not to inhale too deeply. The sickly sweet stench reminded him of rotting corpses, purulent wounds, and gangrened limbs.

The air shimmered with Black Magick. Invisible bands closed around him, but he blasted them out of the way with power of his own. Chris drew closer, weaving his magic with Joshua's into a shield that surrounded them. They crested a rise, and the paddock finally came into view.

One of the stallions was up on his hind legs, screaming and pawing the air. His mare stood guard over their foal. The month-old filly lay on the ground, still as death. Six other horses milled about, neighing up a storm.

Joshua slowed as he drew near, suspecting a trap, but the only thing surrounding him was tainted air. Chris sent soothing magic swirling out. When the horses quieted, Joshua holstered his guns, entered the enclosure, and knelt next to the foal, letting his hands hover over it.

"Not dead. Not quite," he muttered and augured magic into the tiny body to fix whatever the dark had broken. Its mother whinnied nervously and kicked at him with her foreleg. He cushioned what would've been a crippling blow to his chest with a blast of power.

"Chris."

"Yeah. Got it. I'll keep momma away."

Joshua worked over the foal and sent purifying energy into her young mind. The only thing wrong with the filly was that she'd come face to face with evil, and it terrified her. When her dark, liquid eyes opened, Joshua urged her to her feet and sent her to her mother's side. The foal couldn't move fast enough, and she buried her face in her mother's udder, sucking frantically.

Chris loosed his spell on the mare, and she curved her long

neck protectively around where her foal nursed. "Glad you were able to save her."

"Me too." Joshua pushed upright from where he'd been hunkered back on his heels. "Let's bring them back to the barn."

"Good idea. It'll be a mite crowded, but nothing's safe too far from the house right now." Chris snapped a lead rope off a fencepost and clipped it around the stallion's halter. "Knew there was a reason I left that on him." He swung onto the horse's broad back.

"Good plan. The others will follow him."

"You going to ride?" Chris asked.

"Nope. I'm walking back. This is getting stranger by the moment. I don't understand it, and if I ride, I might miss something critical. They're fucking with us, and I need to figure it out."

"I'll start walking back this way once I have the herd secured in the paddock behind the barn."

Joshua didn't answer. He waited until all the horses were out of the corral and clipped the gate shut. Dark energy ebbed and flowed around him like a black-tinged tide, and a nasty, dead-thing smell burned his nose and throat. Just when he thought he had a bead on where it was coming from, it switched direction. Every Black Magick practitioner he'd run across drove in fast and hard, lethal from the moment they targeted you.

Was this some kind of warning?

It was pretty clear someone wanted them off the Giraud land. Had Don sequestered something here? Something the other side wanted back?

Joshua counted backward. Almost three months had passed since they killed Don. Maybe whoever it was had been waiting, biding their time, hoping the grieving widow would pull up stakes and move somewhere life was easier, like Salt Lake City. Dark mages were never known for their patience—or their stealth. Likely whoever was manipulating the strings had grown tired of killing time.

He stopped walking and powered up his magic to run wide open as he spun in a circle. At least it brought one answer. The putrid feel was strongest toward the main road, which wasn't a surprise. The big question was what they were going to do about it.

Leaving was out of the question. If there was something here the Alchemical Council—or worse, the Dark Angel—was willing to harass them over, it must be important.

And well-hidden, since he hadn't sensed the slightest hint of evil since they consigned a cache of Black Magick books to mage fire.

He took off at a lope and met Chris about a quarter mile from the house. "I know that look." Chris punched him in the arm. "You have a determined gleam in your eyes."

"Shit! You're worse than a wife."

"That too," Chris agreed affably. "I came up with something myself. Try this one on. Someone's trying to scare us off. For whatever reason they don't want to kill us, although that's never been a stumbling block for dark mages before."

"Pretty much how I put the puzzle together too." Joshua picked up the pace. "We need to see if Breana remembers anything at all that might shed light on why dark mages would want us gone from here."

"Or why they've gone squeamish about just moving in and knocking us off."

"We're pretty hard assed." Joshua grinned. "Maybe the fact that we managed to kill Alistair, one of their strongest mages, is giving someone pause."

"Maybe so. They've never been overly brave, but their magic's so strong, they never needed to be. I was wondering if maybe they want Breana—alive—and got tired of waiting for us to leave."

Almost as if she'd heard her name, Breana called, "Soup's on," from somewhere near the house.

Even the sound of her voice sent a little thrill down Joshua's spine. What he wouldn't give to crush her against him and bury his hands in her thick, blonde hair. She had eyes like a restless ocean, and a body that was tall and muscular, but with curves in the right places.

Chris shot an appraising glance his way, and Joshua shuttered his longing fast. His next words were quiet, careful. "Why would you think the dark wants her?"

The other enforcer shrugged. "Conjecture. They want something. I suspect this morning was just the leading edge of a real shit storm heading our way."

Joshua agreed. While it was darkly encouraging that he and Chris read the clues the same, they clearly needed help to stave off a full-on attack. He was just about to suggest raising an alarm to see if any other enforcers were close enough to ride to their assistance when another idea struck him.

He whistled, mimicking a raven's call.

Chris nodded approvingly. "Yeah. You always had an affinity for animals."

"Goes along with my healing ability." Joshua whistled again, and a large, coal-black raven winged out of a clump of aspen trees. It settled on his shoulder, gripping hard with sharp talons. When Joshua extended his arm, the raven walked down it until it stared right at him with beady, avian eyes.

"*What?*" the bird chirped.

Part of Joshua's magic was the ability to converse with just about any animal. It was how he'd managed to heal the filly so quickly, by reaching into her mind and reassuring her nothing had actually hurt her.

*"I seek information, my winged brother. If you could fly far and wide and bring me back what you see, I'd be in your debt."*

The raven bobbed its feathered head. *"I will take others with me."*

*"Many thanks. Be cautious. I fear evil lurks on the boundaries of these lands."*

*"My kind already know that."* The raven used Joshua's forearm as a springboard and flew off cawing what sounded like wry laughter.

"How about the wolves and coyotes and mountain lions?" Chris asked.

"They could help," Joshua agreed. "Remember when Don urged that group of mad wolves to shun darkness and return to their natural manner of being?"

"I do. They'd be natural allies."

The men walked into the cleared area around the house. Breana stood by the steps with a tentative smile on her face that faded once she got a look at their expressions. "That bad, huh?" She pressed her full lips together into a frown. "Come on in. Breakfast's getting cold. Whatever it is, we'll need fuel to face it."

Joshua followed everyone else into the house. It might be safer for Breana to send her into town, but he couldn't stand the thought of being parted from her. He curled his hands into fists and shook sense into himself. If being in Salt Lake City would keep her from harm—

"I'm not leaving here." Her voice, harsh and resolute wafted toward him.

"Stay out of my head, woman."

"I'm going to the outside pump so's I can wash up." Chris

turned and trotted back down the steps. "Looking like the two of you need a spot of alone time."

Joshua walked into the kitchen, ready to launch an argument —laced with compulsion—to change her mind, but Breana was already planted dead in front of him, hands on her hips.

"Whatever this is," she said, spacing out her words, "we're in it together. I will not have you banish me to somewhere else while you fight my battles."

He opened his mouth, and was surprised to feel her magic surround him, holding him silent.

"That's right." She quirked a brow. "I'm a witch. Never forget it. And a damned strong one, now that I'm not having to divert my power to protect myself from Don."

Joshua could've broken her enchantment, but he didn't want to. The feel of her power blanketing him was like a balm. It smelled like her—honey, and amber, and vanilla. Jesus, but she was beautiful when her ire was up. Color rode high on her cheekbones, and her hair swirled around her face, curls having escaped her braids. Pale as summer wheat sheaves, even her hair glowed with the power simmering around her.

Breana glowered from her spot next to the stove. "The smart move would be to conserve our power and use it against the dark," she informed him archly, and her spell fragmented around him.

"I only wanted to keep you safe." He held onto the two-foot space between them with difficulty. And laced his hands together behind his back to lessen the temptation to extend his arms to her.

"I know. But I'm not a young, green witch. I don't need protection. My last count, we were three against goddess only knows how many."

"That occurred to Chris and me too. I raised the ravens. And

I can summon the other animals to our side as well, but I'll only do it as a last resort. I don't want them to die in a war that's not of their making."

Her eyes widened. "You have that magic. I knew Luke did. And Sam."

"Not as rare as you might think. Like most skills, if you're good manipulating earth and fire, you can cultivate it."

"About it not being the animals' battle." She closed her teeth over her lower lip. "You're wrong about that. This is everyone's war. If we lose, the world will turn into a place none of us want to live in. Not the animals, and not us, either."

Joshua nodded to himself as anger buffeted him. The dark wouldn't leave breathing room for any who didn't sign on with them. The only reason it hadn't happened yet was because they weren't strong enough.

"Don't forget the battle that's brewing between the North and the South," Breana went on. "It was the reason we decided to move Coven headquarters in the first place. If war breaks out in this country, it will spawn enough chaos and anarchy to strengthen Black Magic far beyond our wildest fears."

"All true, but we can't do much about that. Let's get through what we're facing today."

Breana dropped her hands to her sides. "Coven enforcers' word is law. You can force me out of here. I couldn't say no to a direct command from you, but please don't make me leave. Use my skills." Her voice faltered before she pressed on. "I've lost so much. I can't stand to lose anything else, and this is my home. It's all I have left."

Joshua's heart cracked wide open. He wanted to tell her that they could make a life together, one where he'd do his damnedest to wipe out the misery she'd lived through, but he shielded his thoughts and started to tell her that he and Chris would take her request under advisement.

Chris burst into the room, and Joshua's guns found their way into his hands. Power surged, and he gritted out, "Whatever it is, let's go get 'em."

Chris held his hands up. "Put your guns away. The reason I raced in here isn't because of something bad—for once. Hester Thorne's just pulling up the drive with a wagon and a team. Damn! She's a sight for sore eyes. I love that old witch."

Breath rattled from Joshua's lungs, and he holstered his revolvers. Hester was Abigail's grandmother, and one of the most powerful women in the Coven. She'd been living in San Francisco for the past several decades.

"But that's wonderful news!" Breana pushed past him, grabbing a cloak from a hook near the door and wrapping it around her shoulders. "Someone's looking out for us," she added. "We need Hester's ability. Abigail was going to invite her and her husband to stay with me for a while, but I don't sense his energy. He's been ill for years, and he must've passed over. Could be why she's here. See you outside." She bustled through the door.

Joshua stared after Breana. "Maybe someone's looking out for us," he muttered, "but Hester might not want to stay once she finds out what we're up against."

"You don't know her very well," Chris countered. "She's one tough, old bird. I can't see her running away from a contest with evil. Have you ever met her?"

"Only once, but let's get out there so I can renew my acquaintance." Joshua strode from the kitchen, using the back door this time, with Chris flanking him.

Hester had jumped down from the wagon's high seat, and she and Breana were hugging each other. "So glad you're here."

Breana pushed out of their embrace. "Thank you for believing in me."

"Och. Doona fash yourself. Abigail, she told me everything. Ye're not evil, any more than my granddaughter." Hester's Scottish accent was thick as warm honey. She stood straight, her head even with the top of Breana's shoulders. White hair streamed down her back and shoulders, and a pair of sharp hazel eyes—dead ringers for Abigail's—regarded the group standing in the yard.

"Nice to see you again." Chris bowed.

Hester rolled her eyes. "None of that, young man." She hugged him soundly and then moved to Joshua. "I've met you, but only once I believe."

Joshua inclined his head. "Good memory. I've heard a lot about you, Hester Thorne. All of it good."

"Flattery won't buy you a pot to piss in," she announced.

"Then I won't waste my breath on it." Joshua bit back laughter and held out a hand. Hester clasped it warmly.

"Now that we've got the meet and greet part out of the way —" Hester swept her shrewd gaze over them "—you've got big trouble out there. Took a whole pile of magic to make me and the team invisible enough that evil didn't bother us. What in the goddess's name did the bunch of you do to piss off the dark?"

"Nothing beyond what Abigail likely told you," Breana retorted.

"Then we need to put our heads together and figure this out." Hester leveled her attention on Breana. "There coffee inside?" At her nod, Hester transferred her sharp eyes to Joshua and Chris. "See to my team. They need a good rubdown, water, and feed."

"You got it." Chris started on the nearest harness.

Joshua didn't move quite fast enough because a jolt of magic swatted him in the ass, and he started to laugh. "Yes, ma'am." He moved to the far side of the team of four and went to work.

"That's better. Follow along now," Hester told Breana and trotted toward the kitchen stairs. "We got us a battle to plan. No time to waste."

*"Told you."* Chris used shielded mind speech.

*"She was one of the Coven's founders, wasn't she?"*

*"Not sure about that, but one of the original members for sure."*

*"Damn good thing she's on our side."*

"I was just thinking the same thing," Chris muttered. "All the tack's off. Let's get the horses into the barn, so we can find out what light Hester can shed on things."

A black blur caught Joshua's attention, and a raven flapped frantically toward him. It didn't waste time with his shoulder, but perched atop one of the horses, who whinnied its displeasure and stamped the dusty ground.

*"You have to come now,"* the bird announced.

"I heard that." Hester materialized out of the air next to Joshua and held out her forearm. The bird bent its head and touched its beak to her extended arm.

*"I'm waiting for you. Hurry."* The raven bobbed its head.

Joshua eyed Hester's horses. They didn't look so done in they couldn't be ridden, so he bolted atop one of them. He didn't mind riding bareback, and he could use magic in place of a bridle. Chris took another of the mounts, settling himself astride its broad back.

"Breana!" Hester called.

She hurried down the steps and vaulted onto the third horse. Hester took the fourth, the one the raven had used for a platform. The bird spread its wings, flapping hard, a black streak against the pale winter sun.

Ready for anything, Joshua mentally urged his horse to gallop after it.

# CHAPTER 3

Breana pulled power to stay atop the mare racing after its three teammates. It took all her attention until she found a balance point. No matter what happened, she was glad to the bottom of her soul to see Hester. The other witch had mentored her centuries ago when she was young, just coming into her power. One of the few things Breana had been grateful about when Don succumbed to wickedness was that Hester wasn't around to see it.

The older witch would've ferreted Breana out of her self-imposed isolation and known immediately something was wrong. Before she could do too much nosing around, Don would've found a way to kill her.

*I don't know that.*

Insight slapped Breana hard.

Don might've tried to do away with Hester, but the outcome was far from certain. Breana had been protecting Hester the same way Joshua just tried to protect her. Hester likely didn't need anyone watching out for her. In a direct confrontation with

Black Magick, she might prevail. She was hundreds of years old and hard as tempered iron.

*And I have a few tricks up my sleeve too.*

Over the two years between when Don embraced Black Magick and his death, she'd hunted for ways to annihilate him, weaving her bright power in with the sorcery he'd tried to shove down her gullet. The combination was startlingly potent—and harder than a runaway train to control. Desperate times required desperate means, though. She'd pull out every skill at her disposal if it meant keeping all of them alive.

She smelled evil before she saw anything. The rolling land, dotted with scrub oak, dried up grasses and spiny sagebrush plants didn't look any different, but the air felt heavy, foreboding. Animal shrieks and screams mingled with outraged cawing. She draped power about her, a shield against what threatened them.

*"Don't take time to think—about anything."* Hester projected her mind voice. *"Kill as fast as you can."*

Adrenaline flooded Breana, and she threw her power wide open. Soon they'd be at the road junction. Wolf howls, mountain lion snarls, and coyote yips escalated. A huge flock of ravens closed from the west, flying in a tight vee. Her horse topped a rise, and she instinctively drew hard on reins that weren't there.

The ground ran red with blood. Animals lay in grisly pieces. Those still on their feet fought their brethren that had been turned by wickedness. The air crackled with static and stank of sulfur and brimstone. A man stood in the middle of the road, arms raised over his head, chanting in demonspeak. Dark hair flowed past his waist, and he was shockingly handsome, so beautiful, she had a hell of a time tearing her gaze from his silver eyes and finely etched features. A black robe was belted at his waist, leaving his chest bare. Broad shoulders tapered to a narrow waist.

She wanted to race to him, touch his gleaming gold-toned skin, find out what was under those robes.

"It's a spell," she gritted out loud to steady herself. "Fight it."

*"Never mind any of that. Kill!"* Hester screamed into her mind.

Breana wrenched her gaze from the godlike dark mage. Power blazed from Chris, Joshua, and Hester. Over a dozen sorcerers ranged behind the one that had captured her attention. The men were dressed in snug-fitting leathers and they fought back, lobbing power to meet the magic hitting them head on. The air crackled with lightning when bright magic collided with dark. Wraiths with their red-rimmed charcoal eyes and blood-red talons crowded thickly from all sides. The rotten meat stench of them nearly drowned out all the other noxious scents pounding her nose until nausea heaved in her gut.

Joshua drew one of his revolvers and drilled a line of bullets straight down a dark mage's chest. Blood welled, but the wounds closed almost as soon as they'd formed.

Would the silver mixed with iron do its work? Or would Black Magick trump its power? Breana didn't wait around to find out. She hummed, drawing on her reservoir of dark sorcery, letting it grow to killing velocity. When she raised her hands, she barked a spell in demonspeak and let her power fly directly at the mage Joshua had targeted.

The man's eyes widened in horror, and his flesh bubbled and smoked, bursting into bits of bone and sinew as his body exploded.

Joshua glanced at her, his expression indecipherable. He opened his mouth but before he could say anything, Hester yelled, "So long as you broke that glass open. Do it again."

Power danced through Breana, so intense, maintaining it

took every shred of her ability. She focused on the next mage, relieved to let the lethal power flow out through her fingertips. Killing released enough pressure to allow her to live in her body. Wraiths rushed her, but they couldn't get close. Neither could a phalanx of mad wolves. Apparently her power formed a perimeter they couldn't penetrate.

*Good to know.*

Action unfolded around her, but she was so intent on her next target, the rest of the world narrowed to nothing. The scope of her universe constricted to a place where drawing power to kill was everything. The only thing.

Summon power, let it build, kill. Then do it again. And again. She targeted wraiths, mad wolves, and the dark sorcerers. Equal opportunity death.

Sometimes the men hastened things with their guns. Sometimes not. It didn't matter. Nothing did but the heady rush of bloodlust rampaging through her veins and tightening her gut into a burning nest of vipers. She became a goddess reaping destruction, and it felt exhilarating to fight back. Every one of those bastards she killed made up for a little piece of what Don had put her through. If he hadn't trifled with evil—embraced it with his whole being—she'd never have learned about Black Magick.

She was panting, and sour smelling sweat ran down her sides. She'd never opened herself to dark power like this. It sickened her, made her want to rip her skin from her bones, but if it got them through today, her revulsion was a small price to pay.

A shadow fell between her and her next victim. She snarled, lips drawing back from her teeth, intent on annihilating whatever stood in her way.

"I suspected you longed to switch sides." The stunning man who'd first caught her attention strode toward her, hands raised, power pulsing from them. The perimeter that stopped everyone else didn't even slow him down, and he kept right on moving until he was only a few inches away. "This proves it. You're using our power against us. I command you to stop."

"Command all you want," she growled. "I hate you. I loathe everything you stand for."

"Sheathe your power." Compulsion wrapped her in bands so tight she struggled to breathe, and she grappled with her throat.

"Never," she gasped.

The bands constricted even more.

Hester moved in from one side, Joshua and Chris from the other, chanting in Gaelic, but they couldn't get close enough to help. Their magic boomeranged back at them when they sent it to break the dark mage's hold on her.

Breana gathered breath around the place her throat was almost shut. She reached deep and imagined black strands weaving with bright ones into a magical rope. Once she had it anchored, she knotted it around the cord joining her to the mage and focused all her magic on the point where the two came together, willing her creation to defeat his hold on her.

Lines of strain formed in his handsome features. Rather than fight her, he switched things up and dark, seductive heat rolled off him. Against her will, her gaze focused on his face, his body. He let the robe drop from his shoulders, and breathing turned into a battle for entirely different reasons.

His body was perfect. Muscled shoulders, well-formed arms, and a hard, flat stomach. His dark nipples pebbled into hard buds of lust, and his long, lean legs could've belonged to a Greek statue. She tried to avert her gaze, but her eyes were drawn inexorably up those dynamic legs to his thick, rigid cock. It stood out from his body, springing from a tangle of dark curls.

He ran tapering fingers up his shaft and augured his gaze into her.

Like a moth drawn to fire, a moth that had no chance at all, her body responded, breasts growing heavy and a pulse pounding between her legs. Don had suckered her into sick sexual games with dark beings he conjured from the gates of Hades, but she'd been far from a willing participant.

*I'm not willing now.* Her inner voice was harsh, but she ignored it.

Sexual hunger roared through her, crescendoed, and crashed, sweeping her along with it.

"That's right." He stroked himself harder. "Come close, little one. Sheathe your power and come to me. I could make you very happy."

She looked for the others, but they weren't there. No one was. Not the mad wolves, nor the wraiths. A black bubble surrounded her and the dark mage. "Where are we?" she gasped.

"A place between the worlds. It's safe. Private. Just for us."

Panic gripped her, pushing the lethal sexuality back, but only a little. "I—I have to get back. The others need me."

His face crinkled into what might've been a smile on anyone else. "They're doing fine without you. More than fine. I'm ashamed my minions comported themselves so poorly, but you my dear—" he reached for her with the hand that wasn't stroking himself "—you have warrior blood. A worthy opponent. And you'd be a hell of a lover. We could set the world on fire."

Breana sucked air raggedly into her lungs. Her body wanted one thing, but her mind knew it was wrong. Sex with whoever this was would brand her irrevocably. She'd never be able to return to her life—or to being a witch.

"That's right," he crooned, obviously having been inside her head. "But why would you want your old life—any of it? Sex with me kicks whole new worlds open. Better ones. Places your magic will expand beyond your wildest imagining. I could make you strong."

His words mirrored what Don had said when he was intent on seducing her into wickedness, and her lust turned to ashes. With her mind her own again, she narrowed her eyes and took a step back from the sorcerer.

"Who are you?"

"Do I need a name?" he countered. Intuiting something had broken his hold on her, he quit teasing his cock.

"Not really."

She quested about. There had to be a way back, but what and where? Could she figure it out with him breathing down her neck?

"Fuck me and I'll see you returned."

The lie jangled against her power, and she snorted. "If I fuck you, I'm lost forever. I may have learned Black Magick, but the only reason was to destroy my husband. It never snared me like it did him because I saw the downside."

"Really? And what was that?" He quirked a dark brow and reached for his robe, settling it back across his body.

She wanted to scream at him to let her leave, but she sensed she'd get farther if she could earn his respect. "Unlike my late husband, I value my soul. Never felt like bartering it—for anything."

"I was like you once."

Breana bit her lip hard. "Of course you were. Every sorcerer begins with White Magick.

"Once you open yourself to—"

"Save your breath." She crossed her arms under her breasts, still frantically working angles to free herself. "I spent two years listening to my husband—someone I once respected—leveraging every angle he could think of to get me to acquiesce. He corrupted his own child, for god sakes. Do you think it wasn't tempting to give up everything then? Knowing I'd get my child back? Knowing she'd love me again?"

Breana's voice shook with emotion. While the man focused on her words, she gathered power. Now that she could breathe again—and wasn't fighting throwing herself into his arms—it was easy because the blended magic still ran strong through her. She'd only get one chance. She had to get away from the dark mage. Unlike Don, he was compelling enough, she'd give in eventually.

Worse, the mage without a name knew it, which was likely why he wasn't pressing her harder. What felt like a cat and mouse contest could quickly morph into a vulture and its cornered prey. She had to be gone before that happened.

At the corners of her mind, she felt a slight tug.

*Hester.*

Breana would know her energy anywhere, and it gave her exactly what she needed: direction and focus. An anchor in the world she'd left behind. With a mighty heave, she thrust everything she had into a conduit arrowing right for the old witch's beacon.

The dark sphere imploded around her and the familiar world —the one she'd left—formed again. Magic blasted her from three sides as the others built a barrier around her.

"We got her back!" Joshua screeched.

"Told you it would work."

Hester sounded so smug, Breana almost laughed. She remembered that tone all too well.

"Let's not tarry," Chris said. "Back to the ranch house. It's a more defensible position."

Breana started toward the others, but their magic held her in place. When she gazed about, they were the only ones left standing. All the sorcerers lay dead, and the animals who could leave were long gone. Wraiths never stuck around. The ones who sustained wounds folded in on themselves and vanished. The rest would've left when it was obvious they couldn't win. Only thing left was their carrion stink.

Wolves, coyotes, mountain lions, and ravens lay scattered in heaps across the road and surrounding scrub forest. The scene made her heart hurt, and she sent up a prayer to the goddess for all the innocents who'd lost their lives in today's senseless slaughter.

A blast of power moved from the top of her head to her toes, examining every cell. Breana sucked it in, let it cleanse her. Witch enchantment scoured every corner of her body, her mind, and her spirit. The truth and purity of it made her ashamed she'd played in the filth littering Black Magick's sandbox.

With shame came defiance. She hadn't had a choice. Not really.

Breath whistled from between Hester's clenched teeth just before the barrier holding Breana at bay frittered away to nothing. "Och, and I guess 'tis safe enough," the old woman muttered.

"Me? You're worried about me?" Breana turned incredulous eyes on her mentor.

"'Twasn't but an hour ago ye were looking a hell of a lot like one of the devils we fought," Hester countered. "Not that I wasna glad to have the boost from your power, but once we're back, I expect a full and complete account as to why ye've become so handy wielding Black Magick."

Breana glanced at Joshua, but he was suddenly busy with the horses and looking anywhere but at her. She nodded sharply and rounded up her horse, vaulting atop its back. "Gladly."

They galloped back to the ranch in silence. Breana still couldn't believe she'd broken free from the man who'd kidnapped her. Surely her power didn't rival his, but she'd played him, manipulated him, and taken advantage of a weak spot. Maybe he really did want her for a lover. It was the only explanation for why he hadn't murdered her on the spot.

And taken her soul.

A shudder tracked down her spine and her hands shook. Bodies weren't meant to contain both magics, and she'd pay for today's decision—probably for quite some time. She risked a glance at Joshua. He rode slightly ahead of her, his face hard as carved stone. If even Hester, who knew her better than anyone, felt the need to test her, he must view her as hideously damaged.

Before, he'd been sympathetic about Don's fall from grace. Today would change all that. It had to. Nothing like watching someone you thought was on your side wielding power that made you cringe and filled you with revulsion and white-hot rage.

A raven winged its way toward them and landed on Joshua's shoulder. She felt the burst of magic as he spoke with the bird, and a hint of a smile formed on his chiseled lips before the creature flew back the way it had come.

Her first guess was the bird had thanked him for their assistance today. She buried her hands in the horse's mane, trying to get warmth back into her fingers. Rain spattered down from a gunmetal sky, and she girded herself for what would happen once they got home. She had nothing to hide, and even though she felt dirty and used, she'd invite them to set a truth spell before she answered their questions.

The fence line around her property flashed past, and she joined with the horse's mind, suggesting that now would be a good time to stop. Once it did, she slid from its back and led it to a stall in the barn where she made certain it had feed and water.

"I'll finish up here."

Joshua's voice was gruff. It startled her because she hadn't heard him come inside the barn.

She opened her mouth, but he shook his head. "Just get on into the house. I'll be along presently. All of us want to know why the Dark Angel singled you out."

Her heart stuttered in her chest, and she grabbed the top rail of a stall to remain upright. "D-dark Angel?"

Joshua stopped what he was doing with the other horses and came round to face her. "You didn't know? I figured you met him during the months Don parlayed with Black Magick." Joshua's magic speared her, obvious and exacting. Clearly he wanted absolute honesty.

Breana's eyes felt wide, hot, gritty, and she forced herself to blink—and to breathe. "No, I didn't, but it's probably just as well," she muttered. "If I had, I'd have been so immobilized by fear, I'd probably still be there."

Feeling like she'd been drawn and quartered, she gathered the fractured pieces of her mind and plodded out of the barn toward the house. Every step jarred her until she wanted to crawl out of her skin, but she kept going across the yard and up the steps. She'd fought like hell to stay one step ahead of Don. If the Dark Angel had her in his gunsights, she may as well drink poison and be done with everything.

This wasn't a skirmish she could win.

# CHAPTER 4

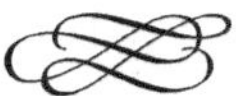

*B*reana sat heavily at the dining room table and dropped her head into her hands, enveloped in hopelessness so profound, she didn't even try to talk herself out of it.

Chris was slumped in a chair at the far end, sipping whiskey from a bottle, his brown eyes sad, but determined.

Hester bustled in from the kitchen. "Here." She thrust a mug into Breana's nerveless fingers. "Drink it down. All of it."

Breana felt the spell the minute she touched the mug, but trust for her mentor ran deep, and she tipped the bitter liquid into her mouth. It burned her lips and throat at first, but once she began swallowing, it warmed the desolate place her heart had become. When the cup was empty, she looked up and met Hester's relentless, hazel gaze.

"Thank you."

Hester nodded curtly. "Thank me with the truth of things. I was across the country, not on a different world. Why didn't ye write to me? Surely things werena so desperate, ye couldna have smuggled a letter out of your home."

Breana placed her hands palms down on the table. "I was ashamed. I didn't want you to know." She swallowed hard. "And I worried Don would hurt you. He threatened to murder anyone I told. Don't you understand?" Breana's voice broke and she fought for control. "I love you. You're the closest thing to a mother I've ever had, and I couldn't bear to have you look at me with disappointment streaming from your eyes just like it is now."

Joshua padded silently into the room and pried the whiskey bottle away from Chris. Tipping it back, he drank deep before handing it to the other enforcer. Rather than sitting, he crossed his arms over his chest. "She didn't know who it was," he said without preamble.

"How could ye not know?" Hester demanded. The words stabbed Breana like little darts. A truth spell dropped thorny folds around her. Even though she'd planned to invite Hester to set one, that the old witch assumed she wouldn't be forthcoming without it stung.

Breana rose slowly to her feet, hands still splayed on the tabletop, and narrowed her eyes to slits. "I won't beg, nor will I grovel. Yes, I learned Black Magick. I admitted it when I confessed after Luke, Sam, and the others killed Don. My plan was to use my blended power to destroy Don. Once that was done, I figured maybe I could save my daughter."

Without giving any of them a chance to weigh in, she hurried on. "I know it was wrong. Knew it at the time, but I did it anyway, and—" she leveled her gaze at each of them in turn "—given a choice, I'd do it again. If the situation was the same."

Hester crooked two fingers her way. "Keep talking. Ye're far from done."

Breana's mouth twitched into a bitter smile. "No one knows

that better than me. One of the things I discovered was I could weave our magic with…the other. It wasn't easy. Took months of practice, but the result was incredibly potent—and hugely difficult to control." She tossed her head back. "You saw what it could do today. First time I actually used it in front of anything but a mirror."

"Wasn't that how you tried to kill Don, after we brought you the news your child was dead?" Joshua asked, his tone unreadable.

"No. It's what I should've done, but I was so distraught I wasn't thinking straight. If I'd turned his power against him, the whole next day would've unfolded very differently." She took an uneasy breath. "If it's all the same to everyone, I'm going upstairs. Maybe I don't deserve anyone's trust anymore, but having all of you stare at me as if I've grown three heads is more than I can take just now." She turned to leave, but she hadn't gotten two steps before Hester's voice stopped her dead.

"Not so fast, sister. We have things to discuss that require your presence."

"Fine." Breana spun, hands fisted at her sides, waiting for judgment to fall on her head. She'd expected Coven justice to hammer her, just not quite so soon.

"Where did Andras take you?" Joshua asked.

"He never would tell me his name," Breana murmured. "Now I know why. As to where he took me, I have no idea. He said it was another world."

"Were those his exact words?" Hester persisted.

Breana thought about it. "No. What he said was it as a place between worlds."

Hester's hazel eyes narrowed in understanding, and her brogue thickened. "Och, 'tis why ye were able to return. Had it truly been another world, ye'd still be by his side and lost forever."

"Did he…?" Joshua's voice faltered and color rose from the open neck of his leather shirt. "I mean, did you…?"

"No. But I wanted to." Defiance stiffened her spine, and she tightened her fists until her hands ached.

"'Tis why he dinna kill you outright," Hester said. "But the bad news is if he wants you that badly, he willna give up, and there isna anyplace to hide you from him."

"I found my way back today." The words sounded petulant, sullen, but she couldn't take them back.

"Because I built a path," Hester pointed out. "I felt you latch onto my energy the moment I reached for you."

Breana waited. Hester had something to say, but she'd reveal it in her own time.

The older witch furled her snow-white brows. "Aye, and ye know me well, just as I know you. The end of things is ye canna use Black Magick anymore, no matter how noble the cause. If ye do, 'twill act as a beacon to summon Andras. Doona delude yourself. He's lying in wait, figuring the pull of his power will be too seductive to resist. He's the next thing to immortal, so he can afford to be patient."

"What happens when we're attacked again?" Breana demanded. "Do I just sit back and allow the slaughter of innocents?"

"If you can't stem the tide with your natural, Goddess-given gifts, that's exactly what you do," Joshua thundered, his hazel eyes on fire with something terrible to look at. He turned away, slamming out of the room.

Chris exchanged a pointed look with Hester before vaulting to his feet and following the other enforcer.

"Nothing good can come of anything from the other side."

Hester's voice was soft. "Look at the havoc it's causing with the two men who just left so they wouldn't fry you with mage fire."

Breana kept her mouth shut and her mind shuttered. Not much point in telling her mentor that she'd felt like an Old World goddess channeling lightening as the mixed power ran through her. She'd felt hideous too—scarred beyond reckoning —and some of that part had yet to dissipate. But surely if a mage brought a pure heart into battle, the type of magic they used wouldn't matter.

"Look at me." Hester's voice was stern.

"I will, but I'm not your acolyte anymore."

"You never were, merely a witch I mentored. 'Tisn't important right now. I recognize that mulish look ye get. Somewhere beneath the spell ye've woven round yourself to keep me out, ye're thinking there's a workaround. A way to use the magical blend ye spent so long perfecting."

Breana opened her mouth, but Hester waved her to silence. "I willna argue about how well it works. Your power saved this day for us, but what I'm saying is ye canna continue to use it. If ye do, 'twill corrupt you thoroughly. 'Tis like dancing with an adder, thinking ye'll be nimble enough to jump aside when it strikes. And ye'll be lucky a time or two or three, but there'll come a time when your luck runs dry, and then the dark power will hold you in thrall, and there'll be no coming back from it."

Hester's nostrils flared. "Ye've grown beyond where I can tell you what to do, but hold what I've said close. It made me glad when Abigail suggested I come here after I lost Michael, the one, true love of my life. At first I thought I'd be fine by myself. The days, they went along, but the nights grew long with his side of the bed so cold and empty. I gave it some thought once Abigail and Luke left, but coming here made sense, and now that I'm here I understand more. The goddess doesn't make mistakes. She sent me where I was needed."

Breana's heart softened. She walked to where Hester sat and wrapped her arms around her from behind. "I'm sorry for your loss. Michael was a good man." She hooked the neighboring chair out with her foot and dropped into it. "And I believe you about the consequences of using Black Magick. I still play host to its filth, and while I was in the thick of things, my body felt like it was on fire from the inside out."

"But wielding it held you in thrall."

It hadn't been a question, but Breana answered it anyway. "You'd know I was lying if I didn't admit as much." She paused a beat. "Andras said he was once like us. Do you know his story?"

Hester narrowed her eyes. "Aye, that I do. But if there's even a shred of sympathy anywhere within you for that viper, lose it now. He's nasty and totally unprincipled. Ye canna believe a word that rolls from that beautiful face, and tumbling into his bed will—"

"I know that," Breana broke in. "Even when I was so hot I could barely think, and he made me come where I stood by just looking at me, I understood full well I couldn't let him touch me, so we can skip that part of the lecture."

A corner of Hester's mouth curved wryly. "Thank the goddess for small things, eh? Why do ye want to know about him?"

"So I'll have something to work with next time he shows up."

"Good ye believe that part. If he dinna plan to claim you, ye'd be dead." Hester's Scottish lilt retreated to its normal cadence. She reached for the whiskey bottle Chris had abandoned and took a long pull. "There are many fallen angels, but Andras is the most wicked of them all."

"Surely not worse than Satan?"

Hester shrugged. "Satan may be many things, but he dinna pick up the banner to rule those who practice Black Magick. Andras did."

"I'll stop interrupting." Breana belted back some whiskey. It strengthened whatever was in the concoction Hester had made for her.

"When I was a young witch, back on the Isle of Skye, humans valued witchcraft. It would be years yet afore the Church painted us as a threat. Back then, their focus was on fallen angels like Satan and his ilk. Black Magick was around, but it was implemented in grottos and cellars. No one admitted to its practice because it was akin to a death sentence. Courts back then were different. If someone was suspected of unnatural acts, they'd be summarily hung." She dusted her palms together.

Breana scrunched her face into a frown. "I scarcely need a history lesson. You're trying to figure out how to tell me something."

"Of course I am." Breath whistled past Hester's pursed lips. "I met Andras when I was but sixteen. Had no idea what he was. All I knew was he was irresistible with those silver eyes and long black hair. I was scarcely a maid, but sex was still new enough, I wanted him with a fury gifted only to the young."

Breana leaned close, silently urging Hester to continue.

"Of course I asked him about himself, and what he told me was close enough to true. Most of it, anyway. He said he was a mage. That he'd been born before the first Crusade and had cut his teeth battling against the Church's incursion as they tried to stuff their god down everyone else's throats."

"So far, so good, eh?" Breana muttered.

"Aye, indeed. What he failed to mention was he'd put out a call to gather dark mages from their hiding places. Andras had big plans, and recognized the strength they could have if they banded together. If not for him, there'd be no Alchemical Council, no Black Magick Assembly. But all that happened long after I first met him." Hester made a face and shook her head hard enough to loosen white hair from her bun.

Breana couldn't find a subtle combination of words, so she just asked outright. "Was he your lover?"

"Aye, for a few months. He's one of the reasons I left Scotland. Once I fully recognized what he was, I tried to end things—many times, but his power was seductive enough to draw me back—even against my free will. The Coven was the only thing that saved me. I couldna tell the other witches about him, but I'd lose myself in their rituals and gather my resolve to break free."

"I imagine he's stronger now than he was then," Breana mumbled.

"Much. If he'd commanded his current level of mastery when I knew him, I'd have been lost forever. He feeds off the ranks of acolytes he's drawn to him, and he's immeasurably more potent than he was more than four hundred years ago."

"Other than the obvious, what made it so hard to leave?"

"I figured love would bring him back to our side." She snorted balefully. "He was working the same supposition, but from the other angle. His. If I'd remained, he would've won eventually. I know the feel of his power, though. It was the main reason I could find you earlier."

"Guess his magic shines brighter." Breana rolled her eyes. "Never mind. Of course it would."

"I started hunting for you the moment I realized what happened," Hester said, ignoring Breana's comment. "After that dinna work, I searched for him."

"Do you think he recognized you?"

"Och, that I do. 'Tis why he dinna fight harder to hold onto you. He may have fashioned himself as the Dark Angel, but beneath it all, he began life as a man, and men doona take it well when ye walk away from them. He loved me. And I suppose if I were honest, I loved him, yet I hated him too. 'Twas what allowed me to run from him, and to build a life without him."

"What if he'd walked away from Black Magick?"

Hester's eyes brimmed with bitter knowledge. "Don't ye understand, child? Once enough dark power runs through you, ye can never get away from it. It roots itself in your soul, in the very fabric of your being. The only way out is death. When I truly understood that, I also recognized I had to leave. He'd never eschew his magic for a life with me. Not because part of him didn't want to. Because he couldna."

"What if there's a way to wrap our power around the other? So we could still use its enchantment, but not damage ourselves?"

Hester nodded knowingly. "There it is. That's the workaround I couldna quite see in your mind earlier. I've never known such a thing to happen."

"Do you think it's possible?" Breana persisted.

Hester narrowed her eyes in thought. "I doona know. Seems like if it was, one of us would've figured it out long since. Why are ye considering that route after what I've told you?"

"Because we need an edge. I haven't detailed the hell Don put me through, and I'm not going to, but if we don't cut them off now, we'll lose our chance." Fury set Breana's teeth on edge, and an unnatural energy burned bright.

Hester gripped her forearm hard and dragged a ruby bright gem out from beneath the neck of her dress. "Look at the stone. Do it now, Breana. That boundary I talked about? The one where ye take on an adder—and lose? Ye're closer to it than I thought."

She hissed, sputtered, and looked away, but Hester kept an

implacable grip on her and moved the ruby to eye level. It pulsed, almost as if it had its own heartbeat.

"Look at the stone," Hester repeated. "Sink into it. Trust it to purify your soul."

With a ridiculous amount of difficulty, Breana gazed at the ruby. Gears meshed together, and fire exploded in her gut.

Joshua bolted down the front steps. He wanted to crush Breana's skull between his two hands to drive the wickedness from her. All the while riding back, he'd struggled against returning to the battlefield to take Andras on in personal combat. The Dark Angel had corrupted Breana…

*Stop. For fuck sakes, stop,* his inner voice commanded.

If anyone had tainted Breana, it was her dead husband. That was where she'd learned to wield Black Magick. She'd admitted it—and more than once—but he couldn't stand to listen to her talk about it anymore.

Chris closed from behind him. "Hey, there, brother. Want to hash anything through?"

"Not particularly." Joshua glanced sidelong at Chris.

The other enforcer shrugged and shook rain from his hair. Joshua glanced at the sky, only then realizing it was still pouring.

"Then you won't mind if I help myself to your thoughts." Chris skewered Joshua with brown eyes that meant business.

"Yeah. I mind—a lot." Joshua picked up his pace until he was running full out, but Chris didn't give up.

"When did you fall in love with her?" Chris demanded. "She was married to another man up until a few weeks back."

Joshua halted precipitously and spun to face Chris. "You think I don't know that? And who said shit about being in love?"

"Don't have to. It's written all over you, and the only reason I can come up with for you to be so upset. We don't get emotional —about anything."

"I am not *emotional.*"

"The hell you aren't. You ran out of that house like the walls were falling in on you."

"Can we just forget this conversation ever happened?"

"No. We can't. We've got trouble ahead. Today was just a taste. If you can't stay in the same room with Breana Giraud because of her proclivity to use Black Magick, maybe you'd be better off leaving. Even if Hester pounds sense into Breana and she never taps into that particular vein of power again, you can't be watching her like an overprotective parent. It will cut into your concentration." Chris plowed on without taking much of a breath. "We have to stand together and fight together—"

"Enough. I don't have to hear that from you. Christ! I was a coven enforcer when you were a kid wearing short pants."

Chris bristled, narrowing his eyes to slits. "You'd blow up your friendship with me over this?"

*I'd destroy the world if it brought me Breana.*

Joshua inhaled sharply, blew out the breath, and did it again as he worked to gain control of himself. Punching Chris, or slapping him around with magic, would be just plain stupid.

"Sorry," he muttered. "I'm not myself. It's not that I didn't know she'd learned the dark arts, but being confronted with the reality was way worse than I imagined it would be."

"When did you fall for her?" Chris persisted.

Joshua shook his head. "I appreciate the offer, but I'm not ready to talk about any of this. Not yet."

*Maybe not ever.*

But Chris didn't give up. "Does she know?"

Joshua turned away. No matter how many questions Chris peppered him with, he was done answering them.

"All right," Chris went on affably. "I'll take that as a no." He moved around so he faced Joshua again. "Try this one on, brother. As you already pointed out, you've been around for a long time. She's one of the older ones too, and Don, now he had at least a hundred years on the lot of you. My guess is you've had your eye on her for years, but being a decent sort, you held your distance..."

"Why are you doing this?"

"Because it's eating at you, and you've got to get past it damned fast. We don't have the luxury of you wallowing in self-pity or misery while you sort this out."

"I am not *wallowing*." Joshua felt the corners of his mouth twitch. "Jesus, but you're annoying."

"Yeah, my big brothers told me that all the time. It's where I got all my practice."

"They did a good job, but I need some breathing space. If I'm not back inside in an hour, you're free to roust me out of the barn."

"I put out a call for more of us."

Joshua's head snapped up at the rapid shift of subjects. "Did you hear back from anyone?"

Chris shook his head. "Which is why you've got to be at the top of your game. Shit, bro. If you love her, let her know. Bed her —or chalk her off as a lost cause. Do what you need to and get past this. Next time they attack—and they will, I feel it in my bones—I need to know you're functioning at a hundred percent."

"So all this is self-serving on your part?" Joshua grinned wryly. Kind of like flapping your hands at a lapdog that refused to leave you be, it was impossible to tell Chris to go away and mean it.

"If believing that makes it easier going down, sure." Chris sent a knowing grin skittering across the space between them, turned on his heel, and ambled off.

Joshua stared after the other enforcer. With the intuition native to them all, Chris knew when he'd said enough. Rain ran down Joshua's face, and his leathers darkened from moisture. He loped to the barn and let himself into the warm space that smelled of hay and animals. Grabbing a rake, a shovel, and a wheelbarrow, he mucked stalls while he thought about Breana.

Either he loved her enough to accept all of her. Or not. It was that simple, and he had to figure out which it was. He couldn't ride on two horses. If he wanted her despite everything, he needed to tell her how much he cared. If he couldn't get past her dalliance with Black Magick, he'd have to excise the part of him that longed to hold her in his arms.

"Which is it?" He spoke aloud to anchor his roiling feelings. Breana had been part of his secret hopes and dreams for over a hundred fifty years. If he cut to the truth of things, she was likely the reason his congress with women began and stopped with sex. It had seemed wrong to hope Don would die. He'd actually liked the man—before he trifled with the wrong side.

Joshua hadn't known what Don was up to, but he'd noticed changes in him. Everyone had, but none of them did anything. He loosened his grip on the shovel handle when his hands began to cramp. Among their many duties, Coven enforcers kept witches in line. So why'd they given Don such a wide berth?

When the answer came, he felt like a prime fool. Don must've paid out the slenderest threads of Black Magick to keep enforcers from looking too long or too closely at him. Breana could've blown the whistle, but Don tortured her. Kept her a prisoner, and robbed her of her only child.

Had Andras been the guiding force behind Don's deceptions —and his campaign to keep Breana in line? Was that the reason Andras singled Breana out today? Because he'd laid claim to her when she was married to Don?

Another worse thought surfaced.

Breana had said Don involved her in sexual torture on multiple occasions where she was blindfolded, drugged, and raped. Had Andras been a part of any of those events?

The shovel handle fractured in his grip, disintegrating into large splinters of wood, and he pounded a fist into the wall. He had to pick a path and stick with it, or his thoughts would drive him mad.

"They might anyway," he muttered. "Lots of things I'll never have answers for."

He guided the wheelbarrow outside and dumped it, then returned to the barn. Regardless how many times he instructed himself to give up his dreams of having Breana standing proud by his side, he couldn't do it.

No matter what it cost him, he'd lay out the truth. If she laughed in his face, or her eyes filled with kindness or pity, he'd move on. Best to get that part over with. Chris' assessment that they were far from done with attacks from the other side matched his own predictions.

They had to meet the next volley like a well-greased machine, and he couldn't let his feelings for Breana turn into a weakness that crippled their effectiveness. Determined. Resolute. He pushed his soaked hair over his shoulders and strode out the barn door.

～

BREANA'S CONSCIOUSNESS swirled down a shiny, metallic tube tinged with red. The ruby—or Hester's magic powering it—forced the rest of the world into nothingness. Like when she'd leveraged Black Magick, but without the euphoria. The sound of gears grinding pummeled her until she screamed, but Hester just tightened her grip.

Every cell began to burn, and her body turned into a mass of agony. Hundreds of tiny teeth tore at her insides, ripping, shredding. Breana's eyes snapped open. "Please," she moaned. "Aw, Jesus, it hurts like a bitch."

Hester shook Breana hard enough to rattle her teeth. "What hurts is the dark power being forced out. Once it has its claws in you, it doesna leave without a hell of a protest."

Steam poured from the gem suspended on its golden chain. Breana blinked, disbelieving. How could a simple stone cause such havoc? "What is that?"

"Something I perfected to annihilate evil." Tears formed in Hester's clear hazel eyes. "In my darkest imaginings, never did I think I'd be using it on you."

Blood dripped from Breana's fingertips. Tears coursed down her cheeks, but when they trickled onto her hands, she saw she was crying blood. Horrified, she stopped fighting the baptism of blood and sorcery. If this was what it took to be reborn into the Coven, to be purged of evil, she'd bless Hester until her dying day if it worked. No going back now. The battle raging within her only had one way out. If evil won, her body would end up immolated in mage fire.

Lines of strain carved deep into Hester's face, but she held the gem in place so Breana had to look at it. In truth, now that the casting had her in its grip, Breana couldn't have ripped herself

56

from its enchantment if she wanted to. Time drizzled past. Lots of it. Finally, the desperation to break free lessened. So did the heat and pain.

She tried to tell Hester that her gamble paid off, that they'd won. Before she could form the words, she fell face down on the table as consciousness deserted her.

BREANA CAME BACK to herself in a pool of her own blood with Hester's arms wrapped around her, and the other witch crooning in Gaelic. Chris had hold of one of her hands, infusing healing power.

Joshua stopped midstride in the doorway and stared at the tableau, but his indecision didn't last long because he hurried forward.

"What in the goddess's name happened in here?" He directed his words at Hester, sounding every inch a Coven enforcer. No witch dared not answer, not when an enforcer asked that way.

Hester raised her gaze to meet his. "She dinna believe how deeply evil was rooted within her, yet I saw it clear as day, so I drove it from her."

"How?" Chris asked.

"Why not ask me? I was here the whole time." Breana felt some of her usual gruffness seeping back, and she welcomed it.

"I'm asking both of you," Chris said pointedly. "Now talk."

Hester drew the ruby back from beneath her dress. "This gem focuses energy. It creates a vortex to do my bidding." She paused a beat. "'Tis a tool I built to seek out Black Magick and destroy it."

"Damn near shattered me in the process." Breana straightened her spine, exhaling raggedly.

"Explain what you mean by *tool*." Joshua flicked the gem with a forefinger, but it didn't change at all. "Looks like a garden variety ruby to me."

"It dinna react to you because ye doona host Black Magick," Hester explained, sounding annoyed.

"When I looked at it—" Breana spoke slowly as she tried to describe what she'd felt "—it trapped me, wouldn't let me go. It ate me from the inside out, forced blood out of me." She turned her reddened hands palms upward. "And it was loud. I heard the whine of steam engines and gears so close they might've rolled over me. Maybe they did. Something turned my tears to blood."

"That covers what it felt like to be on the receiving end," Chris said. "What Josh and I want to know is how it works."

Hester closed her lower lip over her teeth. "'Tis mainly fire, but mixed with an ancient strain of earth power. Once it simmers to a fine point, I infuse air through the stone."

"Where'd you find the stone?" Chris demanded.

Hester narrowed her eyes. "Aye, and ye're a canny one. Persistent too. I found this particular gem in a quarry at the north end of the Isle of Skye hundreds of years ago. The goddess led me there one day, and when I woke from my trance, this stone and two others were clutched in a fist. I've kept them with me always. This one and a star sapphire bend their energy to my will. I have yet to figure out the garnet."

"What we spoke of earlier—" Breana selected her words with care—and shielded her thoughts—to keep Hester's relationship with Andras secret. "The goddess gifted you when you had most need."

"Exactly." Worlds of meaning sat beneath that one world, and Breana knew at least one of the stones was how Hester had escaped Andras' grasp.

"Will Breana recover?" Joshua demanded, directing his words to Hester.

"Aye, that she will."

Annoyance flickered and Breana almost censured them for talking about her as if she weren't there, but thought better of it. Neither enforcer had paid much attention to what she just asked Hester. If she was smart, she'd keep her mouth shut and their attention elsewhere.

"Did you know if Breana would live to see the other side of your intervention?" Chris asked.

After a hesitation so long, Breana was certain Hester wouldn't answer, the other witch shook her head. "These things, they're never cut and dried. If I hadna been able to drive the bits of dark enchantment from her, if she'd turned on me—and 'twas close, mind ye—I'd have called for you boys and your mage fire.

The old witch's eyes filled with tears. "'Tis grateful I am, it dinna come to that." She rose to her feet and kissed Breana's cheeks. "I'm going outside to offer my thanks to the goddess who steadied my hand and my resolve this day."

Breana tried to get up, but her head spun crazily. "Thank you, Hester," she called after the woman's straight-as-a-stick retreating back.

Chris let go of her and stood. "We've lost enough to evil for one day. I'm grateful I didn't have to douse you in mage fire."

"That makes two of us." She managed a wry smile. "Where are you going?"

"Why do you think I'm going anywhere?"

"Intuition. You have that look about you."

He leveled his gaze at her. "You and Joshua need to talk. I'm going to make certain Hester didn't expend too much power for her own good, and then I'll be in the barn fabricating more ammunition."

Once the clump of his boots faded, she levered herself upright and staggered across the dining room and into the kitchen where she pumped water, sluicing it over her hands and rinsing her face. She still smelled like blood and evil, but it was the best she could do for the moment.

Joshua followed her, silent as a shade, with an unreadable expression on his stern features.

"Why'd Chris say we needed to talk?" she asked, too worn-down to play games. Breana steadied herself with a hand on the kitchen countertop. Even standing took a ridiculous amount of energy.

"His opinion."

Breana raked her hands through her hair. Pain jangled her already shot nerves as her fingers snagged on tangles, and she planted herself in front of Joshua. "If you have something to say, spit it out. I want to go upstairs and get out of these clothes. They're bloody and they still smell like that abomination who kidnapped me."

Emotion rippled across his chiseled cheekbones and square jaw, and a muscle danced beneath one eye when he clamped his jaws tightly together. "Hard to know exactly where to start," he ground out.

"If it's that difficult, maybe whatever's bottled up in your throat ought to stay there," Breana retorted. She pushed past him and trudged up the steps to her room. She hadn't noticed the reek of evil clinging to her nearly as much before Hester's spell spun her around and spit her out.

She kicked her door shut and went to work getting out of her dress and corset, but her fingers shook so hard, buttons ripped from their moorings and bounced across the floor.

*How could I have sunk so deep into evil and not recognized it?*

When the answer formed, she didn't much care for it. Apparently, she'd lived with darkness so long, it became second nature. Andras wouldn't have slathered attention on her if he wasn't close to certain his efforts would bear fruit. If she hadn't shone like a beacon, emanating sorcery, he'd have killed her and moved on.

She sensed Joshua's energy moments before he pounded on her door.

Breana crossed the room in three long steps and yanked the door open. "I don't want to hear one blasted word about me being half dressed. What is it that won't wait?"

When she stopped spouting fury and looked at his face, remorse smote her. He couldn't have looked worse if he'd spent the last few days visiting Hell. His eyes held a haunted edge, and resolve etched his forehead into a mass of lines.

Breana's hand flew to her chest. "It's Hester, isn't it? She's not a young witch anymore, and she—"

"Hester's fine," he broke in. "It's me who isn't."

# CHAPTER 6

*J*oshua watched Breana stumble across the kitchen and up the stairs without making a move to stop her. He wanted to, but felt tongue-tied, frozen in place. The determination that drove him into the house hadn't included exactly what he'd say, and indecision rocked him. At least a quarter hour passed after he heard her door slam upstairs before he shook himself with strict exhortations to get moving.

She wasn't a maid courting her first beau. For that fact, he was far from a youngster wooing his first love.

*But she is my first love,* an inner voice corrected. *The only woman I've ever looked twice at, longed for...*

*Yeah, worshipped from afar, but now that she's not spoken for anymore, I've turned into a simpering coward.*

It was as good a place as any to start. He'd just spit everything out. If she told him she wasn't interested, that would be the end of it. Probably just as well. He'd hidden behind loving her, used that love as an excuse to not develop any kind of emotional bond with anyone else. In many ways, she'd provided a convenient crutch.

63

He loved her, but she belonged to someone else, and her unavailability freed him up to perform his enforcer duties unencumbered. He flinched at the unvarnished truth in his thoughts, but they drove him up the stairs, and he knocked on her door.

Breana yanked it open quicker than he'd thought was possible—unless she was standing right next to it. With her face set in grim lines, she snarled, "I don't want to hear one blasted word about me being half dressed. What is it that won't wait?"

Joshua opened his mouth, but before he could begin talking Breana's hand flew to her chest. "It's Hester, isn't it? She's not a young witch anymore, and she—"

"Hester's fine," he broke in. "It's me who isn't."

Breana drew her blonde brows together. "Why ever not? You weren't playing host to evil. I'm not trying to be rude, but I don't have the healing gift—not much of it anyway. You'd be better off with Abigail, except she's not here. Or your own magic—"

Frustration sharpened his next words. "I'm not ill. There's something I need to say to you, and you're not making it any easier."

Breana turned away. "If it's about me and Black Magick, save your breath. I still think there might be a way for us to manipulate their power, blend it with ours to strengthen our abilities, but I'm not trying it on my own anymore. Too risky."

"I understand you meant well," he began, but stopped since he sounded patronizing. Besides, it wasn't what he'd come up here to say. He was stalling, and it made him feel about three inches tall.

For once, Breana didn't offer a pointed comeback. She trudged back about and faced him, arms crossed beneath her breasts. He hadn't noticed them, pushed up by the stays she had yet to remove, until right now, and her semi-clothed state hammered him. Heat flooded his chest and rose to the top of his head. It wasn't the only thing rising. His cock pounded to fullness and pressed against his leather breeches.

Joshua squared his shoulders. It was so far from a lover's gesture, he muffled a disgusted snort—and wrenched his gaze from her cleavage to her face.

"Do you remember when I first met you?" he asked.

She scrunched her forehead in thought. "Yes. It was around a hundred fifty years back. You showed up at Coven headquarters asking about a job, and Don outlined our newly formed enforcer cadre. I was working in the herb storeroom then, so I overheard most of the conversation."

"What else do you recall?" He kept his voice low.

"You'd just sailed across the Atlantic—from Germany if I'm remembering."

"And," he prodded.

Her eyes pinched with pain. "Oh, Joshua. It's such an ugly story. Surely you recall it without hearing it fall from my lips."

He wanted to ease her distress, but his story needed retelling, so she understood how anguish and fury had shaped him, created what he'd become.

Joshua began talking, keeping his voice low. Even so, it vibrated with barely suppressed emotion. "It's been long enough, most of the shock value's dropped away," he began.

"Somehow I doubt that, but you seem determined, so I'm listening."

"I came to the American Colonies after watching my parents and brother suffer for months at the hands of a truly sadistic torturer who hated anyone with magic. The man, a cleric, secured my kin in stocks in a public square, letting them wallow in their own filth and giving them just enough food and water to keep them clinging to life. I wanted to run that bastard through, fry him with power, but other mages—those in my brotherhood —held me back. It would've meant my death, and our numbers were already dwindling. That son of a bitch cut off body parts, then staunched bleeding with fire so his victims wouldn't die."

Once the words began, they ran out of him like a river powered by a strong current, unstoppable by anything less than a cataclysm. "Had it been a dark mage who'd captured my family, the brotherhood—and the Coven—would've stood by me, helped me free them, but it was the goddamned Church. The one who brutalized my blood kin wore a black cassock, and somehow that gave him the right to decide they weren't worthy of drawing breath."

Joshua girded himself for the next part, the truly appalling ending. "One morning the stocks were empty. I assumed death had finally claimed my family, but several priests were carrying on something fierce. Sprinkling holy water, igniting pots of holy oil, and screeching in Latin. When I inquired why they were so upset, a woman told me the three magic-wielders had been spirited off during the night. No one knew what happened, but the priests suspected the blackest witchcraft was at play."

"Awk. Dear God. After all that, Black Magick freed them?"

Joshua nodded slowly, painfully. "I'll never know for sure. I tried to find them—and my brotherhood hunted alongside me— but it was as if they'd been wiped from the face of our mother Earth."

Breana placed a hand on his arm. "I'm so sorry. I didn't know that last part. You tore the scabs off old wounds for a reason. What is it?"

"I'm getting there. I booked passage across the Atlantic right after that. Didn't trust myself not to exact revenge if I stayed. I had weeks at sea to insulate myself—from everything. During the voyage, I vowed to dedicate my life to eradicating evil." A bitter laugh burst past his clenched jaws. "What I wanted to do was declare war on the Church, but my mentor back in Heidelberg convinced me that path was folly before I left. Witches and mages were under attack from two sides, you see."

"Sorcery and Christianity," she muttered, making a hooked sign against evil.

"Indeed. And at the time, Christianity was the stronger. It may still be, but at least they've gotten past committing public murder."

"I'm still not understanding why you're picking over old bones." She tugged a robe from a hook and draped it around herself.

"You caught my eye that first day at Coven headquarters in New York. I asked around a bit and discovered you were Don's wife, so I kept my interest to myself." Joshua looked away from her direct blue eyes. "I guess you could say I carried a torch for you. Never got too close to any other woman. It was easy enough. I buried my feelings crossing the Atlantic. Keeping them where I'd hid them proved easy enough."

Compassion streamed from her. "And now I'm not married anymore." She tightened her fingers around his arm. "I'm also not a good bet. I've been touched by the other side. I saw how you looked at me today while we were fighting. Like you couldn't believe your eyes."

"I couldn't." He did look at her then. "Wasn't sure whether to blanket you in mage fire or crush you against me until the wickedness packed up and left. I finally appreciated why Luke begged us to do everything we could to spare Abigail's life when she was possessed by evil. Nothing quite like walking in another man's shoes to understand him."

"The other part of things," she went on, "is I lost a lot of myself in the years after Don embraced evil. He forced me to do repulsive things—"

"But none of that was your fault."

She let go of him and turned to face him squarely. "There were many things I could've done. I didn't do a one of them. I didn't turn Don into the Coven. Or my daughter. I broke my vows to honor and protect the goddess, even at the cost of my own life." Breana looked away. "I'm not proud of any of it, and it's going to take time before I can accept myself again."

Faced by her pain, Joshua's heart cracked wide open. "Let me help you."

Breana shook her head. "Some things you have to do by yourself, and this is one of them. You're a beautiful man, Joshua. Of course I've noticed you. I've wondered how your arms would feel around me, how you'd be to make love with in my bed."

"If you're attracted to me, they why—?"

"Because right now I'm broken. I'm not fit to be anyone's wife, or even anyone's intended."

"I'll wait. No matter how long it takes. Jesus. God. I've already waited years." The emotions he'd rode herd on raced to the fore. He didn't want to hide them anymore. Not from the woman standing before him.

Breana's eyes filled with tears.

Joshua closed the distance between them and gathered her into his arms, crooning in an old Germanic dialect as he held her. He thought she'd fight his embrace, but instead she slumped against him and sobbed as if her heart were breaking.

"You deserve better than me," she choked out.

"Let me be the judge of that." He stroked blonde hair back from her forehead. "I won't be any more obtrusive than I've been. Only difference is you know I'm here for you. I always have been, and I always will be. Unless you tell me to go away."

"Somehow I have a feeling that wouldn't make any difference." She swiped the back of one hand over her streaming eyes.

"Likely not."

He brushed his lips over her forehead, longing to do more. "I said what I needed to. I'll leave you to change and bathe."

"It'll be the goddess's own miracle if I get through a bath without falling face down in the water."

"I have faith in you."

Before his discipline ran stone dry and he moved his hands from her shoulders down her back to the lush curves of her ass, he turned and let himself out into the corridor. He moved down the stairs and out the front door, stopping once he was in the yard.

Hester rose from where she'd been sitting on an upturned round of wood. "Finally told her, did ye?"

Joshua grinned ruefully. "You never did miss much."

"So long as ye remember that, we'll do just fine." Hester put her hands on her hips. "How'd she take it? Will I be performing a wedding?"

Joshua looked away. "Not anytime soon."

"Och, laddie." Hester strode to him and patted his arm. "Give her a wee spot of time. She's lived through hell, and needs to find herself again."

"Funny, but that's an almost exact replica of what she said."

Hester shook her head. "Enforcers. All rough and gritty with magic to burn. Now's a time we need those things. Trouble's on its way. I smell it brewing."

"Did your nose tell you when it'll show up?"

"Soon. Chris is making bullets. He could use your help. I tried, but I havena got a feel for measuring the mixture."

Joshua nodded once and loped toward the barn. He'd no sooner let himself inside when he heard Chris cursing.

"What's wrong?" Joshua rounded the corner and saw the other enforcer sitting on the barn floor, his long legs splayed wide with reloading equipment spread around him.

"Either we ran out of silver powder, or I can't find any."

"Hang on. There's a packet in my saddlebags." He plucked it out and joined Chris on the floor where they worked in silence for a long time, the only sounds the click of shells as they filled them.

Enough time passed, Joshua thought he might get away with Chris not asking anything about Breana. She hadn't rejected him out of hand, but nor had she given him much cause for hope. At least not in the immediate future, and the way things were shaping up, all of them could be dead before too many more days elapsed. His infatuation was transparent enough that even Hester knew about it. If she knew, how many other witches had chatted about it behind his back? Had he become an object of pity, or worse—derision?

The horses whinnied, stamping nervously.

Joshua sent power spiraling outward to see what had spooked them.

"Wraiths." He spat the loathsome word. "Goddammit. I can just about guess who sicced them on us."

"Andras never did take defeat well. Bastard." Chris bolted to his feet dropping handfuls of the newly made bullets into his pockets. Joshua did the same. No time to load his ammo bandoliers.

"Any word from other enforcers?" Joshua asked. "You put the call out earlier."

"Not yet. I'll call again."

Hester bustled into the barn. "Game time."

"Did anyone let Breana know?" Chris asked.

"Och, and a body would have to be both blind and dumb to not notice the stench of the undead marching this way."

BREANA STOOD STARING at the door Joshua walked out of. Letting him go was one of the hardest things she'd ever done, but everything she told him was true. She did need time to come to terms with her sins. Having him by her side would be a diversion, but that was a terrible way to begin a love affair.

The conversation had dragged her far enough out of her own misery that she undressed and stood over the basin and ewer on a stand in the corner of her bedroom. Pale light streamed through gabled windows, and rain pummeled the panes. Water from the basin dribbled onto the floor around her bare feet, and she mopped it with the towel after drying herself.

Breana eyed the bed longingly. Pitching facedown and sleeping would be an indulgence, though. Work waited everywhere. If she didn't get moving, none of them would have anything to eat. She pulled fresh underthings from a drawer and slipped into a chemise and pantalets, drawing her corset back over everything. Once it was laced, she donned a fresh skirt, blouse, and sweater. Damn near everything she owned was black. She'd taken to wearing mourning as a silent protest after Don joined up with the other side.

She sat on the floor to don stockings and lace her boots. Leaning back against a wall, she closed her eyes and sent power inward, assessing what was different. Hester's power had altered things, and her innards still felt flayed and raw. All the places she'd hidden her pain were laid bare, as were the secret spots she'd stored the love she never gave up on for her daughter.

As she took stock, she understood she finally had a chance to be whole again. Without Hester's intervention, it never would've happened. Black Magick had taken root inside her, and it would've grown like a malignancy, eventually outstripping anything good.

*I'll have to tell her.*

Before she went downstairs, she let herself think about Joshua. She truly hadn't realized the extent of his caring for her. Honor had kept him aloof, and she held deep respect for men whose principles were more than concepts. If she ever loved again, it would be someone like Joshua. A man with magic strong enough to match her own. A man whose passions ran hot enough to sear them both. For the first time in a long time, her body stirred naturally. Not as the product of a Black Magick spell.

The waves of desire felt clean—and welcome—and she ran her hands down her breasts and belly. Before she moved beneath her skirts, her nose twitched and she scrambled to her feet, lust forgotten.

Wraiths were closing on the house, the rotten meat reek of them unmistakable. Why hadn't anyone roused her? Were they planning to fight without her help? She gathered her skirts and dashed across the room.

Before she made the door, Andras formed before her in a burst of fire-tinged air that stank of brimstone. He held out his hands. "The wraiths are my special pets, and they're but a diversion," he said smugly. "They're only here to keep everyone else busy."

"Why do they need to be busy?" she asked, her tone acerbic. "What are we going to be doing?"

"It's more a matter of where we're going. You and I are far from done with one another."

"Like hell we're not."

She pulled her lips back into a snarl and swathed herself with her magic. White Magick. At the least, it would burn him, slow him down. She raised her mind voice to summon Hester, but it bounced back, slapping her hard. Stars swam before her eyes, and they watered from the pain.

"Only a raw recruit fails to ward rooms." Andras narrowed his silver eyes to slits, and she felt his magic rake through her wards, testing, assessing. "You're damaged," he crooned. "Never fear, I can fix those places that used to house dark power. They're still there and begging for my intercession."

# CHAPTER 7

*B*reana flinched. Of course he'd notice Hester's earlier intercession right away. Andras followed his words with power that sent a surge of skepticism into her. Bleak foreboding raced in on its heels. Without Black Magick at her disposal, how could she ever dream of staving off the Dark Angel? She wasn't strong enough.

"That's right." His voice was still rich, liquid honey. "Our power far exceeds yours."

"We'll see about that." She was bluffing, but she didn't have much in her arsenal to fight him. He'd clearly mowed through her wards, and her every thought was laid bare to him. Maybe, since he underestimated everything associated with witch power, he wouldn't pay heed to what she did next.

It might not work. Then and again, she might draw a better hand than the one she was staring at.

Breana threw her power wide open and cried for the goddess to fill every nook, every cranny with her grace and energy. A witch's strength lay in her connection to the earth, and Breana invited Danu to hollow her until she held enough magic to challenge Andras.

He watched her, much as a cat might stalk a mouse. A hunter sure of his prey, certain of the outcome, and batting her about with a paw while waiting to land a killing blow. Or in this instance, a transport spell to some other place.

She couldn't let that happen. Once she was gone from this house, she was as good as dead. He'd pour molten power through her, saturate her with wickedness, and this time there'd be no going back. Hester had gotten lucky because of his arrogance. He wouldn't make the same mistake twice.

"Just listen to you," he mocked. "Calling for someone who could give a shit less about any of you witches. I know Danu, and she's nothing but a supercilious bitch. When she's not busy whoring. None of us on the other side ever figured out why you chose her as your deity." Andras rolled his eyes. "I've indulged you in the hope you won't give me as much grief dragging you out of here, but my patience isn't endless."

Breana ignored him, and upped the ante on her pleas to the goddess. She couldn't reach her power beyond the four walls that surrounded them. That might be the problem, but the gods rarely involved themselves in human concerns, no matter how grave the need.

*Believe!* She exhorted. *I have to believe.*

"We're done here. The only one you believe in from now on is me." Andras crossed the room in a flash of light and snaked out a hand to grab her.

Except he couldn't. An incredulous look twisted his stunning features into something hard and poisonous. He made a fist and tried to smash through a shield that had formed around her. It didn't work any better the second time.

Breana added fervent thanks to her cries for help. Danu was

here. She was listening after all, and her magic—mixed with Breana's—formed the invisible barrier. She wanted to spit in Andras' face, ridicule him right back, but she didn't have any power to spare.

The air around her brightened, separating into motes of multicolored light that pulsed with strong magic. The Dark Angel's head snapped to one side as if someone had punched him. Power roared from him in a blaze of red heat. Tendrils of fire drilled through the protections around her, and she batted at places her hair and clothing caught fire. Frantic, she tucked the long ends of her hair beneath the neck of her sweater and gathered power close, shoring up her protective enchantment.

A harsh thwacking sound jolted her, and Andras' left arm bent at an unnatural angle. He struggled, wrenched it away, only to have it bend nearly double again. He bellowed in agony, and a pyre of flames scorched the bedroom's high ceiling. Smoke filled the room until she choked on it.

Since he couldn't get to her any other way, compulsion thickened the air around her until it felt like molten silver, drawing, sucking, pulling her inexorably toward him. Breana ripped her gaze away after she took a step in his direction. Hopelessness rushed in on compulsion's heels, filling her with profound despair. When she realized she'd drawn a blade from where she kept it in a sheath dangling from her waist, her hand spasmed, fingers dropping the knife. Except it didn't hit the floor. Suspended in midair, it worked its way back toward her hand.

"No!" she thundered and the blade clattered to the patterned rug beneath her feet. Desperation jolted her, and she funneled power into a fine point focused right at his neck. She imagined her magic boring through his defenses, bursting the major vessels running to and from his heart. Strength from the goddess cascaded down her spine, adding punch to her spell.

Andras grappled with the side of his neck. Lines of strain corded it, and he made a chopping motion with one hand. "Fine," he growled. "Keep your puny witch magic." He shook his fist at her. "Know this, Breana Giraud. I always get what I want. Sometimes it takes a while, but I never give up."

A harsh boom rocked her back on the balls of her feet, and he disappeared in a haze of fire that left a disgusting burned smell hanging in the air.

Breath rattled from her chest, and Breana fell to her knees, arms extended before her in supplication. "Goddess. You enhanced my power and rescued me from him. How can I ever thank you?"

Words reverberated in her head. *"Keep your heart and mind pure. Believe in your goodness and your power. They're the only things that will save you in the end."*

With a shimmer of golden light, the goddess energy departed. After the pitched battle between good and evil that had played itself out in her bedroom, the absence of any magic but her own was a relief—until she remembered the wraiths.

Where was everyone?

Lurching to her feet, she stumbled to a window and pushed what was left of her power outward seeking information. She'd figured she'd be weak, but she didn't have enough magic left to reach beyond the front fence line.

It was far enough.

Wrapped in a blaze of white light, Chris, Joshua, and Hester were killing wraiths by the score. Andras might be gone, but his pets were still passing out grief.

It didn't matter how tired she was, or how depleted her magic, she had to help. With a quick prayer to Danu to lend her strength, she bolted from her room and down the stairs, half running, half shambling. As she pelted down risers, she remembered when the stairwell had been packed full of wraiths. She'd lain unconscious that day, ensorcelled by her husband who still lived.

Abigail had taken a big chance and called her back. By the goddess, she'd make certain the other witch hadn't saved her for naught. No one realized then just how much Black Magick she still had stored within her.

*Good thing. Abigail would've left me wandering in the darkness, and the enforcers would've finished me with mage fire.*

She raced out the front door, channeling power before her, and hoping to hell it would be enough to cut through a wraith or two. No point being out here if she was nothing but dead weight.

Joshua sensed Breana's energy before he saw her, but he couldn't risk switching his focus away from a veritable army of wraiths. Undead who preyed on the living, they were a true scourge. Breana trotted to Hester's side, and shock raced through him. Pure white light streamed from her. He blinked hard, certain his imagination was out of control.

A knowing grin tugged at the corners of Hester's mouth, and the light surrounding Breana took on more of a golden hue, simmering with witch power as Hester added her magic to the mix. Standing shoulder to shoulder, the women lobbed death blows at the wraiths, and the noxious creatures burst into putrid-smelling fire.

As quickly as they'd converged on the house, the wraiths vanished. One minute there were at least fifty of them, and the next none.

"What the hell?" Chris demanded, breathing hard.

Breana turned to him. "Easy to explain. Andras showed up here. The wraiths were his special gift to keep you busy so he could make off with me."

Joshua focused his power and scanned Breana up and down. She was still glowing, but the numinous light was beginning to fade. Fear gripped him. She was particularly vulnerable to Black Magick right now. What had happened to his family rushed in, and he cast his mage gift in a wide net, testing, checking, making certain the Dark Angel hadn't corrupted Breana, snuck a little evil in around the edges. Hester's intercession was still new enough, it wouldn't take much to offset it.

"No need for that, lad." Hester was grinning like a particularly satisfied cat. "Breana had enough presence of mind to call for Danu. From the feel of things, our goddess answered her plea." Hester's smile faded, and her brogue thickened, as she aimed her next words at Breana. "And why dinna ye call for any of us?"

"I couldn't. He shielded the room I was in."

Breana closed her teeth over her lower lip. Now that she was herself again, exhaustion rolled off her in waves, and protectiveness surged through Joshua. He wanted to hold her close, make certain she found a bed, and stand guard over her until she was well-rested.

"If he shielded the room," Chris' words broke into Joshua's musings, "how'd you escape?"

"I called on Danu, begged for her help. Andras underestimated both of us—rather badly it turned out." Breana curled her lips into a derisive sneer.

"Is he dead?" Hester's question was low, feral. "Now that would be a piece of unexpected good news."

Breana shook her head. "No. Not even particularly badly injured. His parting shot was that I hadn't seen the last of him."

Joshua kept his thoughts to himself, but as far as he was concerned, he wasn't letting Breana out of his sight, even if it meant camping outside her door all night, every night. He balled his hands into fists. Next time the Dark Angel showed his face, he'd be ready for him. In the meantime, they all needed food and rest.

"Come inside." He focused his words on everybody, but kept a close eye on Breana as she trudged across the muddy yard. Rain still splattered everything, just not as heavily as before. Once they were all within, he elbowed Chris. "Let's wind wards around this place, and then I'll get something going to feed us."

Hester came up to him. "So long as ye're passing out tasks, what will I be doing?" she inquired so dryly Joshua muffled a snort.

"If I assigned you something you disagreed with, I have a feeling you'd ignore me."

She looked askance at him, but didn't comment, so he murmured, "Keep an eye on Breana."

"I'd have done that anyway," Hester countered and turned to leave. "We'll be in the kitchen."

"Witches," Chris muttered. "Gotta love 'em."

"We do. Otherwise we wouldn't have signed on as Coven enforcers," Joshua countered. "Now help me set this spell. At least it'll buy us due warning if unwelcome visitors come calling."

He and Chris worked in an efficient silence. Maybe they should leave Breana's ranch, at least for a little while. They could close up the house and not take more than horses could carry. A wagon would only slow them down.

"Looks like we're done with this part," Chris observed.

"Hold up a minute. How would you feel about leaving?"

The other enforcer angled his body so he faced Joshua.

"Hester just got here. She may not feel like traveling again so soon." He inhaled sharply, his nostrils flaring. "If you're thinking another location will make it harder for Andras to find us, I'm not so certain that's true. They track energy as well as we do. If he wants Breana—and it's sounding like he does—I believe we're better off rounding up a few more of us and taking a stand right here."

"Probably wise. I couldn't figure out anywhere close by we could go. The places I consider safe havens are on the other side of the country."

"Come on." Chris clapped him on the shoulder. "Let's see if the women need our help. I'm starving, and the sooner there's a meal on the table, the better I'll like it."

"I'll just do one circuit of the barn and yard, then I'll be along. I know I said I'd cook, but four is too many making food. We'd just trip over one another."

"Excellent! I'd much rather draw kitchen duty than more time in the rain. I'm starting to wonder if I'll ever dry out."

Joshua retraced his steps, power deployed about him like a banner. If Andras or any of his minions were spying on them, he'd track it down and plug whatever hole Black Magick had carved in the surrounding ether.

He extended his arms in front of him, fingertips curved, ready to launch bursts of power at the least provocation. No waiting to see if a disturbance came from friend or foe. After the past few hours, any power he felt beyond his own was suspect.

While he patrolled, his thoughts turned to Breana. He'd never truly believed he had any chance at all with her—until he began to suspect Don was hiding something major from the rest of the Coven. Enforcers kept witches in line, making certain shady witches were culled. Depending on the gravity of their sins, their punishment varied from simple banishment to death by mage fire. One of the problems had been that Don was highly placed in Coven government. Those witches were far more difficult to bring to justice because their magic was more potent, so they did a better job hiding dalliances with evil. Another problem was if an enforcer tossed out an accusation that ended up being wrong, they'd be held to answer before Coven justice.

Joshua had been biding his time, keeping as close an eye as he could on things, but the Giraud mansion outside New York City was shrouded in spells so opaque he couldn't see through them. When Don announced he and Breana would pave the way for the Coven to regroup west of the Mississippi, he'd been met with enthusiasm.

Escalating tensions between North and South over slavery made everyone nervous, and the sparsely settled west seemed like a safer location. Joshua had volunteered to be part of a group of enforcers loosely shadowing Luke as he chaperoned the Giraud's child on her long trek to Salt Lake City.

But things had gone to hell.

The child had been lost to evil, and they'd nearly lost Abigail to darkness as well. Joshua made a hooked sign against evil, and breath hissed through his clenched teeth. He'd made it to the back of the barn. All the horses and goats were resting. A good sign since they'd be neighing, baahing, snorting, and stamping if something wicked were near.

Could he keep his word about giving Breana the space she needed?

Just thinking about her made him ache to hold her, close his mouth over hers, and enter her body. A lust-tinged shudder rushed through him, and his cock sprang to hypersensitive hardness. He ducked inside the barn and found his way to a darkened corner, stroking his engorged flesh.

It had been a while since he'd come. A few strokes should do the job, make it possible for him to be in the same room with Breana without making a fool out of himself. He grappled with the laces of his trousers, and curved his hand around his penis. Teasing strokes gave way to the hard pulls that would bring him off.

His heart thudded against his chest as he worked himself, and a vision of Breana, long blonde hair cascading down her naked body, filled his mind. He imagined her breasts, nipples pebbled with wanting him, peeking through her thick curtain of hair. Would her nipples be strawberry colored? Or perhaps darker, more coppery?

He cupped his balls with his other hand, pressing on the spot behind them that drove him mad with lust. Breana was kissing him now, her full mouth closed over his and her tongue driving into his mouth. She raked her hands down his back, leaving trails of passion with her long nails. The sweet musk of her arousal rose around them, and she ground the heat of her center against his erection.

Joshua panted and gasped as he worked himself faster. Just as he imagined pushing into the scorching heat of her body, semen rushed from him. He came hard and kept jacking himself, urging his balls to empty. When he got his breathing under control, he wiped his hand on a hay bale, and set himself to rights. Small flares of mage fire obliterated any trace of his seed. It would be just plain sloppy to leave anything for an enemy to latch onto and use against him.

At least somewhat confident he could make it through a meal without spending the whole time making cow eyes at Breana, he let himself out of the barn and continued his transit of the yard. He was nearly back at the house when he stopped, probing more intently with his power. The disturbance was subtle, but something didn't feel quite right. The deeper he delved, the more elusive the evil taint became until he was almost convinced he'd imagined it.

Almost.

This puzzle required stealth because the source of the not-right place was aware of him. Nothing shifted so unpredictably unless it was attempting to remain hidden. Joshua sheathed his power, walked a few feet, then spun and blanketed the spot with enchantment. The Utah afternoon shattered around him. Because his power ran wide open, he wasn't shielded, and whoever was wielding Black Magick knew it.

Joshua groped for the edges of whatever was dragging him away, fighting its pull. When he couldn't get a grip on enough of anything to anchor himself in his world, he used the enforcer's special telepathy to alert Chris.

*"Watch over Breana,"* he told the other enforcer. *"Black Magick just nabbed me. I'll get myself shut of this mess and wipe a wide swath through those bastards on my way out."*

# CHAPTER 8

Breana looked up from the skillet she was stirring. Hester had made a fuss about her doing anything, but Breana convinced her that she was better off busy. Idleness would give her too much time to think.

Chris lurched to his feet and was halfway out the door before her fuzzy brain interpreted his action as unusual. "What is it?" she called after him.

"Joshua. Something's happened to him."

"In that case, we'll all go," Hester said, her tone harsh, resolute.

"Hurry," Chris gritted. "These kind of trails go cold fast."

"What kind are those?" Breana moved her pan off the heat to a warming shelf and ripped off her apron, trading it for her still damp cloak.

"You'll figure it out fast enough. Come on." Done waiting, Chris turned on his heels and sprinted out of the kitchen.

Breana exchanged a glance with Hester and hustled after Chris. "Will we ever see the end of this?" she muttered, not expecting a reply.

"Och, if we canna end this, 'twill be the death knell for humankind. They may not like or trust us, but our magic is all that stands betwixt them and their lives falling prey to darkness."

Despair crept in at Hester's words. They were so few. What hope did they have? They'd fight until they died, but—

Hester closed a hand over her forearm, fingers pinching until Breana yelped. "One of the ways they win is by convincing us they're stronger. They're not, or ye'd be at Andras' side just now, not mine."

Breana shook herself, but the blasted blurriness shrouded her mind. She was tired, but she had to get past that. They caught up to Chris. He stood about fifty feet from the back door, hands spread wide, chanting in an old form of Gaelic. Power lines radiated outward from him, and strain made the bones in his face stand out.

Hester looped a hand over one of his forearms, linking her magic with his. Breana did the same, hoping to hell she wasn't so depleted she'd drag energy from their spell, rather than building on it. A high-pitched hum filled the air, and a jagged gateway grew visible before her.

Breana gaped in horrified fascination. This must be a portal between worlds. She'd heard about them, knew they existed, but the magic to command their appearance had always been beyond her star. The opening became more substantial, surrounded by black fire. Questions crowded, but this wasn't a time to ask any of them. Were all other worlds controlled by evil? If not, did magic that could help their cause exist beyond a psychic veil?

"Your mind wanders." Hester's words cut like a bullwhip.

Breana yanked herself back to the present. Black Magick had dragged Joshua through the gateway. Chris' magic had been strong enough to open the fissure once again. If they all poured everything they had into supporting his working, maybe, just maybe they'd get Joshua back unscathed.

Since not much magic remained at her disposal, Breana hooked into anger. Her fury at Don for the choices he made that cost them their only child. Her incredulity that a man she'd once cared about—trusted—could've become so narcissistic as to believe promises of limitless power were worth bartering your immortal soul to the Dark Angel.

The gateway grew larger, brighter, and a rim of red fire joined the black. Like Hester, Breana had an affinity for fire, so she focused her anger at its dead center. Power exploded, and the witch-spawned fire surged upward.

"Aye!" Hester crowed. "More." She pulled the ruby from the folds of her jacket. Magic shot through the gem, right into the heart of the fire. The hum grew louder, more strident, sounding like an enormous beehive. Gears ground, and bright, white steam filled the air, puffing upward to join the flames.

A scene formed within the gateway. Joshua grappled with three demons. One raked its talons down his back. Another had a scaled arm draped around his neck. The third's mouth was attached to his neck, drinking his blood.

Breana's fury ignited, and weariness dropped away. She knew this particular scene from Hell. She'd lived it when Don dragged her into the demon's world, a world powered by Black Magick. The feel of the demons' heat, their dry, scaly skin, and their noxious charnel pit smell came alive again. This batch stood man height. They sported red hides, horns, and sharp, red talons that sprouted from their hands and feet. She'd come across others before that were all black. Nausea burned in her gorge, but she swallowed it back. She could be sick later—when this was over.

Joshua was in this situation because of her. She'd be damned if his love for her would cost him his life. Light fanned out from

Hester's gem, and the sound of unseen gears grew so loud her ears ached.

Chris moved toward Joshua, one determined step after another. Fire rimmed him once he crossed the gateway and Breana started after him amid the stench of burning hair and clothes.

"Remain here," Hester ordered. "We can do more good this way. Keep your power flowing. It supports mine. We must keep the gateway open. The other side will be doing everything they can to shut it with Chris and Joshua on the wrong side."

Breana gritted her teeth until they felt close to cracking. The magic flowing from her to Hester was amplified by the gem, and it circled back through them in a self-perpetuating arc. Good thing because no matter how horrified and determined she was to not lose either enforcer to Black Magick, her power was far from limitless.

Chris reached Joshua and drew one of his revolvers. He shot the demon attached to Joshua's neck first. It let go, hissing and snarling. Joshua drew a gun and pistol-whipped the demon across its horny snout. Fire shot from its little piggy eyes—until Chris shot point blank into both of them, one right after the other, effectively blinding the creature.

Joshua reached behind him, firing blind, aiming for the one choking him. He missed, but Chris pointed right at the demon's temple and fired. Black ichor flowed, and the damned thing let go. The one that had been shredding Joshua's back hissed and snapped before disappearing in a burst of black flames.

"Now!" Hester shrieked. "I'll punch everything I can out of the gem's power. Ye help drag them to the other side of the portal so I can close the goddamned thing and seal it off for good."

Breana sprinted forward, but the closer she got to the

gateway, the harder it was to move. How the hell had Chris managed to power through what felt like a thorny hedge dredged through with glue?

She ignored a million sharp points ripping holes in her flesh and set one foot ahead of the other. On the far side of the barrier, Chris and Joshua pushed and pulled one another forward. When one stumbled, the other took over as lead. They were lined single file. Presumably the man in front took the brunt of the punishment.

"Hurry!" Hester shouted.

A starburst of white light imploded in front of her, but at least it cut through the thorns, and the next half dozen steps were a little easier. They were enough. Amid gnashing gears and smoke so thick she almost couldn't see, Breana reached the fire-rimmed portal and pushed a hand through.

Someone—she couldn't see who—gripped her so hard she thought the small bones in her hand might break, but then Chris and Joshua staggered through the barrier.

"Get down," Hester cried. "On the ground. Now."

Joshua fell atop her. White hot magic rolled over them, singeing the air, turning it so bright she shut her eyes. Gears ratcheted to a crescendo that made her want to shield herself with magic except she didn't have any more. When silence finally descended, her ears rang so badly, she wondered if she'd ever hear normally again.

She bucked beneath Joshua's weight, but he didn't move, so she wriggled out from under him, realizing he must've passed out.

Next to them, Chris groaned and rolled to a sitting position.

Hester strode briskly to where they sprawled on the ground, looking as fresh as if a trainload of power hadn't just rolled through her. She eyed Chris. "Ye did a good piece of work today."

"Anytime, ma'am." He pushed upright. "Shit! That was way closer than I would've liked. We had a skinny little window after we dispatched those three. If we hadn't gotten out of there, another bunch would've shown up—and finished us."

"Doona dwell on what dinna happen," Hester pronounced. "Let's get Joshua inside so we can figure out if we need to do any healing."

Chris dug his hands into Joshua's armpits and hoisted him over one shoulder. Staggering under the other man's weight, he crossed the yard and climbed the steps.

"We could've helped carry him," Breana said softly and followed Chris.

"'Tis better this way," Hester said, flanking her. "Chris faced off against Hell to save his companion. Ye and I can take over once we're inside."

BREANA SAT next to Joshua where he lay in one of her home's many unused bedrooms. Chris had moved him here an hour ago, and she'd shooed him and Hester away. Since none of them had the healing gift, Joshua was as well off with her as he'd be with any of the others. She'd stripped off his leather shirt and cleaned the wounds in his neck and back. A huge, purpling bruise had formed around the front of his neck, like a macabre tattoo. With an assist from her depleted power, the abrasions were beginning to close, and when she bent close sniffing, she didn't detect any purulence.

He tossed and turned, muttering in Gaelic from time to time, but at least he wasn't feverish.

A soft knock sounded just before Chris came into the room. "How is he?"

"Maybe not quite as deeply unconscious as when you laid him down."

"Mmph." Chris moved to Joshua's feet and unlaced his boots, removing them along with his socks. "I was sure glad to see your hand sticking through into that perverted slime pit of a world. Grabbing hold was exactly the anchor I needed."

Breana straightened. "Could you have gotten out without me?"

"I don't know. Maybe." He grinned crookedly. "That's the wrong answer. What I'm supposed to say is, of course."

"No. You're supposed to tell me the truth—even if it's unsettling to hear."

"That's bullshit, brother." Joshua's deep, gravelly voice cut in. "Of course we'd have escaped. Hell, I was choreographing my exit when you arrived."

"Doing a fuckup of a job with it, I might say." Chris' smile broadened. "Welcome back, brother."

Breana bit her lip to keep tears from forming. "Thanks be to the goddess you're awake." She twisted and wrapped her arms awkwardly around him, retreating almost as fast. Heat from his naked chest seared her, and it was frightening how badly she wanted to run her fingertips over his heavily muscled frame—when he was awake. Her ministrations when he was out cold scarcely counted.

He'd said he cared about her, but hugging him was bold, even for a witch. Men liked to be the ones in charge of such things—until a relationship was established, and she and Joshua were a long way from that point.

"Good to be back." Joshua thrashed until he was in a sitting position and dropped his head into his hands. "Whiskey. Aw Jesus, I need whiskey. My head's splitting."

"I have tincture of laudanum." Breana dashed for the door. "Let me put something together. I'll run it past Hester. She's quite the potions expert, and maybe she'll know what's best after your skirmish with Black Magick. When I came back to myself after some of the places Don dragged me, nothing I tried worked…"

Her voice trailed off. She wanted to infuse hope, not instill despair. "I'm babbling. Back soon."

"The worst part was the blood sucking demon," Chris called after her. "They impart something from their saliva that enters the body. It goes away eventually, but the aftereffects can be damned unpleasant."

"Aren't the two of you a cheery bunch," Joshua groused. "Hug was nice, though. You can come back and do that again anytime."

A smile curved her lips as she hustled in search of Hester's definitive energy. The other witch was in a downstairs bedroom standing in front of a collection of gems and gears she'd set up on a table. The gears turned slowly, and light streamed through a circle of gemstones, making them glow one by one. Steam from water boiling atop a small brazier seemed to be what powered the gears.

"Aye?" Hester glanced Breana's way. "How's Joshua."

"Awake, and with a bastard of a headache."

"Not surprising."

"What can we give him?"

Hester made a sour face. "He'll get past it quicker under his own steam. Last thing he needs right now is more magic—from either side."

"How about whiskey—or laudanum?"

"No laudanum. He hasna been conscious long enough, and

we doona want to erode his hold on his senses. So long as he doesna get stinking drunk, whiskey is fine. A hangover will just make his headache worse. If ye're going after a bottle, leave a wee dram here on your way back upstairs."

"Of course. What are you about?"

"Creating fortifications. We need a break, so I'm reworking this machine to shield us long enough to get some rest."

"You'll have to tell me more, but not just now. Is it steam that drives the gears? And are those the gears that nearly deafened me while we were outside?"

"I doona understand the why of it, but whenever something enchanted by the gears has been activated—like my ruby, for example—ye can hear them grind. And 'tis steam mixed with magic that powers them." She made a snorting sound. "Thought ye dinna want to know more right now, and I could really use that whiskey." Hester's tone was pointed, and Breana understood the other witch must be as exhausted as the rest of them.

"Hang on. I'll be back very soon."

Breana stopped by the sideboard in the dining room, poured a jot into a glass for Hester, and took the rest of the bottle back upstairs. The men were deep in conversation, but they looked up when she came into the room.

"More of us are on their way," Chris informed her.

"How many and when?" Breana handed the bottle to the two men after drinking from it.

"Tomorrow night or the day after," Chris replied. "Only one I'm sure of is Sam, but he said he'd rustle up others."

"Yeah, if we can manage to stay boots up until then, we should be fine. I always liked Sam. He's solid." Joshua tipped the bottle and drank deep.

"How'd you end up in a dark world?" Breana dragged a chair over and dropped into it across from the two men.

"Stupidity, or hubris. Maybe both. I suspected they had to be close, and I found them spying on us. Once I located the rent in the ether, I tried to blow it up." Joshua shrugged, looking sheepish.

"More like it blew up in your face," Chris grunted. "What was that crap about *don't worry about me, I'll get out of this mess?*"

"I was working on it." A defensive note roughened Joshua's voice.

"You saved my life when Alistair MacDuff possessed me. Even if you hadn't, no way in hell I'd have stood by knowing the other side had you."

"I outrank you, and that was an order," Joshua growled and drank some more.

"Goddesses' teeth! Would the two of you stop trying to one up each other?" Breana rolled her eyes. "Besides, I didn't think enforcers had a command hierarchy."

"We don't," Chris grumbled. "Not exactly. I'm going to the barn and fall on my face."

"Not a good idea," Joshua cut in. "In case something else happens, we all need to be in the house."

"Pains me to admit it, but I agree with you. I wasn't thinking straight." Chris turned to Breana. "Any preference where I fall on my face?"

"None. Pick any empty bedroom. When Don and I built this place, we assumed we'd have lots of Coven guests." She made a face. "At least I assumed that. He likely assumed we'd be entertaining the Dark Angel and his ilk." She hesitated, but the next words wanted out, so she gave them free rein. "Is it only the dark who maintain other worlds?"

"Of course not," Joshua answered. "On the good magic side, though, the border worlds are closed to the living."

Breana shook her head. "Doesn't seem fair. We could use an army to shore us up."

"Don't discount spirits," Chris said and slipped out the door. "Ask me more about them after I wake up."

"Do you have any idea what he meant by that?" Breana demanded.

"Yes and no. The spirit world is a mixed bag. You can't control them in the same way you interact with the living. Most mages steer clear because of how unpredictable shades are once you've raised them."

She thought they might not have a choice about who helped them—beggars scarcely got to be choosers—but kept her mouth shut about that. "How are you feeling?"

"Like warmed over horse shit, but I'll live." He patted the bed next to where he sat.

Breana hesitated. If she got that close, she wasn't certain she'd keep her hands—or anything else—to herself. Joshua needed rest. So did she. Who knew when the next skirmish would materialize from Black Magick? Focusing on that was way more important than the confusing welter of feelings turning her brain to mush and her nether regions to pounding hunger for the man across the room.

His gaze sharpened, became speculative. "Which is exactly why you should come here. I'd get up, but I'm far from at my best." Without giving her a chance to protest, he went on. "Yeah, I was inside your head just now, and you're right. The next attack is impossible to predict. In the meantime, you felt mighty good when you wrapped your arms around me."

"Maybe we should wait until the rest of this sorts itself out—" she began, her words sounding like the feeblest of protests. Joshua was stunning with his hair like liquid flame and eyes that were shading to gold as he gazed at her. Something wild and untamed flared in their depths, and he bounded to his feet in a burst of magic that must've cost him because it placed him inches from her.

He threaded his arms around her, but the kiss she anticipated didn't come. Instead, he drank her in, his gaze roving over her as if she were the finest thing he'd ever laid eyes on. "I never thought I'd be fortunate enough to hold you, feel you against me."

"If you felt that way, why didn't you ever show up on Beltane or any of the other festivals? Witches aren't exactly known for faithfulness on those occasions."

"I didn't want you that way." His voice roughened. "Not that I've been a monk, but sex just to lose myself in a woman's body lost its allure long ago. Besides—" a soft smile began in his eyes before reaching his mouth "—once I'd had a taste, I'd probably have challenged Don to a duel at sunrise. And gotten kicked out of my Coven enforcer spot for my troubles. There'd have been hell to pay finding another job after that—assuming Don's buddies didn't string me up."

She grinned wryly and snugged her arms around his naked back, delighting in the liquid silk of his skin beneath her fingertips. "Our communities are small," she agreed. "I never figured out how he did it, but Don maintained his good name up until the head-to-head confrontation when you and Chris and Sam and Luke showed up here."

"We already had our suspicions. Didn't take much to stoke the flames, but those aren't the flames I want to feed just now."

He cupped the side of her face in one calloused hand and closed his mouth gently over hers. The kiss was gentle, tentative. It gave her a choice as he teased and nibbled her lips, biting and sucking. Where it was sandwiched between their bodies, his cock swelled to fullness and pressed tantalizingly against her belly.

Breana tightened her hold on him and opened her mouth to his tongue. He tasted of well-aged magic, and the heat of his need rose, filling the air with urgency. He traced the line of her chin with his hand, running his other one down her back to snug her against his ridged flesh.

Her breath quickened as she leaned into him, and her nipples peaked into points of hunger pressed against the naked flesh of his chest. When he jammed a leg between hers, she writhed against him, welcoming the heat from his body, obvious even through layers of skirts and petticoats.

He broke their kiss. "Are you sure?" he rasped. "Do you care about me?"

She struggled for truth. "You're such a beautiful man. Any woman would—"

"Not what I asked," he broke in. "We're not talking about *any woman*. We're talking about you and me."

"I'd be a liar if I said I didn't notice you. And an even bigger one if I said I never imagined what it would be like to sleep with you, but I never let myself hope for a future for myself. I still can't quite believe Don's dead, and I'm free."

"Yet both those things are true. For the third time, Breana. Do you care for me? Could you love me?"

"Yes I care about you, but I don't know if I can love anyone." She straightened and untangled herself from his embrace. "Don't you see? I'm damaged. Broken. I don't know how fixable any of it is, and until I'm whole, I don't have much to offer anyone." She took a shaky breath. "I can make love with you, but beyond that, no promises."

He surprised her by brushing his mouth over hers in the gentlest of kisses. "Then we'll wait until you want me enough to take a chance on a future together. I told you I'd wait for you, and I will. Now get some rest. I'm going to."

Desire still burned bright. It had been so long since she'd made love with someone, she wanted him back in her arms. Wanted more kisses that turned her dizzy with craving him.

"I want you too, darling. Neither of us are youngsters anymore. We can wait until it feels right to us both. You're not as damaged as you think, but me telling you won't help you see it. You have to find that path on your own."

"You're feeding my words back to me."

"I guess I am. It's not easy to chase you out of here, but you'll know when the time is right. I want to make love to all of you—heart, mind, soul, and body. Just having your body, wonderful as it would be, isn't enough."

Warmth smelling of spiced mead moved from the top of her head to the soles of her feet, and she realized he was bathing her in his magic. "Thank you for loving me." Tears were close to the surface.

"I fought it for years, but it was never a choice. Not really. From the first moment I laid eyes on you, you were the only woman for me."

"That's quite a compliment."

"And a good place to stop for now." He walked her to the door, kissed her forehead, and deposited her in the hall, shutting the door between them.

Breana made her way back downstairs. She needed to talk, and Hester had always been a good listener.

# CHAPTER 9

Joshua lay back on the bed. His groin ached with unslaked lust, but his spirit was alight with joy. He closed his eyes and relived every moment of holding Breana in his arms, of kissing her and feeling her nipples harden against his chest. She'd been on the verge of spending when he'd asked if she was certain. It was one of the hardest things he'd ever done—to stop when they were so close to making love.

Part of him kicked himself. Most men would've taken what was offered and sorted the pieces out later. Hell, had it been a hundred years back—or maybe even fifty—he'd have done the same thing.

But not today. And not with Breana. She was too important to him.

He shut his eyes and assessed the reservoir that held his magic. While far from recovered, he had enough to mount a defense—should the need arise. He sent power zinging in a wide arc. The women were downstairs. Chris slept two doors down the hall from him. When he pushed wider, he sensed enforcers moving closer, but they weren't near enough to see who'd heeded Chris' call. If he had his druthers, he wanted Luke's solid magic by their side, but he wouldn't arrive for quite a while yet. He and his wife, Abigail, planned to join the Coven's wagon train moving everyone from the Atlantic coast to the Salt Lake area. It was likely the group had yet to set out. Or if they had, they hadn't been on the trail very long.

His mind was wandering because of the vast amounts of power he'd expended. While not quite ready to admit he'd have been lost without Chris and the women's assistance, the probable outcome wouldn't have been pretty. The demons wouldn't have killed him. No. They'd have tried to turn him. Failing that, they'd have kept him alive and fed off his power. Not so different from what the Church did to his kin.

The hypnotic hum of gears emanated from the room where the women were working. Nothing constant, but the energy flashed off and on. He tried to figure out what they were up to, but it eluded him. He was curious, though, about whatever Hester had ginned up to concentrate her power. Even though she'd remained in the background, he felt positive her magic was what had allowed Chris and Breana to make their way through the negative energy field and into the demon-spawned world just beyond the veil.

He needed rest, but his mind was too busy for sleep to have a chance of claiming him, so he settled for a soothing cadence that focused healing magic through him. His back was still plenty torn-up, and his neck ached from the two-pronged demon attack. The one choking him had held him in place, so the other could feed on his blood, draining his power. A shudder ran through him at the memory of the smarmy feel of Black Magick against his body.

Once he'd done all he could to encourage his wounds to knit

together, it was time to get up and moving. The only reason to remain prone would be if he was asleep. Since that wasn't happening, he was better off working at the myriad tasks that kept the ranch running smoothly. Ranching and farming were nothing if not hard work. Joshua grinned wryly. He'd chosen a life in the saddle. It had its own set of challenges, but at least they varied day by day.

Would Breana want to remain here? Or would she take to life on the road? At least until the children started coming. Maybe they could blend the two. Be vagabonds for the first few years, and then…

"I'm getting way ahead of the curve," he muttered. "She has to make some hard decisions first, be willing to offer up her heart. And trust I'll always care for her."

He got to his feet and pulled his leather shirt off the back of a chair. A quick look convinced him it would take hours with a needle and thread to repair. So much time, it might not be worth it. He fingered the leather where it hung in shreds, shrugged, and put the shirt back on. Sewing was for the dark hours, by lantern light.

From below, the gear noises ratcheted up. They drew him like a magnet, the pull of their magic strong. He strode from the room, aiming for brisk, but barely making half that as he walked down the hallway and the back staircase. The room where the women worked pulsed with light. Brightness seeped around the edges of the closed door.

He stood still for long moments sampling the feel of the power. It was witch—yet ever so much more. He delved deeper, intent on making certain the power was pure and not some perversion of Black Magick. Relief coursed through him. It may not be anything he'd ever felt before, but at least it wasn't evil.

Joshua shook his head, considering the tingling sensation that bombarded him.

What the hell had Hester done to magnify her magic tenfold? Furthermore, was it something the rest of them could learn? Or at least tap into? He reached for the doorknob, but ran up against something that bit back before his fingers connected to the metal. He tried again, but an even stronger unpleasant jab traveled up his arm.

Growing more impressed by the moment, he moved his hand upward. Would the power keeping him from opening the door allow him to knock? Before he got the chance to try, the door flew open with a pink-cheeked Hester on the other side.

"Get on inside. Don't stand there gaping. I need the door shut. Magic's escaping."

She sounded so much like the crusty witch he remembered from before she and her husband went west that Joshua laughed as he sidled through the door. It shut behind him of its own accord. Clearly magic was running the show here.

*So what else is new?*

He peered through clouds of steam that came from a cast iron caldron perched atop a squat, black brazier sitting on the hearth. When he breathed deep, the steam felt like a balm, healing his injuries from the inside. Could the surfeit of magic in the room possibly sense what he needed?

Breana nodded at him from a three-legged stool near the brazier. She employed a flow of magic to direct the steam toward a stack of five gears arranged in descending order. The larger one powered the smaller one adjacent to it. Now that he was right next to them, they weren't any louder than they'd been upstairs. Intriguing, since he'd figured they'd be deafening up this close.

Streams of multihued light swirled around the gears, almost

as if they were gathering momentum. Every once in a while, a tendril of light arrowed from the smallest gear to an array of gemstones laid out on a buff-colored square of tanned deer hide. The magic picked a particular gem, and it glowed softly, perhaps absorbing power.

All in all, the effect was mesmerizing, and soothing in an odd sort of way. "What is all this?" He spread his arms expansively, and one of the beams of light wrapped around him.

"Do ye want the short version, or the long?" Hester looked up from turning the gemstones.

"Tell me enough so I understand. How'd you come up with this magical system? And what exactly does it do?"

"You're living part of your last question," Breana spoke up. "Your back and neck are glowing. By the time you leave here, I'd wager that all evidence of the Black Magick attack will be eradicated."

A quick internal survey validated her words. His neck had stopped aching, and the raw spots on his back didn't throb as intensely. "So this power is intelligent and doesn't need one of us there directing it?"

"Aye and nay," Hester replied. "I designed it to seek out and destroy Black Magick and its aftereffects. It sensed ye'd been wounded, and was quick to step in."

"Keep talking." Joshua gestured with hand.

Hester nodded at Breana. "May as well take a break. I canna talk and keep atop the stones and what they need."

Breana stood. "I'll get something going in the kitchen. Food's been light today. We never did get to eat that last meal. Not sure it's salvageable, but if it's not, I'll start from scratch." She offered Joshua a shy smile that thrust his heart into a stuttering gallop and walked out of the room.

When he realized the entirety of his attention was focused on the door that had just shut behind Breana, he turned back toward Hester. "I'm listening again."

"The first gems came to me," she began, "back on the Isle of Skye. I've always believed the goddess gifted them because I had sore need to escape the Dark Angel long afore he'd taken that title."

Joshua sensed a whole other tale lurked behind those words, but he didn't ask. It wasn't important right now, and this was.

"Once I got to the American Colonies, I dinna use the gems—and the first three were a ruby, a star sapphire, and a garnet—for long years. What Breana and I were trying to do here was add to my collection of power stones. Some seem better at concentrating magic than others, but I'm getting ahead of things.

"When my husband grew gravely ill, and my natural witch power couldna heal him, I remembered the stones and distilled magic through them." Hester narrowed her eyes. "Damn if it dinna work. His heart became stronger. For a while I thought mayhap I'd actually defeated time, but such wasna to be."

"I'm sorry," Joshua murmured. "I recall how much you loved him."

"Thank you." Hester cleared her throat, and when she glanced at him her eyes shone with unshed tears. "Getting on with things, there came a time when the gems alone dinna help, so I rigged up what ye see here. It's grown over time. When I began, I only had two gears, but the resonance of the five worked far better. Mechanism's actually quite simple. Steam drives the gears, and the gears concentrate power that loads the stones."

"Like a magnetic charge?"

"Exactly. It lasts quite a while, but the stones need to be recharged after they've run through a particular amount of magic. Today, I spared nothing, so I ran the ruby dry."

"Could any of us use the stones?"

"Aye—and nay. 'Tis why Breana and I were down here. These gems—" she pointed "—came from Breana's jewelry case. She never had much of a love affair with gemstones, but her husband, bastard that he was, showered her with jewelry. No doubt trying to make up for being a total rogue.

"Some gems, like the garnet, never responded to anything I did to waken it, but it jumped to Breana's command a little bit ago."

Joshua knit his brows in thought. "So it's a multifaceted interface that requires both the gem's energy and the mage's special magic."

"'Twould appear so. As should be obvious, I'm still learning about this."

"If we all had power stones at our disposal," he persisted, "it might make us invincible." Excitement coursed through him. This was the edge they'd always needed in their long running fight against Black Magick.

"Slow down, laddie. 'Tisn't something ye can learn overnight. I've spent years—"

"Yes, but we can profit from your errors. So we'll be that much farther ahead of things since we're not starting from nothing. Other enforcers should be here tomorrow, and—"

"How many and who?"

"I don't know, but Chris might. All he told me was Sam and whoever else he could find on short notice."

Hester returned her attention to the gears. They'd quieted, and she directed a stream of power at the brazier. Water bubbled, steam billowed up, and the gears clattered back into action. Once their power built, light streamed outward again, and she moved the stones around until one began to shimmer with an inner glow.

"'Tis far from precise," she murmured. "Like trying to capture a moonbeam. Betimes none of the gems light. Today, they're more cooperative."

"Maybe they sense we need their help."

"Maybe so. Come close and give this a try. Your magic is different from mine, and ye're a man, so the energy differential will be altered along that dimension too. Start with the stones. Hold each one. Sense their energy. When one calls to you, direct the brazier to spin the gears and weave your magic in with them. The result should envelop the gem ye picked and give you a medium to concentrate your power."

"Sounds simple enough," he muttered, reminding himself that Hester was both accomplished and powerful. If she saw the process as arbitrary, slippery, he'd do well to bring his best effort forward.

BREANA MOVED about the kitchen turning out a meal, but her mind kept returning to Joshua. When she'd thrown her heart open to Hester, her old mentor had listened carefully until Breana ran out of words. Much of what she'd said was that she was scared to share her heart with anyone ever again. Don had hurt her as profoundly as a man could hurt a woman. His slippage into evil had been so unexpected and irrevocable, it changed their life forever.

Dead was one thing. How long would it take before he left her dreams, her memories?

"Never." Hester had answered that question, but it was almost the only one she'd responded to. After the clipped *never*, that almost disappeared into Gaelic, she'd added, "For ye doona forget wickedness of that magnitude. Nor do ye want to. The knowledge of how close darkness is to us all keeps you honest—and vigilant."

"Awk!" Breana looked at the amount of pepper in her mortar and pestle, and realized if she tossed the whole amount into dinner, it would become inedible.

For the next span of time, she chopped, stirred, kneaded, and got her oven up to baking temperature. Only when she had a skillet full of venison and onions, bread baking, and greens bubbling in hog fat did she let her thoughts drift again. Hester hadn't told her what to do, but Breana hadn't expected she would.

It wasn't as if she didn't know Joshua. She'd known him for years, but hadn't viewed him in a romantic light because for most of that time, she'd been reasonably happily married. What was between her and Don hadn't been perfect, but it was better than what many couples had. At least they'd respected one another, and cared enough not to run roughshod over each other's sensitive spots.

Until Don made a deal with darkness.

"If it's fear that's holding me back," she said to the empty kitchen, "what am I most afraid of?"

She winced at her bald-faced question. The likelihood of Joshua joining forces with Black Magick was slim to none, so there'd be no repeat of the disaster she'd lived the last two years. Was the problem that she didn't know if she could return his love?

*Not just his. Anyone's.*

*So was I planning to live out my life alone?*

The question stopped her cold. She'd never envisioned herself as a maiden aunt type. She was still young enough to have more children, and she'd always wanted a houseful of them.

Carolyn's birth had been hard, but she'd recovered from the damage.

*Whoa. Hold up there. I have no idea if he wants children. In truth, I don't know how he plans to live. If he wants to settle somewhere, or if his peripatetic existence is etched into his blood.*

She thought about it. She'd enjoyed her wagon journey across the country, but could she live without a permanent home for years on end?

No answer came.

She stirred supper and checked on her rolls, giving them a shot of magic to hurry things along. Once they were out of the oven, she banked her fire, moved the rest of supper to warming shelves, and made her way back to the downstairs bedroom where Hester had set up shop.

Energy pulsed, tangible long before she got to the door. She scented the air, tasting it, and recognized the tang of Joshua's unique magical signature. Hester must've gotten him involved in picking a gemstone.

*Good.*

The more practice all of them had picking and filling power stones with their magic, the faster the process would go next time round. Suspended from her neck by a length of leather, the garnet warmed where it nestled between her breasts, almost as if it sensed her thinking about it.

"Open." Rather than touch the door, she commanded its submission to her needs.

It swung inward, and she walked through, keeping her presence shrouded so as not to disturb Joshua's concentration.

He held a moonstone between thumb and forefinger. The large, oblong gem reflected all the colors of the rainbow, and they bathed his form in reflected light. A satisfied smile wreathed his face, adding to his almost ethereal beauty.

Breath caught in Breana's throat, and she moved farther into the room.

Hester caught her eye and shook her head ever so slightly, so Breana thickened the shrouding around herself, waiting.

"There." Joshua gazed at the moonstone. "It's done. My magic is linked to the stone's resonance." He twisted to face Hester. "You're a genius, madam witch."

"Nay. Just a determined woman who set out to keep her one true love by her side a little longer."

"As soon as Chris gets up, we'll have him select a stone."

"'Tis possible one of these will match up with his energy." Hester was clearly choosing her words carefully.

"If it doesn't, there must be at least one jewelry store in Salt Lake," Joshua replied. "I felt a difference immediately between how the moonstone sat in my palm, compared with the others. Chris—and the other enforcers—may have to dig a bit, but they'll find stones to complement their energy as well."

Breana understood fully. The garnet had come alive in her hand, whereas the other gems were inert. Nothing more than pretty pieces of highly compressed mineral dust.

Joshua tilted his head to one side; magical waves flowed outward from him in violet, teal, and deep green. "Breana. I know you're in here. Show yourself."

She dropped the ward wrapped about her. "Sorry. I didn't want to disturb you, and you were still pairing your energy with the moonstone when I came in."

"You could never bother me. I'm happy to see you."

"I'll take over in the kitchen until dinner's ready." Hester headed for the door.

"No need to do a thing except dish things up," Breana said.

"Then I'll find Chris and get the table laid."

"We'll be along presently." Joshua held the door for Hester. After shutting it carefully, he spun to face Breana.

She closed her teeth over her lower lip and battled an inane desire to throw herself into his arms. Reason squared off against the part of her that wanted him, and she stood rooted in place.

"Breana?"

She loved the sound of her name rolling off his tongue, half prayer, half entreaty. Raising her gaze from the dusty floorboards, she fell headlong into his eyes. Glowing and golden, they called to her, told her without words how much she meant to him.

When he opened his arms, she tossed caution to the four winds, walked into his offered embrace, and turned her face upward for a kiss.

# CHAPTER 10

*J*oshua sensed the change in Breana as soon as he noticed her presence in the room. Higher than a just-freed bird, he rode the crest of his success with the gemstone. Glowing softly, the moonstone pulsed in his hand. To have the woman he loved here to share his victory completed things, made them perfect.

He wanted to ask why she'd changed her mind, but talk could come later. He stroked the side of her face tenderly and absorbed her beauty. Sharp cheekbones lent her an exotic appearance. Unlike many blondes, her skin was tanned a rich golden color from all the outside work she did. Freckles scattered over her upturned nose and cheeks. Her eyes reminded him of the ocean on a stormy day. A deep, vibrant blue, they held gold flecks near their centers.

The corners of her mouth twitched. "If all you want to do is look, we can scoot on in and join Hester and Chris for supper. Before everything gets cold."

"It sounds hokey as shit, but you're so beautiful, I could look at you forever. I used to search out excuses to visit the Coven storeroom when you worked in there. And later on when you moved into the office." He hesitated. "Probably why I noticed before most anyone else when you started keeping to yourself. It was different enough, I wondered what had happened. Even asked Don once."

Breana narrowed her eyes. "Now that's intriguing. What'd he say by way of explanation?"

"That you'd been ill. Thanked me for my concern." He continued to caress her cheek and neck. "I'm ashamed to admit this, but it only occurred to me months later that he'd likely spelled his words to make certain I didn't dig any deeper."

"Maybe between the two of us, we can finally close off that chapter of things."

"No maybe about it."

He tightened his hold on her, loving the lush feel of her curves pressed against him, and lowered his mouth atop hers. Unlike their previous kiss upstairs, this one took off like a restless racehorse that had been penned up for far too long. She threaded her arms beneath his and splayed her hands across his back, drawing him close as she opened her mouth to his questing tongue.

Little panting moans filled air that thickened with the musk of their combined arousal. The moonstone was sandwiched between his hand and her back, and it pulsed with heat. If he looked at that hand, light would probably be streaming through it. She tasted sweet as he plumbed her mouth with his tongue, like honey wine rich with flower scents.

One of her hands traveled upward, and she wove her fingers into his hair. Her hips squirmed against his erect cock, and he positioned a leg between hers, glorying in the hunger they shared for each other. Now wasn't a time to do much more than tap the surface of that craving, though.

She snaked a hand between them and curved her fingers around his unbelievably sensitive ridged flesh. He groaned and pushed into the heat of her palm while she spread her legs wider and rode his thigh. Their kiss deepened, and she pushed her tongue into his mouth, sparring with him as she bit and sucked his lips. Pressed against his chest, her nipples felt like agates, and the moonstone throbbed in time with their lust.

She gripped him more firmly as he thrust into her hand, treading a ragged edge of control. Her hips settled into a tight rhythm, and he moved the hand with the moonstone between them. Too many layers of clothing to burrow beneath so he cupped her sex. Light indeed flowed through his fingers as he pressed his palm over the sensual juncture between her legs. She stroked him harder, and the leather of his trousers grew warm from friction.

Magic pounded from Breana in visible waves, and she cried out as her body dissolved in release. Though he tried to hold back, her arousal stoked his own to a white hot inferno. His favorite sexual fantasy, the one where he held Breana in his arms, had finally come true, and his body took over with a mind of its own. Semen juddered from him, urged on by her hand.

Gasping, panting, they clung to one another until their breathing slowed. "I haven't come that way since I was a maid." Breana laughed, and it warmed him.

"We'll see if we can't find a bed before long." He smoothed hair back from her flushed face, pleased beyond words at the evidence of her passion for him.

She fumbled with the laces of his pants.

"I can clean myself up," he protested.

"But then I wouldn't get to lay eyes on that wonderful cock." Her blue eyes twinkled merrily as she left his embrace long enough to pull a towel from a chest of drawers.

By the time she got back, he'd finished the unlacing job, but he didn't protest when she drew his still-hard cock from his trousers and wiped both him and the inside of his pants. Her fingers felt heavenly where they touched him, electric with promise.

"I'd love to take you upstairs—" she licked her tongue over lips swollen from their kisses "—but we should make an appearance in the dining room. The others are probably waiting on dinner for us."

"Food's not a bad idea." He winked lazily. "We'll need fuel for later." Even as he said the words, he hoped the *later* he'd just alluded to would be lovemaking, rather than a pitched battle with Black Magick.

"Your hand's still glowing." She pointed. "That moonstone really, really likes you."

"How do you know it doesn't like you?" he countered, grinning. He wondered if he'd ever stop smiling. Joy ran through him so hot and bright, he couldn't contain it all.

"Because when I picked it up, it ignored me. Come on, Venison's waiting. Fresh rolls too."

"Thank you. The words feel mighty inadequate, but—"

She placed a hand over his mouth. "Whatever are you thanking me for? I should get down on my knees and worship a man who still wants me, knowing what I've done. Or failed to do." She twisted her mouth into a scowl.

"I was thanking you for taking a chance on me. On us. Can't be easy after how badly you were betrayed." He narrowed his eyes to slits. "Don't beat yourself up too much over Don. Even if you'd tried to rat him out, he'd have used that quiet tone of his and told people you'd gone over the edge. It's not unknown for witches who are old to burn through so much power, their minds end up touched by madness."

Breana shook her head sadly. "That never even occurred to me, but likely you're right. Regardless, he wouldn't have gone down easily. He'd become a master at hiding what he was, and once that Salem witch showed up—with her evil stashed inside my child—he made himself invincible."

Joshua dropped the moonstone into a pocket. "I know I brought him up, but let's not talk about Don. Not right now. What tipped the scales about me?"

Scrunching her forehead in thought, she pressed her lips into a thoughtful line. "It boiled down to either going through the rest of my life afraid to let any of myself out of hiding ever again."

"Or?"

"Or taking a chance on living fully, completely. I've always liked you. More importantly, I've always respected you. Those are good ingredients for a beginning."

"I agree. Caring and respect are a solid foundation." Joshua turned solemn. "I will never, never give you cause to lose that respect." He took a breath. "And I'll hold out hope that in time you'll return my love." The words weren't as hard to get out as he'd feared they'd be.

"I'd say there's a strong chance. I stopped believing in myself somewhere during the long saga with my husband. Your faith in me will go a long way toward me being able to trust myself again." Color rose to her face, and she looked away. "Before we get too serious for words, how about dinner?"

He glanced at the brazier. "Do we need to bank that?"

Breana shook her head. "No. It's powered by magic. If you were to lay your hand on it, you'd find it barely warm. Surprised me, since it drives the water to boiling."

Joshua latched a hand beneath her elbow. "It would be an honor to escort you to the table."

"You sound hopelessly old fashioned." She let him guide her out into the hallway toward where the scents of supper beckoned.

"Well, I was born over two hundred years ago, so I have every right to be *old fashioned*. Besides, I've never courted a woman before. Not seriously." He stood aside to let her enter the dining room first.

When he walked in, Hester and Chris broke into ribald sounding cheers. "We heard that about courting." Chris sent a knowing grin skittering across the room. "Looks like I've lost my bunkmate. Be warned," he told Breana. "He snores after he's had too much to drink."

Breana shrugged. "Likely I do too. If I was drunk enough, I'd never notice." She glanced around the table. "Looks as if you two started without us."

"We weren't sure ye'd show up at all." Hester smiled warmly. "I can make plates for you."

"No need." Breana headed for the kitchen amid a rustle of skirts.

Joshua stood awkwardly, not wanting to sit before she did.

Hester looked pointedly at him. "Sit down. I was describing the power stones to Chris. Show him your moonstone, so he can get the feel of how gems blend with mage power. I was trying to demonstrate with my ruby, but it will come easier with yours."

He dug the gem out of a pocket. It still streamed bright, white light when he held it in his palm.

Chris' brown eyes widened. "Wow! I can feel the power from all the way across the room. What did you do to it?"

"Not sure I understand exactly, but I used the contraption Hester invented to mingle my energy with the stone's. What you see—and feel—is the result."

"As soon as dinner's over, I want to find out if any of the

gems like me enough to do that. How long does the enhanced power last?"

"Depends how much ye ask of it," Hester replied.

Breana pushed the kitchen door wide and swept through with two steaming plates in tow. She set one in front of Joshua and the other where she planned to sit, right next to him. "What do you want to drink?"

"Whatever you're having is fine."

"We're running low on damn near everything, so maybe just water." At his nod, she returned to the kitchen, and he heard the pump creak as she worked it.

"Any word from the other enforcers?" he asked Chris.

"No. Now that you bring it up, seems odd to me. I figured they'd check in when they got closer."

Breana set tumblers filled with cold water in front of their places, sat, and began eating. Joshua tucked into the food too. He was hungry, and Breana's cooking was always a treat, considering the lack of access to many ingredients city-dwellers took for granted.

"This is really good."

"Thanks." She smiled mischievously. "Magic covers my blunders nicely."

"Back to our brothers—" worry pinched the corners of Chris' eyes "—maybe that's the first thing I'll do once I have my own power stone."

"What?" Joshua asked. "Try to reach them?"

Chris nodded.

"While you're seeing if any of the stones blend with your energy, I'll look for Sam and them. It'll be a good opportunity to find out how well the stone extends my mage gifts."

Once he began eating, he realized how hungry he was, and for the next while, he shoveled food into his mouth. Worry about the other enforcers nagged him. Not that they couldn't take care of themselves. They could. But they should've told someone if darkness waylaid them. It was one of the enforcers' unspoken rules.

*Always let someone know where evil lurks. In case you fall prey to it, others will pick up the banner.*

His fork scraped china, and Breana asked, "Would you like more?"

He did, but his sense of unease about why they hadn't heard from Sam had done nothing but increase over the course of the meal. Worse, the moonstone had begun to hum. He didn't know the stone, or its moods, but the tenor of its vocalizations sounded like a death chant.

Joshua focused on Hester. "Does the ruby communicate with you?"

The old witch nodded. "Och aye. No one but me can hear it, and it produces quite a few patterns, depending on how it wants to get my attention."

"You're worried," Breana said.

"Yeah." Josuha nodded. "We should've heard something from the other enforcers by now."

"Go." She made shooing motions with one hand. "Do what you need to. We've got things under control here."

Joshua pushed his chair back. He bent and kissed the top of Breana's head, then strode from the room. The stone quieted, almost as if it knew it had his attention, and didn't have to expend further power nagging him. A wry grin split his mouth. Somewhere between an early warning system and a badgering mentor, the moonstone would take some getting used to.

Almost as if it divined his thoughts, the damn thing pricked him through his trousers. He opened his mouth to tell it to stop, but shut it with a *clack*. The stone was sentient, and it wouldn't do to get off on the wrong foot with it.

He let himself out the front door and walked down the porch steps. Light was nearly gone from the day, and the western skyline had taken on a purplish-black cast. The temperature had dropped, and the air felt chill and raw, but at least it had quit raining.

Joshua extracted the moonstone from his pocket. It all but jumped into his questing fingers, so it obviously wanted to be useful. Hester hadn't mentioned that part, but maybe it didn't work quite that way for her. Mage power and witch power were different.

He focused his magic through the moonstone and called for Sam. The other enforcer didn't answer. Joshua tried several different methods of calling on the stone to amplify his native ability, but none of them worked.

As an experiment he was almost certain would fail, he pictured Luke's energy and sent out a telepathic signal to him.

The other enforcer answered almost immediately. *"Joshua! I thought you were still in Salt Lake."*

*"I am. It's a long story, brother. So long as I reached you. Where are you?"*

*"On a train headed for Council Bluffs to meet up with the Coven wagon train."*

*"When does it leave?"*

*"Maybe a week from now. Depends when we all show up and how fast we can buy the rest of what we need."*

Joshua thought about the geography of the United States. *"Are most of the Coven arriving by riverboat up the Missouri?"*

*"Maybe two-thirds. Abigail and I originally planned to be with them, but we ran out of time. My old teacher is with us, and it took a while to*

*get his house buttoned up so he could leave." Luke paused a beat. "How is it we can communicate over such a great distance? I don't need to know everything, but please, brother, tell me you haven't joined up with the dark side." Luke's concern was palpable, even via telepathy.*

*"Stand down. It's not Black Magick. Hester is here. The reason I can converse with you is because she designed a contraption that concentrates our power via gemstones."*

*"Oooh!" Abigail's mind voice cut in. "I know about that invention. Actually helped grandma fine tune some of it. Never could find a gem that sang to me, but I haven't given up looking."*

*"Goddess be praised it's not evil at work. Now that's out of the way —" relief rang beneath Luke's words "—why'd you call me through our link?"*

*"We've got trouble. Dark Angel trouble. Sam was on his way here, but he dropped out of sight. I tried to reach him several times telepathically. When I couldn't, I was experimenting to see how much punch my new power stone had." Joshua balled his free hand into a fist. "Good to talk with you and Abigail, but I have to get back to figuring out what happened to Sam."*

*"That's not sounding good," Luke snapped. "Too bad I'm not closer, but since we've established you can reach me this way, keep me up to date."*

*"Will do."*

The deep, pinkish glow that had illuminated his stone faded after Joshua dismissed the telepathic link. He stood in the yard and sent his power in a wide arc, using the stone to amplify his ability. The difference hit him with all the subtlety of a runaway freight train. His senses were enhanced to an almost painful degree, and the scents and sounds of the night bombarded him.

He smelled mountain lions on the prowl not far from the barn. Coyotes too, holding silence for once as they too tried to figure out how to get into the rich bounty behind the barn's four, stout walls. Mice, rabbits, marmots, and rats scurried this way and that. Night was their time, and they were making the most of it.

Joshua experimented with modulating how he pushed power through the stone. Different frequencies yielded different information, and he hunted until he found one that brought the taint of wraiths and mad wolves running free. Not close, but not all that far away, either. If a dark sorcerer showed up, he could fan the evil creatures into attack mode damned fast.

He decided to try to reach Sam one more time before he went inside and joined Breana. Thoughts of holding her tight against him filled him with longing, and his cock bolted upright, straining against the laces of his leather breeches. He'd see they had a proper bed this time, and he'd take his time undressing her, kindling his mage light to be sure not to miss even the smallest part of her wonderful body—

*"Brother!"* Sam's strained voice raked across Joshua's mind like a buzz saw.

He snapped to attention, his lust scattering like ashes. *"Sam! Talk to me."*

*"Four of us. Surrounded. Maybe twenty miles south of you. Just off the main road."*

*"Chris and I are on our way."*

Before he was even done talking, Joshua raced for the barn, calling Chris as he ran.

# CHAPTER 11

Breana stood next to Chris in Hester's workshop, walking him through the various stones laid out on the square of tanned deer hide. So far, the emerald showed the most promise, but an opal ran a close second.

"What do you think?" she asked Hester.

"Doona ask me," the old witch countered. "I'm not the one going to be pairing my energy with it."

"Good point. Old habits die hard, and I'm used to taking direction from you." She turned her attention to Chris, but before she could say anything, his eyes widened and he spun on his heel and raced out of the room as if the dogs of Hades were after him.

"What in the nine hells?" Breana exchanged glances with Hester.

"Whatever it is canna be good. Come on. If we want to be part of this, we need to follow him." Hester scurried after Chris, barking a command to seal her workshop from dark forces once Breana cleared the doorway.

By the time they caught up with the men, they were

saddling horses. "Good you're here. Saves time." Joshua was all business, and he sounded grim. "Sam's in trouble. Him and three others."

"They're the ones who were on their way to help us, so we're all coming," Hester said, staring Joshua down. "Not up for discussion. Ye'll need all the magic ye can gin up, and Breana and I have freshly-charged power stones."

"Damn it!" Chris groused. "Another few minutes, and I'd have had a stone of my own."

"You can get back to it later. Jesus, I'm glad we made more bullets," Joshua said sharply and climbed the ladder to the loft. When he came back down, bandoliers crisscrossed his chest, and he tossed a matching set to Chris.

*Assuming there is a later,* Breana thought sourly and busied herself readying a horse. Hester did the same.

"My guns are in the house." Chris sprinted out of the barn.

"Mine too." Joshua shouted after him. "Grab all of them, and I'll secure the barn."

Breana led her horse into the yard and vaulted atop its back. No gun belts or bullets for her. Not for Hester, either. Witches stuck with magic.

Chris pelted down the steps, four revolvers tucked in the curve of his arm. He handed Joshua's over before holstering his own and springing onto his horse.

Breana wove a quick spell to ward her house. It wouldn't keep something serious like the Dark Angel out, but it would at least slow him down.

Hester directed her mount to Breana's side. "I can help with that spell." Magic arced from her, and the house disappeared in a foggy cloud with smoke-tinged edges.

Breana gasped. "Your ruby did that?"

"My word, it certainly did." Hester looked surprised. "Damn

if the stones aren't growing stronger. It appears there's power in numbers with these things."

"Or your machine's getting better at what it does," Joshua suggested. "Let's ride, people. Twenty miles is a long way."

Hooves churned through the muddy yard as they took off, heading for the main road leading east to Salt Lake and west into mountainous desert. Breana gazed at Joshua's back where he sat arrow-straight in his saddle. Earlier that evening, she'd been close to going after him because he'd stayed outside so long. Once Chris had settled on a stone, she would've. While the stones fascinated Breana, Hester was the logical one to direct Chris through pairing one with his energy.

In truth, she'd been looking forward to joining Joshua in the dark yard. To winding her arms around him and inviting more kisses. Once their lips touching wasn't enough, she'd planned to lead him to her bedroom. Just like Chris had to wait for his stone, she'd have to wait to make love to the man who sang to her soul and made her heart ache with wanting him. Once she'd let go of the wall she'd erected around her heart, she was close to certain she could fall in love with him.

Fury roiled through her as she rode across the night-dark terrain, mage light suspended to light the way for her horse. Goddamn Black Magick and its practitioners all to Hell. They'd stolen enough from her, and she'd be damned if they'd rob her of her next chance at happiness.

The horses settled into a canter. A full out gallop would tire them long before they got close enough to help, and this wasn't like the eastern part of the country where they could trade out spent horses for fresh ones when they rode through towns. Joshua hadn't said which direction they were headed, but it scarcely mattered. They'd have to rely on what they had to hand. Salt Lake was the only city for hundreds of miles. Having a horse break a leg would mean doubling riders on another—and it would slow their pace considerably.

*"Which way?"* She sent in mind speech.

"South." Joshua's words carried back to her. "No magic. When we get closer, we'll ward ourselves. Won't give us much of a leg up, but I suspect we'll be badly outnumbered, and any advantage is better than none."

Shielded, power shrouded down to nothing but a faint glow, Breana set her teeth in a tense line and rode hard. She worried about her horse navigating in the dark without her mage light for assistance, but there wasn't any help for that. They stopped twice at creeks to water the horses and walk them a bit until they stopped blowing hard, and then they pressed on.

She sensed Black Magick long before she saw anything. Apparently, the gem felt the disturbance too because the garnet sounded a warning, pricking unpleasantly where it lay against her chest.

Joshua wheeled his horse hard right off the faint track they'd been following. How he'd known just which of the barely-there trails to choose was a mystery, but the enforcers all had an interconnectedness. Something to do with sharing the Coven founder's blood when they were initiated. Much of what enforcers did was cloaked in secrecy, so competing magic couldn't dilute their effectiveness.

Mad wolves howling reached her ears about the same time the stink of wraiths made her gorge rise. *Crap!* The dark had launched a full out attack, presumably to keep Sam and the others from joining up with them. The thought turned her blood icy cold. What had the Dark Angel planned that required keeping them segregated from assistance? Clearly something ruthless enough, he was willing to pull out all the stops to ensure the other enforcers never made it to her ranch.

Chris and Joshua halted, beckoning her and Hester to draw close, their horses nose to nose in a tight circle. "Not far now," Joshua said. "We ride another half mile, then come out blazing. By my count we face over a hundred mad wolves, an army of wraiths, and at least two dark sorcerers driving them."

"Ye have the link." Hester drew her mouth into a harsh line. "Did we get here in time?"

"Yes and no," Chris said. "Sam and Cory are still alive and kicking. Ben's dead, and Tom's not good."

"Got it." Breana nodded sharply. "Let's get moving. Maybe we can save Tom. He's a good man. Steered clear of Don afore anyone else suspected anything."

"He came to me with his concerns," Joshua concurred. "But there's no time for that story now." Wheeling his horse around, he kicked up dirt and clumps of sagebrush, riding fast and true into the danger that faced them.

Pride swelled in Breana, and she urged her mount after him. Joshua oozed courage. It never occurred to him to put anything but his best effort forward, no matter the risk to himself. She vowed to be a worthy mate for him. She may have fallen off the straight and narrow once, but never again. From now on, she'd do what was right, no matter how hard the path. Don might have punished her by turning her over to demons, but at least it would've been a clean end. Not one that mired her in crippling guilt and recriminations.

Wraith stench swelled, and wolf howls grew louder. Magic flashed in front of her as Chris and Joshua dropped their warding and showed themselves.

"Remember your stone," Hester exhorted. "You're not used to working with it, but follow its lead."

It was a timely reminder. Breana wasn't used to using the garnet, and it hadn't occurred to her now, but she threaded her power through it before she revealed herself. A break in thickly growing aspens led to a large circle, obviously cleared by someone. She fired her mage light, and an obscene stone altar came into view. About three feet tall, it was splattered with blood. Human bones scattered around it told the only tale she needed. This was one of the places sorcerers sacrificed humans, feeding on them to augment their evil powers. She'd heard of such things, but never laid eyes on the evidence—until now.

The garnet pulsed hotly against her skin, and she looked up in time to see a mad wolf lunge through the air. Power flew from her fingers and the thing didn't just fall into a heap, it vaporized into blood-colored bubbles and foam.

Her eyes widened with surprise. Clearly, she didn't need as hefty a dose of magic next time. If she conserved what she used, it would go farther. More wolves closed on her, with wraiths ringed behind them. Surrounded, she couldn't see beyond the fell creatures trying to cut her off from everyone else.

Fury boiled hot, filling her with righteous indignation. Nothing mattered but killing. So what if sorcerers made more wraiths and mad wolves? At least she'd make a dent in their numbers. The garnet sent a wave of what felt like delight skimming through her. It liked the idea of mowing through wickedness.

Meantime, her horse whinnied, shying crazily in its attempt to not get too close to death closing in from all sides. Breana flicked a finger. The small motion loosed enough power to annihilate two wolves. Pulling hard on her reins, she drew the horse around in a circle, killing as she went. Most of the wolves lay either dead or dying when half a dozen wraiths rushed her, and the horse decided it was done. Bucking, rearing, it launched a campaign to unseat her, so it could run like hell as fast and as far as it could from the carnage. Diverting a small amount of energy into a calming spell didn't alter things one whit. The horse was terrified, and it wanted to be gone. *Now.*

Breana was breathing hard, but exhilaration roared through her. She was going to win this round, but not if she had to ride herd on her mount. Linking to its mind, she bound it with power and cut a deal. She'd dismount, and he could run, but not far enough he wouldn't return when she summoned him for the long ride back.

*"Thank you, mistress."*

"Don't get yourself killed," she called after it.

*"Don't plan to."* A whinny told her he'd made it through the wraiths. No wolves left. Not in her sector since she'd killed them all.

Fire scored her side, and she wheeled to face a huge wraith. With their red-rimmed, charcoal eyes and blood red talons where fingernails used to be, they were gruesome to look at. Add in the reek of dead things rotting on a hot day, and the undead scared the crap out of most everyone they went after. Some of their favorites were their own relatives. Blood called to blood, first and foremost.

Flames puffed from her assailant's mouth, and Breana did a double take. Since when had they turned into dragons? Last she knew, fire flowed from their hands, not their mouths. In the moment indecision stayed her hand, the thing immersed her in flames. Gasping and choking, she rolled on the ground, desperate to quench the pain as Black Magick chewed holes in her clothes and charred her hair.

Breana rolled to a sit, spewing destruction in a wide arc. Wraiths folded in on themselves, vanishing in puffs of noxious smelling, gritty smoke. Some of her hair still burned, and she sent magic to suffocate the fire. Hands extended, she made certain every wraith in the immediate vicinity had been vanquished. Only then did she pat down her head, and tuck what was left of her braids beneath her clothing.

*Where's everyone else?*

She peered through the smoky murk, but didn't hear battle sounds. Nor did she see anyone else. Now that she thought about it, she hadn't seen anyone since she began to fight. Reluctant to raise her mind voice—and give away her position—she scented the air. Was she still in the same place she'd begun, or had Andras somehow spirited her back to one of the worlds controlled by darkness while she fought?

If he had enough power to pull something like that off—and presumably he did—that would be just like him. Sneaky and devious. Keep her too busy to notice and push her over a psychic edge into goddess-only-knew where.

"No!" She banged a fist into her open palm. "I refuse to be manipulated like that." She waited for a snarky response, but was met with nothing but silence. Smoke that had nothing to do with wraith fire rose from the ground. Deep gray and black, it shimmered, reflected in her mage light.

*At least my magic works here.*

Breana shook herself. The only reason she thought she might be elsewhere was because Andras had spirited her off before. Her imagination was working overtime.

*But then why can't I hear anyone else?*

Heedless of exposing herself, she sent power zinging in a wide arc. The garnet urged her to do more, push harder. When she did, the blackness around her shattered, giving way to a familiar moon and stars. The battle she hadn't heard rose around her, and she rushed forward, intent on helping. What had happened while she was encased in that cocoon? Whose doing had it been? Had her own magic created the bubble to keep anything else bad from getting in?

*Doesn't matter. I can sort things out later.*

Before she could figure out where she was needed most, Hester shrieked. "There ye are. Get over here. Now."

Breana ran toward her mentor's voice, sidestepping two wolves who jumped her from both sides. Power ran through her like high-voltage lightning, and she reveled in her new-found magical strength. Before, she'd been too busy killing to truly appreciate that she'd tapped into a well that felt bottomless. Likely it wasn't, but she could do ever so much more than she'd ever been capable of before, and it made her feel invincible.

Better yet, this power felt clean, not like something clawing her to shreds from the inside.

A wraith had its spectral arm wrapped around Hester from behind. Others held her on both sides. The air crackled as bright magic collided with dark, and the scents of ozone and brimstone burned Breana's nose. An enormous wraith, seven feet tall at least, kept trying to close its mouth over Hester's to steal her soul, but the old witch hissed, spit, and writhed like an alley cat.

The only thing missing was fire. Why wasn't this bunch using it?

Breana took aim at the one that had Hester in a chokehold. It crumpled into nothingness as its head rolled from its misshapen shoulders. With barely a pause to draw breath, she cut through two of the four still holding Hester captive, annihilating the one that had been intent on sucking the life's breath from her.

Jesus. God, but their stink became intolerable when they died. Her stomach rebelled in protest, and bile splashed the back of her throat, but she swallowed it back. The last two wraiths, sensing defeat, melted into darkness and Breana rushed forward, wrapping her arms around Hester.

"Thank the goddess and all the bloody saints you're all right. Why didn't you call for me?"

"I did. Ye'd vanished. I suspected foul play, but was too sore pressed myself to go after you." Hester's voice held reproach—and relief—as Breana hugged her in the middle of a bloody circle of carcasses. Some had been wolves, but many were unrecognizable.

"Yeah, I didn't realize I was inside some kind of shielding just a little bit ago. Did you kill something besides wolves?" She pointed at a lump of flesh with bones sticking out of it. "Where are the enforcers?"

"I killed whatever attacked me," Hester replied grimly. "Kill first, ask questions later, but not all of them were wolves. The men have to be over there. How's your power holding up?"

Breana grinned, feeling fey, wild. "I have plenty. Thank you a million times over for discovering a new source for us."

"Ye can thank me by getting out of here alive. We're far from done."

Breana trusted Hester's instincts. The woman had kept herself alive for centuries, against steep odds from some of the tales she'd spun. She gazed around them. "Nothing left here to kill. Let's join forces with the men so we can get out of here."

A sharp cracking noise jolted her from the soles of her feet to the top of her head just before the ground disintegrated beneath them. She and Hester scrabbled at earth as it whizzed past, but nothing she grabbed onto held.

"What's happening?" she screamed, to make herself heard over the cacophony around them.

"Not sure. Nothing we can do but ride it out," Hester yelled back. "Whatever ye do, doona let go of me."

"I don't plan to."

## CHAPTER 12

Joshua worked with the moonstone on the fly. Since he'd never fought using its power to augment his own, everything he did was an experiment. He worried about the women. At first they'd all been together, but battles had a way of separating people. He scanned the area again, but the smoke and fire were too thick to see very far. Leaving Sam, Chris and Cory wasn't possible—not until they had the upper hand. As a compromise, he searched for witch energy, gratified when it burned into his mind. Breana and Hester were slightly to the north behind a curtain of flames. From the feel of things, they didn't need any help, but he vowed to work his way toward them as soon as he could.

Tom still clung to life. At least they'd been able to move him away from the worst of things and erect a protective shield around him. He was unconscious, which was probably for the best, otherwise his injuries would hurt like hell. And no one could spare magic to patch him up.

Ben was, indeed, dead. To keep the dark from feeding on him, turning him into cannon fodder to enhance themselves,

Joshua had doused him in mage fire. The man didn't need a clean death, but this way, they saved his remains from being desecrated.

Sweat ran into his eyes, and the reek of evil soured his stomach. He wanted to call Breana with mind speech, but that would pinpoint her location for the sorcerers who'd thrown this party. They'd yet to show their cowardly faces. He silently exhorted her to be careful. Losing her now, when she was almost his, would be intolerable. Too horrible to even consider.

They had a life to live together, goddammit, and he'd pull down the gates of Hell to make sure they got their chance at happiness.

A ball of wraith fire hit him square in the chest. It brought his awareness zinging back to their enemy massing around them, and he diverted power to extinguish the flames. They'd killed scores of wolves, and even more wraiths, but the dark mages behind the attack remained stubbornly out of sight.

"Pay attention, brother!" Chris shouted.

"We've got to smoke the sorcerers out," Joshua screamed. "Otherwise this will never be over."

"Agreed." Sam pushed matted blond hair with singed ends behind his shoulders. "These bastards will just keep coming unless we can knock a hole in what's driving them."

"Just how do you plan to accomplish that?" Cory sidled toward them, fighting his way through three wraiths. Something dropped out of a tree as he walked under it, and the enforcer cursed roundly. "Shit. Crap. Fuck." He stripped something that was black, snakelike, and a foot long off his arm. "Well, I'll be goddamned. Giant leeches. Where the hell did these come from?"

"Does it matter?" Sam quirked a blond brow. "At least they don't fight back very hard."

Cory crushed the thing under his boot heel and it splattered his leather-clad legs with black blood.

The sharp stink of poison made Joshua's nose prickle unpleasantly, and he sent magic zinging to Cory's lower legs. "That's why they don't fight back," he growled. "They have a different way to kill you."

"First one I've seen," Chris muttered. "Maybe it was the only one."

"In a pig's eye," Joshua shot back.

"No more stepping on them." Cory rolled his brown eyes. "How are we going to trick the masterminds behind this into showing themselves?" Unlike the others, he kept his black hair short, shorn close to his skull.

A harsh, grinding noise filled the air. When Joshua searched the ink-dark landscape for its source, he saw a volcano of dirt spin upward about fifty yards away. Riding on instincts, he pushed power hard, and sensed Breana and Hester traveling away from him at unheard of speeds.

"New plan," he said tersely. "But it'll solve the other problem too. I wager those bastards just shanghaied the women. There's a hell of a big hole in the ground. If we hurry, we can jump through before the gateway closes."

"Any idea where it leads?" Sam asked.

"Does it matter?" Joshua countered and took off at a gallop for where dirt and rocks still spewed skyward. It would be a neat trick to use the same portal, but if they hurried—and he employed the stone's magic to mask their energy—it just might work. He hoped to hell Tom would remain undisturbed, but they were too few to station a man next to him. Besides, the likelihood of wraiths and mad wolves staying once their masters left was thin.

He waited until Sam, Chris, and Cory were on either side of

him and draped a protective shield around all of them. The hole in the ground stopped throwing dirt skyward. They had to move now, or the women might be lost forever. Not that they weren't enterprising—and it boded well they were together—but he wanted Breana back by his side before anyone harmed her further. She'd suffered enough.

Savage protectiveness beat a track from his toes to the top of his head, and he barked. "Now."

The four enforcers jumped into profound darkness. Joshua pushed power ahead of them, hoping to hell it would blend well enough with the women's energy to fool whoever stood at the bottom.

What kind of world would they come out in? If they got very lucky, maybe they could kill enough of the dark sorcerers to make a difference. Enforcer energy pulsed near him, and they fell faster. The smell of wet earth and roots trumped evil. He filled his lungs over and over with air that wasn't tainted by wickedness. The moonstone approved, thrumming hotly from the pocket he'd dropped it into.

Time dribbled past. He'd been to other worlds before, but never one that took this long to get to. Sam's magic flared as the other enforcer pushed at the edges of the funnel surrounding them. It splintered abruptly, and Joshua barely had enough time to cushion their fall to heat-packed black earth.

Cory pounded a fist into the baked dirt and bounded to his feet. "Damn if it wasn't illusion."

"Which means they know we're here," Sam said somberly. "And they were keeping us in stasis as long as they could." He scrambled upright and spun in a circle. "Anybody recognize this place?"

Narrowing his eyes, Cory scented the air. "Nope. Never been here."

"Me, either," Chris said.

Joshua curved his hand around the moonstone, urging it to find Breana. The gem didn't respond for so long, he started to wonder if the sorcerers had somehow managed to spit the women out elsewhere. He drew the gem out and held it between his thumb and forefinger, turning to see if it changed at all depending which way it pointed.

"What is that?" Sam asked, his tone lined with suspicion.

"Something Hester cooked up to concentrate power. Works like a champ, but there's a process to link your energy with it."

"Almost had one of my own." Chris shook his head. "Another half hour and I'd have been set."

"It'll still be there for you," Joshua said grimly. "Just make certain you get back to claim it."

"So we can't all use the same stone?" Cory asked.

Joshua shook his head and moved the moonstone to the one spot it had shown a faint flicker. "This way. We can talk more about it later."

He fanned power ahead of him and ran fast, every sense on high alert. The cracked, black dirt beneath his feet was studded with rocks, and the playa extended as far as he could see beneath a sickly violet-gray sky. Three suns perched a few degrees above a distant horizon, but they didn't move much, and it was hard to tell if they were rising or setting. Thank the goddess the air was breathable. Thin, but at least it wasn't poisoned. He'd been to dark worlds where he had to divert magic to take a breath.

He urged his legs to pump harder, not understanding why no one from the other side had risen up to stop them. Sam had drawn into the lead, and he skidded to an abrupt stop. A harsh, tearing noise filled the air, and the dirt in front of them split, disgorging demons. Joshua's not-quite-healed wounds throbbed painfully, remembering his last fight with them.

Light blazed from the moonstone. It wanted to fight. When Joshua pointed it at the nearest demon—seven feet tall with three eyes across its hairy forehead, cloven hoofs, and a long, curving red tail—the thing charged him. And exploded mid-leap.

*It can't be this easy.*

To test the gem's destructive path, he swung it toward the next demon. It got close enough to shower him with grisly bits of bone and sinew when it burst.

"I am definitely getting myself one of those," Cory muttered. Power blazed from his hands as another demon fell. Not in bits, but dead was dead.

Mostly because of the moonstone, six demons lay scattered around them in as many minutes. No longer a threat, they seemed to be it for the welcoming party.

Driven by urgency and a bone-deep knowledge that they had to get the women out of this world before the Dark Angel—or whoever was behind this—moved them to yet another location, he sprinted forward. Every sense was honed to its sharpest edge as he searched in all possible directions.

The moonstone's initial faint glow flickered and died out. He stopped and turned in a full circle, concentrating intently, but the stone didn't rekindle. It pulsed in his hand, like it wanted to tell him something, but he didn't understand its language.

Not yet.

"They're not here." Sam spoke flatly.

"My take too," Cory chugged alongside them.

Joshua felt as if he was being ripped in two. Remaining in this world made no sense, but if they left, how the hell would he ever find Breana again?

"Maybe they left on their own," Chris suggested. "Hester is goddamned strong. More than capable of getting them out of here."

"I'll stay here," Joshua said. "Do more digging around—"

"Bad call," Sam cut in, his voice rough. "We stay together, and I say we go back." He eyed the other men. Chris nodded curtly. So did Cory. Enforcers operated by consensus vote. Joshua could refuse to leave, but maybe he was letting his heart lead, rather than his reason.

"Look." Breath whistled from between Chris' teeth. "I know you love her, but we have a better chance of finding her together. If you stay here by yourself, power stone or no, the dark will eat you for lunch."

Sam frowned. "You and Breana?"

"Why not?" Joshua bristled.

"You took that wrong," Sam said. "I was just surprised is all. Congratulations, brother—"

"No time for that," Cory spoke over Sam. "Game's over here. Let's go before we have to fight our way past another demon attack. Hope to hell Tom's still alive."

Power rose, blanketing them, and Joshua girded himself for whatever ugly surprises lay in wait. His soul screamed for Breana, but she wasn't here.

*I'll find her,* he vowed to himself. *No matter what it takes, or how long. I'll find her.*

BREANA'S FALL ended in a spine-crackling thud. It would've been worse had she not pulled power at the last moment to spare herself broken bones.

"Oomph. Knocked the breath out of me."

"Doona get too comfy." Hester's acerbic words almost made Breana laugh. It was vintage Hester to understate the obvious.

"What next? How do we get back?"

Hester rolled to her feet and offered Breana a hand, dragging her upright. "We doona *get back*."

"Huh? Why not? Surely you're not suggesting—"

"Shut up. We have to leave now afore we canna escape, but we're going to do something unexpected. 'Twill at least give us a fighting chance. Keep hold of me. In fact, take my other hand. Ye'll know this chant. Follow along."

Breana indeed recognized it after the first two Gaelic words. They were opening the gates into the lands of the dead. How they could get there from where they were now was a mystery, but she trusted Hester and wove magic in with hers.

White light flickered around them, but didn't blaze up like she was used to. Clearly something about this world stymied witch power.

"Keep it coming," Hester hissed through clenched teeth. "Mind link to that garnet. I tell you, child, there's no time to waste. They're headed our way."

Long years had passed since Hester called her *child*. She felt impending disaster closing fast. The stink and feel of Black Magick made her skin crawl, and she reached for her power stone pushing magic through it. The circle of light burst into brilliant blue-white luminance, and the demons' world vanished in mist.

When she tried to breathe, her lungs constricted. Wherever they were now—maybe a space between borderworlds—had no air. Or not much. She imagined bits of air and laced them into a mat around her nose. It helped, but only a little. She wanted to ask Hester how long they'd be in this airless void, but didn't have the breath for words.

Finally, when her vision was shading to a gray haze, the air thickened. A spate of Gaelic burst from Hester thanking Danu for ceding safe passage.

Breana's lungs stopped burning, and they came to a stop on a spongy surface, surrounded by thick, gray mist. Hester kept nattering in Gaelic. "Och aye, and I know this place. We could've ended up in far worse. Follow me."

Watching where Hester placed her feet, Breana crossed a marshy, swamp to higher ground. The mist grew still thicker until she could barely see the other witch a few steps ahead of her.

"I didn't realize you could travel from their borderworlds to our own," she said.

"Neither did I." Hester turned and drew close enough for Breana to see the triumphant grin on her face.

"You threw the dice?" Breana squeaked, incredulous.

"Mayhap not quite so bad as all that. I'd read this was possible. Just never tried it myself. Never had reason to." She sucked in a breath and blew it out. "Wipe that shocked look off your face. We had to get out of there. Of course we could've returned to our starting point, but they'd have just captured us again. This made much more sense. They willna have any idea at all what happened to us, plus I'm hoping to rustle up a few allies while we're here."

Now that she was getting over her shock, curiosity took over. "Are all the border worlds linked?"

"I doona believe so, but the paths of the dead have many entrances."

"Can sorcerers come here?"

"They can, but the power burns them, so 'twould be a last resort." Her grin took on a feral aspect. "The Dark Angel may well want you, but I wager not badly enough to risk his own precious hide.

"Let's be quick about this," Hester went on. "We mustn't tarry long here. The place drags at the living until ye lose all will to live and fall into a sleep from which there's no wakening. Have ye never been here afore?"

Breana shook her head. "The idea always gave me the creeps, but now that we're here, it's not so bad."

"Och aye, but 'tis." She let go of Breana's hands. "Wrap your fingers around the garnet, and keep your mind sharp. This will take but a few moments."

Breana drew out the garnet. Simply touching it cleared her mind, and she understood how muzzy she'd become. As Hester summoned a drawing spell, Breana recalled what she knew about the realm of the dead. Spirits craved the warmth of living flesh and engaged in any amount of nefarious dealings to draw them close enough to sidle up to, sucking the will to live from them. Their proclivity to steal from the living was the main reason Arawn, god of the dead, had erected barriers to keep his flock contained.

Spirits flowed toward Hester, but maintained a respectful distance—no doubt a byproduct of the other witch's spell. Breana wound a ward about herself to keep them at bay. And not a moment too soon. Their cold, disturbing energy pushed against her, seeking a way in.

She had to get through this. Had to. Joshua and the other enforcers needed her and Hester.

*Bullshit! I need Joshua.*

Now that she'd made up her mind, she wanted to hold him in her arms, feel his acres of muscles against her body as he claimed her mouth with those hard, chiseled lips of his. Tell him she could love him, care for him.

"Help me." Hester's voice was thin, strained. "I've almost got this, but I need a wee bit more magic to contain these spirits and move them back to our world."

Breana blinked in disbelief. "But that's against the covenant with Arawn. He corrals the dead here so they can't—"

"Spare me quoting the rules chapter and verse. No arguments. Help me. Our need is great, and we can ask forgiveness later."

Long years as Hester's acolyte leapt to the fore, maybe driven by a jot of compulsion from her old mentor, and Breana looked through her third eye. Seeing the warp and weft of Hester's casting, she shored up the weak spots.

"What exactly are we doing with this mass of dead energy?" she asked, breathless from the magic running through her.

"Bringing it back to the spot we left and turning it loose on our enemy. The dead willna have any trouble tracking evil to its roots. Whatever ye do, doona loose your wards."

Breana snorted wry laughter. "You could've skipped that lecture. They're pounding at the gates as it is. Their energy is more tolerable than Black Magick, but not by much."

"Ready yourself. We're leaving."

"I'm more than ready. Let's get this over with."

"Och, child. 'Twon't be over, but we may win a small respite to plan our next set of strategies."

Breana clacked her mouth shut. Black Magick would dog them until the end of their days if they didn't fight back with every weapon at their disposal. And even that might not be enough. Grim determination filled her, and she focused power to draw them back to their own world. If the goddess saw fit to grant her grace—and Danu had every reason not to—she'd be reunited with Joshua there.

Maybe.

*Please.* She raised her hopes in a silent plea. *Please.*

In the meantime, she needed to figure out how to help Hester command their latest allies. Any assistance killing their enemy was welcome, and she'd do whatever was needed to maximize the shades' potential. She hoped they'd have a moment to sort things out once they emerged, but you couldn't count on anything when you faced off against the dark.

She suppressed a shudder that ran from her head to her toes and tightened the power wrapping her in brightness.

# CHAPTER 13

Joshua knelt by Tom's side. His healing magic was stronger than the other enforcers', plus he had the moonstone to help out. Mercifully, the dark army had left, and Tom was by himself. The enforcer was still unconscious, and Joshua labored to draw him back.

Chris hunkered next to them. "Anything I can do?"

"I don't think so. He got a whopping dose of their saliva when they chewed the crap out of his shoulder. I've done what I can to mend that, and the dark taint is leaving, but it's slow."

"We need to hurry it up." Sam stood over them.

Joshua sent a gentle strand of power into the comatose enforcer. He was closer to the surface, close enough he might break through soon left to his own devices. That was better than forcing things.

"Why?" He glanced up at Sam. "What do you sense?"

"Can't put my finger on it. Not exactly, but something's got me stirred up. Feels like ghouls are walking on my grave."

Tom groaned, and his blue eyes snapped wide open. He struggled to sit, but Joshua held him in place, hands on his shoulders. "Easy, brother. Take a few breaths and center yourself."

"Did we thrash those fuckers?" Tom asked, his voice thick and gravelly.

"For now, but they may well be back, and we need you ready to fight."

"Then let go of me. Hard to get a straight breath flat on my back."

Joshua rocked back on his heels. A wave of cold rolled over him, so eerie and unexpected it drove him to his feet. "What the hell?" He twisted in a circle trying to figure out where the sensation originated.

"Yeah." Cory scrunched his face into a mass of concerned wrinkles. "It's not Black Magick, but it still feels off. Like something that shouldn't be here."

"That's it." Sam drove his fist into a nearby tree. "I knew I recognized that particular vibration, but it's been a hell of a long time."

"Recognized what?" Joshua beat back exasperation. Sam wasn't always the clearest communicator.

"It's the dead. Someone punched through into the paths of the dead and let them loose."

Joshua's eyes widened. "Aw shit. All of them? That could be worse than Black Magick."

"Doesn't feel like all that many." Sam tightened his jaw.

"What I want to know is who loosed them," Cory muttered. "And why."

"They're harder than a greased pig to control." Tom rolled onto hands and knees and levered himself upward. His brown hair was caked with blood from where it had fallen across his wounds, and his leathers were stained red too.

Joshua moved his gaze from one man to the next. "How many

of you have herded them before?" Tom, Sam, and Cory nodded. All three wore resigned expressions.

"Got to send them back where they came from and patch up the rent between the worlds," Sam said.

"About the size of things," Cory agreed. "Not that I don't appreciate a challenge as much as the next enforcer, but we've got our hands full. All we need is for sorcerers to pop back up while we're herding shades."

Joshua sucked in a tense breath. What he wanted to do was find Breana, not take a side trip to the paths of the dead, but fate seemed determined to keep him so preoccupied he couldn't tackle his top priority. The cold prickling across his skin grew even more pervasive, and he grabbed the moonstone. Rather than pulsing hotly like it had done when he faced demons, it acted sanguine, as if nothing out of the ordinary was afoot.

*Maybe it's running out of juice and needs another stint with Hester's machinery.*

He wished he knew more about how the power stones worked.

"I need all of you," Sam said, his voice just shy of a command. "I'm going to open a pathway from here. When the shades show up, we'll chivvy them through. If we have everything ready, it should go fast. Come on, brothers. Let's nail this."

"I'm on it." Chris strode to Sam's side. "Always up for learning new tricks."

"How you doing?" Joshua asked Tom. "You could sit this one out and let your power come back up to snuff."

"Nah. I'm good. Feeling more like myself by the moment." The tall, rangy enforcer sent a cocky grin Joshua's way and made his way to where Sam stood.

Joshua let go of the moonstone, dropping it back into his pocket. It wasn't doing much good anymore since the shades weren't products of Black Magick, and he worked power more effectively with both hands free. The faintest of scents threaded with the bitter cold surrounding him. He sniffed the air, his nostrils flaring, to make certain not to miss anything.

Breana!

He'd know her scent anywhere. It might've been his mind playing tricks on him because he wanted to see her so desperately, but the special wildflower and musk mixture he associated with her grew stronger.

A swirling vortex opened in front of Sam as the enforcer fed power into it, widening it into a funnel to send the shades packing. Chris and Cory added their magic to the mix, and the gateway stabilized, glowing blue-white. Despite Tom's smug words about helping, the power spitting from his hands was more show than anything else.

Joshua sidled between Sam and Cory. "Do either of you sense witch power?"

Sam shot a pointed look his way. "Could use a little help here. We can hunt for the witches once this is done."

Shame pricked Joshua, and he dug for the right frequency to augment Sam's whirling funnel. The bitter cold intensified, and a cloud of shades hastened toward them. Joshua marshaled his magic, ready to send it auguring into the flock of dead.

"Wait until I tell you," Sam cautioned. "We've got one chance to get this right."

"What happens if we don't?" Chris asked.

"We end up chasing them down one by one," Cory gritted. "Takes forever."

Joshua's breath steamed in the frigid air, and his teeth chattered. The ice-rimmed cloud split down its center. Before he had a chance to react, Hester and Breana leapt through in a flurry of ice chips.

Hester took in the enforcers and the power eddying around them, her hazel eyes turning agate hard. "I brought the shades," she announced. "Ye will *not* undo my work. They're here for a reason, goddammit."

But Joshua wasn't listening. He scooped Breana into his arms and held her close. Words wouldn't come, so he hoped the frantic beat of his heart against her ear would tell her how frightened he'd been that she was lost to him forever.

"No time for that, either." Hester thumped him soundly across the shoulder blades. "These shades need a firm hand, and so long as you boys are here, ye get to help."

Sam burst out laughing. "Christ Almighty, Hester, but you're a sight for sore eyes. Just what did you have in mind? Didn't Arawn pitch a fit about you freeing this batch of shades?"

"Never saw him, so I couldna ask." Hester rounded her eyes into innocent balls.

"Funny, same thing I asked her," Breana muttered. "Once I knew what she had in mind."

Joshua hadn't let go of her, but Breana wriggled out of his arms. "Hester really does need a hand. Riding herd on those things is a trick and a half."

The shades surrounded them now, and the air filled with sleet and ice crystals, dancing to a breeze only they felt. Every once in a while, ice particles cut a path through Joshua's warding and scored his cheeks with raw, biting efficiency.

Sam and the others closed off the vortex, and a muted roar rose from the shades. Clearly, they'd intuited they were on their way back to Arawn's prison for the dead, and they hadn't been pleased about it. The air warmed fractionally, moving from Arctic blizzard to dead-of-winter cold in New York.

A group of shades formed a shimmering pack and edged away.

Hester raised both hands. Power flared, catching them, and forced them to stop.

Breana pushed her garnet, suspended on leather around her neck, forward. The gem caught the light from a breaking day, and magic cascaded from it right to the containment circle Hester had drawn around the shades.

"It's been like this since we left Arawn's realm," Breana muttered. "Either the damn things want to feed off my warmth, or they're trying to escape."

"What exactly are we doing with them?" Joshua asked, raising a questioning eyebrow.

"Why sending them after Black Magick." Hester cast a pained glance his way. "I'm surprised ye had to ask. Lend your power, and we should be done damn quick."

"Sketch out the spell," Sam gritted. "Not familiar with that one."

"Ye will be once ye hear it," Hester retorted and Gaelic tumbled from her, taken up by the others at proscribed intervals.

Though Joshua had never thought to mix them quite this way, the dirge for the dead mingled nicely with a compulsion spell, and he added his magic to the mix. Interestingly enough, his moonstone was back in the thick of things, augmenting his natural-born power.

Hester's incantation changed, and a determined expression turned her face harsh and foreboding.

"You're feeding the sorcerers' energy signatures into the shades, right along with compulsion to do your bidding." Joshua nodded slowly, impressed by her strategy. "Smart. Creative use of different magics."

"That's right." Hester broke off chanting. "They'll turn into long range bullets, not stopping until they find a sorcerer—or a wraith or mad wolf—to destroy."

The dead faded away, some singly and others in groups until the grove was empty, and the temperature back to normal. Joshua dropped his hands to his sides. "What happens after the shades locate Black Magick?"

"Further, how can you guarantee they won't assimilate and turn into weapons for sorcerers?" Sam asked, narrowing his eyes to slits.

"If my spell runs true, they have to return to the paths of the dead once their task here is done," Hester said. She closed her mouth over her lower lip. "I've never known a shade to switch sides after death claimed them, but some of the batch we freed might've had an affinity for darkness. All bets are off for those. Magic willna bind them nearly as strongly to my bidding."

"Regardless, it's done now," Cory said. "Nothing to do but sit back and see how the pieces fall."

"Maybe we should at least try to let Arawn know," Sam ventured.

"How?" Hester countered. "Last I checked, the gods scarcely danced to our fiddling. Danu might've helped Breana, but such occurrences are rare indeed."

Joshua needed Breana close, so he wrapped his arms around her from behind, drawing her against him. He wanted to shower her with love, share his heart with her, but for that they needed to be alone. He settled for asking, "What happened to the two of you?"

"Doesn't matter." She leaned into him, turning her head to nestle into the hollow of his collarbones. "Hester had a brilliant idea, and we escaped before harm befell us. Not sure if we could've finessed moving between the borderworlds without the power stones, but we're here, and hopefully the shades will help us."

He held on tight, never wanting to let her go. "It's been a long night. You up for riding back?"

"Not sure if we'll get all the way home, but we need to leave here," she replied, glancing at the blood-soaked ground and piles of dead wolves.

"Agreed. It'll be good to put this place behind us." He ran his hands down her arms, loving how she fit against him, and delighting in the feel of her, warm and vibrant, beneath his fingertips.

Sam whistled sharply and four horses cantered toward them. Another whistle brought two more.

"I need to call mine," Breana said. "I bound him with magic."

Hester whistled, called, and sent magic spiraling outward, but her horse didn't respond. "Bastards must've killed it," she mumbled. "Too bad. I always liked that bay gelding. He was more of a wagon horse than a riding one, but still…"

"You can ride Ben's," Sam said. "I'm going to torch this place with mage fire before I leave. All of you can get moving. I'll join you soon."

"Do you want help?" Joshua asked.

"Nah, I'll be fine." A rakish grin cut through the grime, blood, and grit tracking down Sam's face.

Tight-lipped, Hester clambered into the saddle and headed the horse toward home. Breana didn't need help, but Joshua made sure she was settled on her horse just the same. Dawn turned the eastern sky ruddy as they rode north, and he thanked every deity he could think of for keeping Breana safe.

Sam caught up to them after about half an hour and offered a thumbs up sign. "All done. We could've left them, but I didn't want to take the chance."

"Thanks." Joshua nodded sharply. "Always better to make

certain everything evil is well and truly beyond where they can do further harm."

He'd vowed once to never let Breana out of his sight and failed. Still he didn't quite see how he could've kept his commitment to always stand beside his fellow enforcers and remain by her at the same time. Not unless he trained her to fight by his side. The thought made him smile. She was already a hell of a warrior.

They weren't moving as fast as when they'd ridden to help Sam and the others, but miles still clipped by beneath the horses' hooves as the sun moved higher in the sky.

She dropped back so her horse trotted next to his. "I'm glad you made it through everything."

"I could tell you the same. Don't get so far away from me next time."

She sent a grin skidding his way along with a sidelong glance. "That sounded suspiciously like an order. Enforcer to witch and all that."

"It wasn't. Not exactly." Heat rose to his face, and he tried out bunches of words, none of which exactly fit.

"I'm teasing you. There's a creek ahead. I smell water. So does my horse. What say we stop for a break?"

He deployed power, searching for the unmistakable taint of Black Magick but not finding any evidence of it nearby. "Seems like as good a spot as any. I'll let the others know." Kneeing the horse, he caught up with Sam, who'd ridden ahead with Hester and the others.

A LARGE GROVE of willows provided shelter as they let the horses drink. Breana had hoped for some private time with Joshua. It was the main reason she'd suggested stopping, plus they were over halfway back, and everyone needed a break. While the others sat on the riverbank, she beckoned to Joshua, drawing him aside.

"I'd shield my words with magic—" She rolled her eyes.

"—but witches and mages have awfully keen ears," he finished for her and threaded his arms around her shoulders, gazing into her eyes. His shaded to green in the midmorning light, and she cupped the side of his face in one hand.

"The way things have been going, I wanted to say a few things, and us even making it back to the ranch isn't a given, although it's looking more likely than it was an hour ago." Breana shrugged. "Maybe Hester's idea about deploying the shades will at least buy us a respite."

"Was that what you wanted to talk about? Shades and magic?" His eyes twinkled mischievously and he pressed his body so close all she could think about was how much she wanted him to kiss her.

"No. I wanted to make certain you knew I liked you—a lot— and that it wouldn't take much for me to fall in love with you." She released a breath she didn't realize she'd been holding. It hadn't been nearly as hard to utter those words as she'd feared.

A broad grin lit his face, making him so stunning, she almost couldn't bear to look at him. But she couldn't tear her gaze away, either. "You've just made me a very happy man," he murmured just before he slashed his mouth over hers. A passionate, self-assured male claiming what was his.

She wove her arms around his neck and kissed him back, wanting him with a ferocity that turned her blood molten. When he licked the seam between her lips, she opened her mouth, sucking hungrily on his tongue. He bit, sucked, licked, as she moved her mouth from his lips to his neck and back again. His skin tasted of sweat and magic, and it stoked her lust. Her nipples peaked, becoming hard points of need, and his cock swelled against her belly.

He let his hands rove down her back, nesting one around the curves of her ass as he pulled her against his erection. Her sex slicked with wanting him, and she groaned. Would this be like last time where they teased each other into climaxes? Could they actually finesse something more satisfying?

His breath beat a fiery path down her neck and he closed a hand over one of her breasts, rolling the nipple beneath its layers of fabric. She broke away from their kiss. "The others. We're too close."

"I can fix that."

The honey-rich feel of his magic surrounded her as he sequestered them behind a barrier. He led her to relatively dry ground beneath a small grove of aspen trees, and she began to undo the laces of his pants.

"I can get them," he said, his voice rimmed with raw need. "You're the one with all the layers."

"Not so many." Her breath came fast, and she sat to unlace her boots. She'd barely gotten the first one off when he knelt before her, and drew her stocking down her leg, his movements almost reverent. The heat of his hands on her flesh ignited sparks, and he ran a fingernail up the sole of her newly bared foot.

He fumbled with her other boot, and his mouth followed his hands as he drew her second stocking off. He flicked his tongue between her toes, sucking each in turn. The sensation raced straight up her legs and she jammed a hand between them, so lost in hunger, she didn't care about anything except pushing her body into an orgasm.

Joshua batted her hand away. "That's my job." He licked his

way up the inside of her leg until she wanted to scream with frustration, but she left her throbbing, aching nub alone.

His hands trembled when he pulled the ribbon holding her knickers in place. Rather than taking them off, he laid a hand over her sex, teasing her through the thin fabric. She wriggled beneath his touch and tried to reposition herself so she could grasp his cock where it stood out from his body, hard and proud, but he shook his head and bent to close his mouth over the charged nub between her legs.

He breathed heat into her, and slowly tugged her smallclothes out of the way, stringing kisses across her belly. She slid her fingers under his hair and jammed herself against his questing tongue, wanting the feel of him against her naked flesh more than she'd ever wanted anything.

He swiped his tongue over her sex, licking, teasing, and his hips bucked as he drove his cock against her lower legs. Magic jolted as he mind-linked with her, and the rhythm of his tongue changed as he sensed exactly what she needed. He slipped two fingers inside her and cradled her ass with his other hand, all the while sucking harder, then backing off just before she came until she was wild with wanting him.

He moved up her body and she wrapped her legs around him, fully open for the thrust that would drive his cock home. Inside her, where he belonged. He hovered above her, and his eyes—golden now—bored into hers. "Once this is done," he rasped, "you'll be bound to me. I'll follow you to the ends of the earth. There'll be no escape."

"I don't want there to be."

"Breana." Her name was part entreaty, part prayer. "I love you, woman. I've loved you forever. You're a part of everything I am. I didn't realize how much until I let that part of myself loose."

"I'm glad. I want to be the center of your universe." She pushed her hips upward. "Please. I need you."

In one fluid thrust, he buried himself inside her. She was so primed from his tongue, her body convulsed around him as a climax roared through her.

# CHAPTER 14

The scorching heat of her body almost undid him when she shuddered around his cock. He rode the barest edges of control, letting her climax quiet before he started moving. He wouldn't last long, but maybe he could make her come again. It was a worthy goal. The feel of her around his cock was amazing. She'd stretched to accommodate his girth, moving her legs from his waist to his shoulders to take him more deeply inside her. He wished she was naked, that he could suckle and touch her breasts. Laving her pussy with his tongue had been so sensual, he'd had a hell of a time not coming in his pants. If they'd still been laced, the friction from the tight leather would've been enough to push him beyond the brink of his magically-reinforced control.

Holding himself up on his arms, he gazed at her spread beneath him. Her head was thrown back on her long, beautiful stalk of a neck, and her eyes were closed. Passion splotched her face and chest a lovely rose color, and her erect nipples were fully visible through the fabric of her dress. He was still joined to her mind, and he drew back until only the tip of him teased the entrance to her body. Her lush heat beckoned, but he held himself there for long moments before sinking ever so slowly back inside her.

He wasn't sure how many more times he could do that before he lost it and slammed into her without any restraint at all, but he'd give it his best shot. She felt amazing around him. Better than every fantasy he'd spun about her. He had no idea how many hundreds or thousands of times he'd come with an image of her driving his hands as they pumped his engorged penis.

To finally have the real thing was almost unbelievable.

She tightened her muscles around his shaft and opened her eyes. Warmth and tenderness laced with pure, unbridled heat spilled from her, and she settled her hands on his hips, tugging, wanting him to move faster.

He withdrew and thrust. The dance her muscles did around his cock urged him forward. She slowly, purposely, moved a hand to her mouth and immersed two fingers. When she rucked up her skirts and touched herself with her moistened fingers, rubbing herself, he was lost.

Groaning, he clung to her hips. His body developed a mind of its own and he fucked her, moving as hard and as fast as he could. He felt her next climax seed from the previous one, and joined his energy to hers. When she crested, his balls snugged against his body, and semen spurted from him.

Hot, viscous, burning, it melted his soul. He bent his head and kissed her, breathing her in as the last of his spasms spent themselves. He held her for long moments, catching his breath and savoring how she felt cradled against him.

Reluctantly, he moved his mouth from hers. "We need to leave."

"I know. We got lucky no one bothered us."

He brushed his mouth over hers one last time and pulled his

still-hard cock from her body. After wiping himself with some tufts of grass, he got to his feet and tucked his cock back inside his pants, lacing them up over an erection that didn't want to resolve.

She'd slithered back into her smallclothes and was lacing her boots. Breana stood, frowning. "Where's everyone else?"

"They left to give us some privacy, but they're traveling slow until we catch them up. Sam told me that somewhere between me tasting you and fu—" Joshua bit off the word, not wanting to be crass.

"Oh come on." She moved close and cupped her hand over the bulge in his trousers. "You can fuck me with that any old time you want."

He smiled. "Everything is so new. I want to shield you, protect you—"

"Ensorcel me in a tower and keep the only key?" She winked broadly, and he laughed.

"Keeping you only for me is rather alluring. Are you offering?"

"No. Just tossing out ideas. If you're like most men, you'd want that tower damned close to the kitchen."

"You've got my number, sweetheart." Joshua whistled, and their horses trotted over. He helped her mount, despite her protests, and they cantered down the road, searching for the others.

Half an hour passed before they came into view, but Joshua had been on alert the whole time, scenting the air for evil, and not finding a thing. Breana was his woman now, and he'd protect her come hell or high water, whether she wished it or no.

"Seems odd that darkness would've vanished so completely," he muttered as he pulled his mount alongside Sam's sorrel stallion.

"I was thinking the same." The other enforcer set his mouth in a harsh line. "It's like they're holding back, massing for the next attack."

"Aren't you boys the gloom and doom patrol?" Hester rolled her eyes. "The shades are doing the work I sent them after. It may not buy us much, but the next day shouldna yield any wicked surprises." She paused to take a breath. "Mayhap by then, I'll have stones matched to the rest of you."

"I get to decide first between the emerald and the opal," Chris said.

Breana nudged her horse between his and Sam's. "The way I understand things," she said, "is that if a stone works with your energy, it won't be a match for anyone else." She sent a questioning glance Hester's way.

The older witch shook her head. "Wish I knew. Working the ruby and star sapphire to focus and concentrate my own magic was one thing. The stones appear to have a synergistic effect. Mine are stronger now that ye and Joshua have stones. 'Tis anyone's guess how potent they'll be if three more join the mix."

"Four more," Tom said. "I've always admired your magic, but you never could add."

"I was being conservative," Hester informed him, her tone haughty. "We might not have stones to hand that are a match for everyone."

Joshua smothered a grin that wanted out. Hester was backpedaling to salvage her pride. He didn't blame her. No one liked their mistakes waved in front of their faces. He glanced around them. They'd rejoined the main road between Breana's ranch, Salt Lake and points east and west of them. Soon, they'd be home.

Home.

He liked the sound of that, and it surprised him. He'd never wanted a home. Not since the Church turned his original one into a shambles. For a moment, he wondered if he was becoming soft, losing his competitive edge in the long-running conflict against sorcery, devil worship, and Black Magick. In a flash of stark insight, he understood the most important thing in his life was Breana. Loving her, watching over her, making sure their children were safe—no matter what was happening in the world around them.

He wheeled his horse hard right and down the lane leading to the ranch.

"Nice to be back here," Sam said. "I was sorry I had to leave so soon last time."

Something rattled in the back of Joshua's memory. He didn't want to make Sam uncomfortable by asking after the woman he'd mentioned visiting in New Orleans, so he just said, "Where were you when you intercepted Chris' call for help?"

"Subtle." Sam whistled low. "You should've been an ambassador—for a country that's under fire."

Joshua dismounted and came around to Breana, holding out his arms. She tossed a leg over the back of her mare and slid into them. After a quick kiss, she sprinted toward the house. "Got to get some food cooking," she called over one shoulder. "You men eat a surprising amount."

"Right behind you." Hester dashed nimbly after her.

Joshua loosened his saddle and chucked it over a fence rail. The other enforcers were similarly engaged. Chris led the horses toward the barn. Cory and Tom trudged across the yard, stopping at the pump to sluice cold water over their hands and dust-caked faces.

"You never did answer me." Joshua kept his voice low, the words pitched only for Sam.

"I was close when he called, else I wouldn't have heard him, but you already know that. Nevada territory, give or take a few miles. "Didn't stay long in New Orleans. The woman had married and she already has at least two little ones. I didn't even let her know I was there once I saw her and her husband."

"I'm sorry."

Sam turned the full force of his blue gaze on Joshua. "Don't be. If what was between us had been worth it, she'd have waited. I told her I'd be back, and I always keep my word."

Joshua started to say that five years was a long time, but Sam must've intuited his words because he said pointedly, "You waited over a hundred years for another man's wife. I wasn't gone that long. My lady friend didn't believe in me, so we wouldn't have worked. Once we'd made love, I assumed she'd be faithful."

Joshua's head snapped up. "Are you certain one of her children isn't yours? That might explain—"

"Absolutely certain," Sam cut in. "I know how to control things like that. It's why none of us have packs of bastards roaming the countryside."

"You have such a golden-tongued way with words." Joshua bit back a snort. He clapped Sam on the back and said, "Come on inside. Say, since you appeared to know about my, erm, interest in Breana—and Hester knew—was it common knowledge?"

Sam drew his brows together thoughtfully. "Maybe not exactly common knowledge, but nor was it as well-kept a secret as you'd hoped. Can I stand as your best man?"

They trooped up the broad front steps, wiping travel dust from their boots on the mat before stepping inside. "We haven't discussed formalizing anything—yet," Joshua said. "She's still in mourning for her child."

Sam lowered his voice. "She lost that kid years back. As soon as Don turned it to the dark."

Joshua stopped and switched to shielded telepathy. *"She never gave up hope of reclaiming her. The death we crafted in mage fire killed any possibility of that."*

*"Don't worry. I'll keep my mouth shut, but the sooner you legal things up and start producing babies of your own, the better things will be for Breana. Nothing like a babe in your arms to lessen the hurt from losing another."*

*"I'd have committed bigamy fifty years ago if she'd wanted me."* Joshua grinned and switched to speaking aloud. "Whatever the lady wants is how we'll do things. I smell food."

"Maybe if we're lucky everything will be done by the time we get there."

Joshua slugged him in the arm and headed for the kitchen.

"I heard that." Breana greeted him with her arms elbow-deep in flour.

"None of this guilt by association." Joshua broke into a grin. "I'm here. What do you need help with?"

She closed her teeth over her full lower lip, making him think about how those lips felt pressed against his. Lust ignited every cell from his toes to his head, but he forced himself to focus.

"I'm here too." Sam mock bowed. "At your service, Mistress Giraud."

"Hester's in the workshop with Chris, Tom, and Cory. Maybe you could show Sam where it is so he can get rolling with a power stone of his own."

"I don't need an escort." Sam jerked his chin back the direction they'd come from. "Powerful magic's coming from the end of the first floor." He screwed his face into a grin and glanced at the tented-out front of Joshua's leather breeches. "If I leave the two of you alone, will dinner molder and die for lack of attention?"

"I'll see it doesn't." Breana was clearly trying to sound firm, but she was smiling.

"Holler if you need any of us, but I won't hold my breath. What I will do—" Sam spun to face Joshua "—is wager you a twenty-dollar gold piece you don't make it through dinner preparations without dragging Breana upstairs."

Joshua quirked a brow. "So I get the gold if I win."

"Yup." Sam dug the coin out of his breeches, tossed it in the air, and palmed it again. "If you lose, my lucky coin stays right here with Papa."

"You're on!" Joshua held out his hand, and Sam shook it before trotting out of the room.

Breana had finished kneading the biscuits and was rolling and cutting dough. He checked the oven, prepared to add more tinder, but it seemed close enough to baking temperature. From there, he lifted lids on pots sitting on the stove, stirring and tasting. She hip-butted him out of the way and opened the oven door, sliding her baking trays inside.

"There." She dusted floury hands together amid a shower of white particles. "Nothing to do now but wait." She batted her eyes in a come-hither gesture. "The bet was we'd go upstairs. No one said a thing about the kitchen table, or the floor, or—"

His cock throbbed painfully, pressing against his tight-laced pants. "You, woman, are pure temptation."

"Did I hear a complaint?"

"No, ma'am. Never."

"Good, cause it's going to get way worse." She reached beneath her skirts and tugged the ribbons of her knickers. When they slid down her legs, she stepped out of them, and he realized she was barefoot. Breana knelt in front of him, and undid the laces of his pants. Drawing his cock into her hands and rubbing the sensitive head with her fingertips, she bent her head and took him into her mouth.

The lush wetness of her questing tongue as it swirled around him threw his heart into triple-time rhythm. He wanted her with a fierceness borne during long years of holding himself back. Of watching her on Don's arm, and wanting to kill the other man.

She teased him with her lips and tongue, biting, sucking, milking his shaft with her hand while she took more of him into her mouth. With a groan he couldn't quite stifle, he buried his hands in her hair and gave himself up to sensation spilling through him. He wanted to immerse himself in her sex, but he couldn't have withdrawn from her mouth if a tornado had run through the house.

She tightened her hand around him, and his hips thrust with a mind of their own as semen juddered from him in sheets of ecstasy that rocked him to his core. She sucked and swallowed until his body quieted. With a grin that wouldn't have been out of place on a Siren, she let go of him, got to her feet, and sashayed over to her work table. Facing away from him, she rucked up her skirts, baring the creamy globes of her ass as she bent over the table.

The golden mat between her legs was spiky with her juices, and her invitation obvious. He surged forward, still-hard cock in hand, and drove into her, burying himself full-tilt. She rocked back toward him, and he reached around her, rubbing the seat of her woman's pleasure while he plumbed her from behind.

She placed her hand over his, showing him the rhythm she needed. He withdrew and thrust. Because he'd just come, it was easy to pleasure her, but he took his time, walking her along a fine edge, but backing off when she closed on release. Her body trembled beneath his, finally escaping his hold on it as her muscles clutched him, contracting rhythmically.

He considered a second orgasm, but decided to save himself for later when they were upstairs in a real bed. He moved his arms until they were tucked beneath her shoulders and bent forward to kiss the nape of her neck before withdrawing and cleaning himself up.

Breana pushed her skirts into place and shinnied back into her underclothes, tying the pink bow with a flourish. "There," she said breathlessly, and grinned. "You get the gold piece, and we got to have fun anyway."

"Best part—" he bent over the stove, moving things around and taking the biscuits out of the oven "—is we didn't ruin dinner."

"Best part? You might want to try that one again." She thumped her chest with a finger.

"Bad choice of words, sweetheart. The best part is you. Take it easy while I carry dishes to the sideboard."

"I'll go let everyone know it's time to eat. Been mighty quiet from back there. Hope that machine of Hester's didn't go south on her."

Joshua watched the provocative swing of Breana's hips as she walked out of the kitchen. That she wanted him with a need as great as his own thrilled him. She'd finessed their skirmish in the kitchen, and he'd never see the room in quite the same way again.

Laughter rocked him. Before they were done, he had little doubt they'd christen every nook and cranny of the farmhouse. Don may have moved here with her, but they'd stopped having sex before they relocated.

He was her first lover here—and he'd be her only one forever more.

Would she want to marry right away? Or had he been right about respecting a mourning period for her child?

*Guess I'll have to ask her to find those things out.*

His practical nature said they should wait until this latest clash with Black Magick played itself out, but the part of him that had lusted after her forever didn't want even one more day to elapse without her as his wife. Once loosed, the depth of his emotion shocked him. He hadn't thought he was capable of wanting anyone as badly as he craved Breana.

*I was wrong.*

He'd kick the earth off its axis if it threatened his love. Nothing would ever harm her. Not now. Not ever. He'd see to it personally.

# CHAPTER 15

Breana and Hester worked together companionably, cleaning up after the meal everyone had shared. The men had retired to the front porch with a bottle of port and cigars from Don's stash of Havana tobacco.

Breana glanced Hester's way. "You never did share much in the way of details about the men and their stones. Is Tom the only one who doesn't have one?"

A troubled expression crossed Hester's face, intensifying the lines across her forehead. She switched to shielded speech in Gaelic, which told Breana she truly didn't wish to be overheard. *"No reason I could tell why the stones dinna take a shine to his energy, but they reacted in a way I've never seen afore."*

Breana stopped washing dishes in water she'd heated over the stove and turned toward her mentor. *"Say more."*

*"It happened twice, until Tom refused to try again. Said he wasn't cut out to have a power stone."*

*"What happened twice,"* Breana pressed. *"I can't read your mind. It's shielded too closely."*

Hester shook her head. *"Not sure as I can label it. The machinery worked like it always does with heat and smoke, and the stones took on a glow—until he held them in his palm for a short time. Then they winked out as if they'd checked him over and decided they dinna wish to be associated with his energy."*

*"Did he act uncomfortable?"*

*"Nay. Not terribly."*

Breana narrowed her eyes to slits, thinking. She'd only met Tom a handful of times. He'd shown up at Coven headquarters about a year before she and Don left for Utah Territory. The harder she thought about it, the hazier the details became, almost as if someone—or something—didn't want her to remember.

But he'd avoided Don toward the end. And Joshua had said something about Tom confiding concerns about her erstwhile husband.

Hester dropped her shielding. "Let's get these supper dishes done. I'd like to lie down for a while. We've been at one thing or another for well over twenty-four hours." She blew out a tired-sounding breath. "Hell, I was exhausted when I drove my wagon and team into your yard. Never did get around to unloading the wagon, and I'm not going to do it now, either."

"It's actually pushing forty-eight hours, now that you mention it. I'm tired too, but in a weird, spun-out kind of way." Breath whistled from between her teeth as she turned back to her sink full of lye soap and water. "Chris ended up with the emerald. How about the other two enforcers? I'm actually glad to see those gemstones of mine going to good use."

"Sam paired with the opal. The corona of pearls all but leapt into Cory's hand, and they turned the most amazing pinkish-orange, like an overactive sunset."

"That other." Breana was hesitant to say anything about Tom out loud. "It's worrisome."

"Not much we can do about it right now. He's had plenty of chances to attempt something nefarious, and never acted on a one of them."

Breana considered that as she pulled the drain and pumped cold water over the soapy dishes. She warded her next words. *"You're thinking he's flirted with evil, and isn't sure quite which side of the road to walk on."*

*"We worked together too closely and too long. That's exactly it."* Hester's gaze bored into her. *"So long as he hasna fully given in, I'm not thinking we have much to worry about."*

*"I don't agree. The dark sorcerers could use him as a conduit. He's a weak link, and I'm not sure we want him around here. Goddesses' teats!"* She raked her wet hands through her hair. *"We have enough trouble without courting more."*

*"It's not as if we truly know anything. Regardless, nothing to be done about it until we've all had some rest,"* Hester spoke firmly. Grabbing a flour sack Breana had turned into a towel, she attacked the pile of clean dishes.

A thought slammed into Breana, spurring hope rather than fear. *"It's possible we're overreacting. Tom hosted evil when they attacked him back at the battle. Joshua had one hell of a struggle calling him back from darkness. There just might be enough taint left to bother the stones."*

"Not likely. The stones attack dark power, drive it out, heal it."

"Maybe they were wrong about Tom," Breana persisted. "Magic doesn't always act the same way. Lots of different things can intervene."

"We willna solve this one till we know more. On a more pleasant tack," Hester went on as if they hadn't just been discussing evil incarnate. "Now that Joshua has declared his longstanding interest in you, will I be calling the goddess's blessings upon your wedding promises?"

Breana froze mid-swipe and clutched her dishtowel before it fell to the none-too-clean floor. "It's too soon," she squeaked, cleared her throat, and tried again. "We need time."

Hester set the last of her stack of dishes on the sideboard and hung her towel on a hook. When she turned to face Breana, she'd crossed her arms beneath her breasts. "Why? He's known what he wants forever. 'Tis only ye who are newly come to the game." Her expression softened. "I've known you for many a long year, and ye were never well-mated with Don. The two of you came to a place where ye lived peaceably enough—until his infatuation with evil gained a toehold. Why not take a chance on true happiness?"

"Because I want to be sure that's what's in store for us. He's a good man. It'd be a damn shame if I let him down."

"Pretty words." Hester cast a knowing look her way. "Better said afore ye offered up the pleasures of your body. Now that your flesh has been joined, it tempts fate to remain unmarried."

"Then how come so many of us couple willy-nilly at Beltane and the other solstice and equinox festivals? No one's running about saying they have to solemnize those relationships."

"'Tis something entirely different. Those men and women aren't in love. They're having sex to ensure the land remains fertile. Joshua's adored you for as long as I've known him."

Breana tossed her head. "You may think you're my mother, but you're not, and I refuse to be railroaded into something this important. I need to do some soul-searching and figure out what I want. After that, he and I need to talk. Maybe now's a good time to at least make a start on the figuring out part. I've been so swept up enjoying his charms, I hadn't paid anything further much heed. Think I'll take a walk. I'm too wound up to sleep."

Hester crossed the kitchen and gave Breana a quick hug. "I'm here if ye need me, child."

"Thank you. Get some rest."

"I will."

Breana let herself out the kitchen door. A glance at the sky told her the afternoon was all but spent. Dinner had been generous, so she could probably get by without making supper. She strode to the fence line and wandered toward the springhouse, a place she'd avoided since Don used it as a storehouse for books so wicked they made her skin crawl. The books were long since gone, burned in mage fire, but she'd taken to storing food in the house's generous root cellar. Her excuse had been that it was closer—if not nearly so large. In truth, she hadn't wanted anything to do with the springhouse.

Not quite sure what drew her, she approached the small structure, half-buried in dirt and sod to keep things cool. At first she thought the low murmur tickling the edges of her hearing was an artifact of leftover dark energy, but voices formed as she drew near. She warded herself, being as unobtrusive as she could. It wouldn't do to have a magical flare announce her proximity. Because she kept things low key, her shielding wasn't perfect, but it was as good as she was likely to get.

She crept closer, one stealthy step at a time, and focused her power to amplify the conversation unfolding in the springhouse. Andras' voice was unmistakable, and her stomach clenched with dread. She assumed the other man had to be Tom, but the cadence of his voice was wrong. Her eyes widened and she choked back a gasp.

*Cory.*

The man having a tea party with the devil was Cory, an enforcer she'd always respected. How could he have hidden his dalliance with evil so thoroughly?

*Don did.*

The thought stopped her cold. What she should do was turn the other way and quietly alert the others. Five—six if you counted Tom—against two were decent odds. They'd prevail.

*I will do that, just as soon as I see if I can't learn something.*

She leaned closer, listening intently. Maybe Andras would reveal enough to give them a true edge. The possibility filled her with chilly resolve. If they could put their battle with Black Magick behind them forever, she and Joshua could make a life for themselves without always having to look over their shoulders. The corners of her mouth twitched into a reluctant smile. Maybe she wasn't as far from a decision about him as she'd led herself to believe.

"Lure the woman outside," Andras rasped. "Come up with some believable pretense. Maybe you can use that new stone, the one that's making my skin burn just being near it."

"What do you need her for?" Cory asked. "She's a decent sort."

"Why I want her is no business of yours." Andras' words weren't any louder, but they crackled with command.

A shudder ran through Breana. Apparently none of Hester's shades had targeted Andras, or if they had, he'd trounced them.

"Bring her outside and walk to the far side of the barn. Your horse went lame, and you want her to take a look at it. If you don't like that excuse, come up with something on your own."

"What happens then? She'll know I jumped sides when you show up, and I don't lift a finger to help her."

"Your problem, but I could fix it by killing you once you've served your purpose." Andras chuckled nastily. "Besides, it's not important. Once I get my claws into her this time, she's never coming back here. I've taken a fancy to her."

Cory barked laughter. "You'd do better taking an alley cat to bed. That one'll scratch your eyes out and roast your balls on a stick over mage fire."

"I wasn't aware witches controlled mage fire," Andras replied coolly.

"They don't. It was just an expression." Breana could almost imagine him shrugging. "Your funeral, fellow. Anything else before I do your bidding?"

"Yes. Your presence is required at our normal meeting place north of Salt Lake. Leave here immediately afterward. Your next set of instructions will arrive via one of my minions sometime before midnight. Wait for him, and carry them out."

"That's it?"

Breanna knew Cory well enough to hear the barely restrained anger beneath his words.

"I'm not used to repeating myself."

Breana shook herself out of the semi trance she'd fallen into listening to the men plot her kidnapping. What the hell had Andras promised Cory to induce him to switch sides? Don had received vast sums of money, willing spirits to service him, and a fawning attitude from highly placed sorcerers like Alistair MacDuff. It sounded as if Cory hadn't negotiated nearly as rich a deal for himself. Or maybe he had, and Andras was reneging.

*What a surprise. Evil not keeping its word.*

She would've laughed, but then they'd know she was only a few feet away. She backed away, quietly, carefully, until she'd put a respectable distance between herself and the springhouse. Then she turned and ran, letting her magic skitter to nothingness in the brisk breeze as she pelted up the steps.

Her first stop was Hester's bedroom. She'd picked one of the downstairs rooms not too far from the one she'd staked out as her workshop. Breana shook her awake and began to talk before the other witch had her eyes fully open.

Hester listened, looking more and more thunderstruck.

"Och, terrible news! I'm not understanding why those pearls aligned themselves with Cory, but 'tisn't important. We need Sam and Joshua. Chris too." Hester sprang to her feet, still fully dressed. "Knew there was a reason I dinna bother stripping off these duds."

"I'll reach Joshua and tell him to bring the other two. Where?"

"My workshop. It's easier to ward."

Breana raised her mind voice, aimed just for Joshua. *"Meet me in Hester's workshop. Bring Sam and Chris. No one else."*

His reply was immediate, lined with concern. *"What happened?"*

*"Tell you when you get there. Come now."*

Breana ran down the hall after Hester, who'd already left. By the time she got to the workshop, the brazier was crackling as Hester built up the fire. Pounding footsteps announced the men would be there in no time. As soon as they showed up, Breana shooed them inside, closed the door, and sealed it with magic.

"What the hell is wrong now?" Sam growled.

"We were just getting into that bottle of port." Chris grinned.

Joshua draped an arm around her shoulders. She leaned into him briefly, and sent a questioning glance Hester's way.

"Room's warded," Hester said, "but use telepathy and shield that too."

After a sharp nod, Breana outlined what she'd heard outside.

*"Cory?"* An incredulous look spread over Sam's face. *"I can scarcely believe it of him. Shit! I damn near raised him after his parents died. There has to be some rational explanation."*

*"Like what?"* Joshua demanded. *"He apparently didn't ask for directions when Andras instructed him to show up at wherever their normal meeting place is."*

*"So long as we're discussing enforcers,"* Chris inserted. *"Why isn't Tom here? Is it because the stones rejected him?"*

*"We can't afford to take a chance on anyone we're not sure of,"* Joshua said, his voice tight with tension. *"We also don't have much time to chew the fat. Breana, when Cory comes looking for you, go with him. The rest of us will deploy ourselves and be close enough to do some good when Andras shows up."*

A feral grin split Sam's face. *"We're going to take on the Dark Angel, huh? I like it."*

*"If we could manage Alistair MacDuff, I bet we can send Andras straight to Hell."* Chris chuckled.

Joshua elbowed him. *"As I recall, brother, you spent most of that particular episode unconscious."*

*"Did not. I fought him good—before he figured out how to get his blood inside me. Things didn't go so well after that."*

Hester clapped her hands sharply together. *"We need a plan after Breana trots out of here with Cory."* She turned her unrelenting gaze on Breana. *"And ye, Missy, will need to take verra close care not to let him see into your mind. Not a thing."*

*"Got it,"* Breana snapped through gritted teeth. *"I'll do what I can to stall him too."*

*"Excellent. We may need the time."* Hester seized a short blade from a nearby table and grabbed Breana's hand, making a quick slice at the base of her thumb. Once she'd done the same to her own hand, she held the wounds together.

*"You and I were bonded this way years back,"* Breana protested.

*"Aye, child, but I wanted it good and fresh. In case we have to hunt you down from...elsewhere."*

Her words made a chill course down Breana's body, turning her blood to icy sludge. Surely it wouldn't come to that.

*"I'm still linked to the shades,"* Hester went on. *"I've already*

*summoned them to my side. Some will come, some not, but they're on their way."*

"Brilliant!" Joshua crowed. *"We can marshal their energy to help bind Andras."*

*"Let's hope it turns out to be that simple,"* Chris muttered.

A sharp knock at the door snapped Breana's head around. *"That'll be Cory,"* she said. *"Act normal. We were all reloading our stones' energies."*

Hester blew out a breath. A welcoming smile blossomed on her face and she sent a bolt of magic to open the door.

Cory stepped inside. "Not that I had to look very hard, what with the huge infusion of magic concentrated in here, but what are all of you doing? And if it has something to do with the stones, why didn't someone call me?" Mild reproach ran beneath his words.

"I did look for you." Joshua shrugged. "Actually, you showing up is timely. Chris was about to hunt you down. We're recharging the stones and letting them get to know one another better."

"Hopefully, they'll help make us a more effective fighting unit —if they all amplify the same frequency," Sam cut in.

"Once we learn how to manage them." Chris grinned ruefully. "Handling my emerald is like trying to tame a tornado."

"Get your stone out—" Hester made come along motions at Cory with one hand "—and we'll get things cracking. Once they're all fully charged, I plan to move things outside where we have some room to test what they're capable of."

Cory dug a circlet of half a dozen pearls from an inner pocket. "I'm up for recharging these, but then I'd hoped for Breana's help with a different project—at least for a while."

She rounded her eyes, all innocence, as she glanced his way. "What might that be?"

"I was just down at the stable. Think my horse has gone lame. You've got a good way with animals, and I'd sure appreciate it if you could take a look at him."

"Me?" Breana shook her head in what she hoped looked like disbelief. "You've got me confused with Abigail. Healing was never my forte. Hester, maybe you could take a stab at helping his stallion."

"Maybe so, but animal doctoring was never up my alley, either."

Breana kept a close eye on Cory, wondering what he'd do. What gambit would he come up with next to induce her to leave the house with him?

He shrugged and placed the pearls on the square of deer hide. "First things first. If mine's the only one that needs another shot of power, let's get her done and we can go outside and practice."

"What about your horse, brother?" Chris asked.

"Damn if I know. Not sure if riding him is a good idea just now. Come on, Bree. Maybe just a quick peek before we get heavy into practicing with the stones? Then if there's something I can do—maybe a poultice or some kind of magic—he'll have time to heal up before we need to go somewhere."

*"Agree,"* skittered across her mind, barely there, but a quick eye flash from Joshua told her who'd sent it.

"Sure." Breana nodded briefly. "Don't expect miracles, but of course I'll do what I can."

# CHAPTER 16

Joshua watched Breana walk toward the barn with Cory, chatting good-naturedly. He handed her credit for her acting skills. The other enforcer would've had no reason to believe she suspected a thing.

Hester gestured the group to the far side of the house. Power swirled around her in a blue-white maelstrom, and the air grew chill as the dead gathered forces, using Hester as a central point. The cold was so pervasive and unpleasant, he wondered how the witch stood it.

"Work with me to contain their energy," she ordered the men. "They willna be worth nearly as much if Andras knows they're here."

Joshua tossed a shield around the massing shades and chafed impatiently. The thought of Breana being on her own for as much as a moment with Andras made his skin crawl. "We need to get moving."

"Give her some credit," Hester hissed. "I trained her. I know what she's capable of. She can hold her own until we get there.

We're waiting until we have a few more shades, and then we'll move. They're arriving faster now."

"It's like they attract one another," Sam muttered.

"Yeah," Chris said. "They do."

The back door slammed, and Tom pelted down the steps. "What the fuck?" he demanded. "I was dead to the world when I felt this unholy cold. Why are the shades here?"

Joshua groaned inwardly. He'd forgotten about Tom, and he felt like an idiot for his oversight. He should've spelled the other enforcer so he'd remain asleep until this was over.

Tom narrowed his shrewd blue eyes and sifted thick fingers through his unruly, brown hair, pushing it out of his face. "None of you trust me," he blurted. "Because of the stones. For that matter, where are Cory and Breana?"

"Seeing after Cory's horse," Joshua answered. He took a measured breath. "You're right about the stones. It's possible they were reacting to some residual defect Black Magick left in you, but when I had a similar problem they healed me. Regardless, magic is persnickety, and I'm willing to wait that one out to make any judgments. In the meantime, I'd take it as a kindness if you went back inside."

"A *kindness*, is it?" Tom glowered. "You're gearing up for a fight. Looks like you need every able-bodied man. My magic's close to recovered. Don't make me sit this one out. Please."

Something about his tone caught at Joshua, and the man's words rang true, but then Don's had too.

*I never asked Don pointblank if he'd been turned by evil.*

"This isn't a decision for me alone, but we need to figure things out fast. Breana's been gone for at least ten minutes." He faced Tom squarely, focusing a truth spell. "Have you parleyed with the dark?"

"Of course not," the other enforcer sputtered. "That's occasionally happened to witches, but never to an enforcer. Not that I know about anyway."

"I say we include him. His words dinna tangle in your spell." Hester spoke from the center of a widening ring of glimmering shades.

"Thank you." Tom inclined his head. "I've never let you down, Hester Thorne, and tonight won't change that."

"How about the rest of you?" Joshua looked from Sam to Chris.

"I'm good with including him," Chris said brusquely, and Sam gave a thumbs up sign.

"Looks like you're in. Don't make me sorry," Joshua told Tom, then directed his next words at Hester. "Are enough of those godforsaken dead here to do any good?" He shivered and tugged the lacings of his leather shirt to snug it against his body, but it didn't make him any warmer.

Hester nodded, her mouth set in a terse line. "Aye. Let's go."

"Someone fill me in," Tom said. "What are we doing?"

Sam clapped him on the back. "We're off to fight Black Magick, brother. Same as always. So long as we're both alive at the end of things, I'll give you the grisly details later. Glad to have you here. I couldn't believe you'd been turned."

Joshua was done waiting. He took off for the barn at a dead run with the others behind him. Tom would either help them— or not. How he comported himself today would determine if he remained a Coven enforcer or met his end in mage fire. Right along with the Dark Angel.

Destroying Andras filled Joshua with cold delight. He'd battle the Dark Angel and send his sorry hide to Hell nine different ways. He kept power flowing to contain the shades, but the closer they came to the barn, the less likely they'd escape detection. Anything that lowered the air temperature to below freezing was impossible to sequester for very long—with any combination of magic.

He raised his hands to summon maximum power and linked to the moonstone that he'd moved to an upper pocket. He didn't want to have to hold it in one hand because that would dilute his ability to work power. Bright light flashed from the far side of the barn followed by a harsh, tearing noise.

He pushed his legs to greater speed. That had sounded a hell of a lot like a gateway forming between worlds. "Cory, you goddamned son of a bitch," he screamed. "You better do something to keep her on this side of that portal or I'll hunt you down like a dog, and you'll find your end in mage fire."

BREANA SENSED Cory's nervousness as she walked by his side. The other enforcer was usually pleasant, mildly flirtatious, and a bit of a ladies' man. Because she couldn't resist, she asked, "Everything all right, Cory?"

"Yeah." He kept his eyes on the dirt ahead of them. "Why would you ask?"

She shrugged. "I don't know. You just don't seem quite like your normal self. Probably worried about your horse. You broke him from a colt as I recall."

The enforcer smiled, but it looked like the gesture cost him, judging from the tense set of his shoulders. "Indeed I did. You've got a good memory, Bree."

They reached the barn and she started to go inside, but he said, "Lancer's around back."

"How about if you bring him inside?" She stood with the door propped open. "I can hang a lantern so I can see better. We're losing the light fast out here."

It was a reasonable suggestion, and she didn't wait for him to reply, just went into the barn and kindled a lantern with a quick shot of magic. The carbon oil flamed bright and clear, and she hung it from a hook, readied her magic, and waited.

The horses in the barn whickered nervously, which set the goats to *baahing*. About the only creatures not making noise were the chickens. It shouldn't take long for Cory to lead a horse in through the barn's double back doors. When a few minutes had elapsed, she got serious about drawing power and shielding herself with it. To hedge her bets, she called Danu.

The goddess had helped her once. Maybe she'd take pity on her again.

Tension thrummed through her, turning her stomach into a writhing mass of snakes. Where were the others? Had Andras sabotaged their plans somehow?

*Stop it! I fought him by myself once. I can do it again.*

Maybe her thoughts were sheer bravado, but they settled her, and she drew the garnet outside her top, gratified to see rosy light stream through it and illuminate a circle around her.

The back barn door slammed against its stops and she girded herself. Andras' peculiar scent, brimstone mixed with cologne he applied far too liberally, stung her nose. The horses stamped and whinnied, kicking against their stall doors. The goats set up a fuss too. Animals were vulnerable to evil because of their enhanced senses. She'd have reached into their minds with calming spells, but didn't think she could spare the magic.

Andras strode into the barn, coming to a stop a few feet from her. He cocked his head to one side. "Odd. You don't seem surprised to see me. I know—" he clapped his hands together in an obscene parody of sudden understanding "—you're pleased I'm here."

"Don't flatter yourself. Where's Cory? And his horse? Or were those just handy excuses to persuade me to come out here?" She screwed her face into a scowl. "I resent you culling good men from our ranks and turning them into bastards."

He shrugged. "Resent all you want. It won't change things. We offer a superior package. Better benefits. It's good to work for us. You'll find out soon enough."

"Oh really?" She fanned magic more deeply about herself. "Why's that? I have no intention of becoming a dark sorcerer. I had plenty of opportunities—offered up by my late husband. I wasn't interested then, and nothing's changed." She bared her teeth in a snarl. "I'll kill myself before I sign over my soul—or my power—to someone like you."

"Think you're too good for Black Magick? Hah!" He sneered, showing his teeth back at her. "I'll break you and enjoy every minute of it. We'll see if you're still so high and mighty this time tomorrow."

The horses pitched into full rebellion, neighing and kicking their stalls. One of the goats ran past Andras. He shot it with a jolt of Black Magick, and it fell onto its side, making piteous little groaning noises.

"You goddamned, fucking bastard." Breana focused power to kill the creature, put it out of its misery.

"Maybe you're the fucking bitch," he simpered. "You killed it."

"I don't revel in others' suffering." Fury burned white hot, and she spread her hands, channeling the garnet's power. "I say we end this now. You want me. Come and get me. Otherwise go back to your perverted, twisted world. I'm sick of this, and I'm not playing anymore."

"And that, my dear, is why I picked you to be my mate, my queen. I love your spirit. You're beautiful when you're all fired up, and I have to possess that energy. Make it mine." His eyes glowed like quicksilver, and his golden skin took on a russet hue as power roared through him. He drew a hand downward, and a fire-rimmed gateway ripped open.

The noise almost deafened her, but she couldn't clap her hands over her ears. She needed them to focus her power. The minute the gateway formed, it pulsed and shimmered, exerting a pull that dragged at her, sucked her toward it.

"No!" She planted her feet. Using magic, she drew a length of halter rope from its slot on the wall, looped it around herself, and tied it off to one of the many hooks lining the barn's roughhewn walls. Her next act was instinctive. She had no idea what impact it might have, but she grabbed the burning lantern and heaved it into the pulsating vortex.

A resounding boom filled the barn, like crashing thunder but a hundred times worse, followed by a flash so bright it seared her eyes. The portal winked out, and the horrible dragging that wanted to suck her into oblivion ceased abruptly.

The horses went mad. One bashed a hole in the barn's back wall and raced out into the night. The others smashed interior walls, trying to follow the one lucky enough to escape.

Shock blossomed on Andras' finely chiseled features, followed by fury. Clearly, he hadn't expected her to destroy his gateway. "You fucking bitch," he snarled. "I can build another one, and this time I won't hesitate, I'll chuck you through the second it's open."

The temperature in the barn plummeted.

Shades.

"I think not," she shot back.

"Best listen to the lady." Joshua waltzed through the door

with Hester by his side. Shades surrounded them. Tom, Sam, and Chris followed, herding the shades from behind.

Freezing cold had never felt quite so welcome, and Breana untied her tether rope. "Nice of you to stop by." She flashed a grin at Hester and Joshua.

"I may have lost this round," Andras growled, "but I'll be back. I won't rest until you're mine." His form took on a wavery, insubstantial aspect.

Hester barked commands in Gaelic, and the shades surged forward, surrounding Andras. He tossed bolts of Black Magick, but they were impervious to it. Death had a few advantages, and that was one of them. They probably couldn't smell the sulfur reek, either.

Breana choked around a thick place in her throat where her stomach threatened to rebel. At least the remaining horses had found a way out with the goats hard after them. The animals weren't any fonder of the shades than they'd been of Black Magick. She felt her way forward with her power, seeking how to slot it in with Hester's casting.

Sparks flew where their magic collided with Andras' desperation to create an exit for himself. For long, heart-stopping moments, it looked as if he might make good on his escape. Only the barest outline remained when Joshua planted himself right in front of the Dark Angel. Holding the moonstone in front of him, he chanted in Gaelic.

Breana recognized the incantation, and she added her voice to his. Hester's hand was apparently holding the shades in place. Left to their own devices, they'd have scattered to the four winds. Anything rather than returning to Hell. Hester said she'd bound them to her will, but Breana had her doubts how effective that would be. Lots of possibilities for escape existed between here and the borders of Arawn's world.

His exit stymied, Andras spun to face Joshua, his handsome features drawn into a rictus of fury. "You think to stop me? Puny mage." Fire flashed from his hands, but the moonstone diverted it.

"We'll see who's puny," Joshua shot back.

Sam hurried to his side, his opal gleaming hotly. Unlike the moonstone that glowed pure white, it held a reddish hue, laced with violet.

"Go ahead," Andras taunted. "All of you tin soldiers line up. Easier for me that way." He barked a word in demonspeak and black fire raced up Joshua's arm, circumventing the moonstone's magic, and igniting his leather shirt.

Joshua thrust the burning garment against a hay bale, and smoke joined the stench of sulfur, brimstone, and ozone. Sam focused a stream of mage fire, but it bounced off whatever Andras had shielded himself with. A low, keening moan rose from the shades as they drew in closer, drawn by any kind of heat. They couldn't escape, either, and were clearly making the best of it.

Breana jumped between Joshua and Andras. "You will not hurt him," she gritted out from between clenched teeth. "Your fight is with me. I'm the one you've targeted."

"Isn't that tender?" Andras leered at her but aimed his next words at Joshua. "How does it feel to hide behind her skirts?"

"I'm not hiding." Joshua strode between her and Sam.

The barn door slammed hard, and Cory waltzed in. Breana's eyes widened. She spun, aiming a killing blow right for his midsection. He twisted out of the way, and a hay bale behind him burst into flames. Breana withdrew her magic, and the fire died as quickly as it had kindled.

"You!" Andras pointed a long-nailed index finger at Cory. "You should've been long gone."

"It appears I'm not." His gaze roved over the others. "Before any of the rest of you try to kill me, this was an undercover operation. I'll explain everything later. Come on men." He grabbed Chris with one hand and Tom with the other. "Let's fry this son of a bitch with mage fire and be done with him once and for all. I know his weak points now. So long as the shades have cut off his exit, we're golden."

Breana stood shoulder to shoulder with the enforcers, Sam on one side and Joshua on the other. Cory's words had pinged true off her magic, but that didn't mean much for someone imbued with dark powers.

"My count of three," Joshua growled.

"You think I'm just going to stand here and let you have your way with mage fire? Think again." Andras sent power zinging toward Hester.

Breana felt it slice through the old witch's wards like a hot knife, and Hester slumped to the floor. Fear for the woman she loved like a mother curdled her stomach. Trusting the men to level the Dark Angel with mage fire, she bolted to Hester's side, falling to her knees next to her as she hastily built what she hoped to hell was an impervious ward around them.

*Ha! Hester's ward was solid. That wasn't the problem.*

*Doesn't matter, I have to do everything in my power protect her.*

The clean, copper scent of mage fire filled the barn and it lit up brighter than midday. Black Magick clashed with it, and sparks filled the barn, igniting whatever they touched. Breana bent over Hester, running her hands over the other witch. Her heart was still beating, but she was torn up inside, her lungs punctured.

Bloody froth bubbled from her lips, and she moaned, obviously in pain.

Running on instinct, Breana drew Hester's ruby from the folds of her dress. She touched the garnet to it, heartened by the flare of wine-colored light that kindled and then traveled the length of Hester's body, settling over her chest. Breana invoked a healing chant, instructing the magic to fix what was broken and to work fast. She pushed as much power as she could muster into her spell and was rewarded with the gnashing of gears. Hopefully, that meant the stones were spinning their enchantment—and saving Hester's life.

The firefight behind her flashed and flared. Andras wasn't going down without a hell of a fight, but she couldn't take her attention from Hester. She gripped her hand. "Goddammit. Fight. I will not lose you over this. Come on, Hester. Live. Do it for me."

Holding Hester on this side of the veil was selfish if she was mortally wounded, but Breana had lost enough. She thought Hester squeezed her hand, but the movement was faint, and she might've imagined it. Bending close, she spoke right into her ear in an archaic form of Gaelic, Hester's native tongue, exhorting her to not give in. To not become another casualty of Black Magick's stain.

"Besides," she murmured. "You have a wedding to perform. It wouldn't feel right to have anyone but you officiate. You're the closest thing I've ever had to a mother."

Hester's eyes flickered open. The bloody sputum around her mouth wasn't forming anymore. "Exactly what I was waiting to hear." She struggled, trying to sit, but Breana held her in place.

"Hush. Not yet. You were all but dead."

Hester opened her mouth to reply, but a huge *whump*, followed by the sound of a voracious fire chewing through magical ether, drowned out her words. The brightness intensified until Breana shut her eyes, but she still saw the light from the men's combined mage fire through her closed lids.

"Hold him down," Sam screamed.

"Got him," Joshua yelled back. "Aim your mage fire to follow my knife blade and finish this."

# CHAPTER 17

Joshua focused a stream of mage fire, using his moonstone to amplify it, while keeping a close eye on Cory. Sam was one of the Coven's undercover enforcers. There were only a dozen at any given time, and it seemed unlikely Cory would've taken on an assignment Sam didn't know about. Regardless, Cory's own stream of mage fire, augmented by his pearls, sprayed toward Andras right along with everyone else's.

He spared a glance at Breana, kneeling by Hester's side, and muttered a quick prayer the crusty old witch wouldn't die. He had the healing gift, but annihilating Andras took priority—over everything.

At first none of the mage fire penetrated the Dark Angel's wards, but he'd given up trying to run out on them. Probably couldn't spare the power. He'd stopped taunting them too. Despite his bravado, something in his silver eyes told Joshua the man fully expected this to be his last fight. He'd been genuinely surprised to see Cory. Furious too, but he'd been wise enough to not waste energy on recriminations.

"Aim your fire at his hands and feet," Cory said tersely. "His wards are thinner there, and once you're through, you can work the flames in toward his core."

The steady stream of black-bordered flames ceased as Andras frantically recrafted the power protecting him.

Cory stepped forward. Mage fire blasted from his raised hands right at Andras' chest, far less protected since the Dark Angel had moved his focus to his hands and feet. Cory's fire projected handily through what was left of Andras' shielding over the central part of his body.

"You always were a stupid, arrogant bastard," Cory grunted and added more mage fire.

Joshua offered Cory points for staunch tactics. Apparently, what he'd revealed about weaknesses in Andras' shielding was true. When the Dark Angel reacted as predicted, Cory struck hard and fast.

Joshua didn't hesitate. He sent his own power winging after Cory's. So did Sam, Tom, and Chris. The combination should've brought the Dark Angel to his knees. Instead, he changed form, morphing into a seven-foot-tall, red-scaled demon, with a forked tail, horns, and cloven hoofs. His mouth sported two rows of wickedly sharp teeth, and black fire spewed from it.

Mage fire surrounded the demon but couldn't penetrate its scales.

"What now?" Joshua asked tersely.

The shades hissed and spat at the demon, but even they moved back, giving it space. Suddenly Joshua understood why Andras had focused his power at Hester. Without her magic guiding the shades, they'd soon become rudderless and leave.

"One of you has to take over the shades," he yelled.

"Me," Tom said, his voice grim as the dead he'd just

volunteered to ride herd on. "I've done it a time or two before. Can't hold 'em forever, though, so work fast."

Joshua gauged the distance between himself and the demon that had been Andras. He had no doubt what stood before them was the Dark Angel's true form. Fallen angels became demons, so it made sense.

The demon vomited more fire, and edged away from them, his intent clear. He might still be doing his damnedest to inflict maximum damage, but he'd be gone the second he saw a clear path.

Joshua surged forward, using his power and his body to forge a path through the demon's protections. The dead parted, offering him clear passage, but they'd never posed a serious problem.

Sam closed behind him, hard on his heels, offering his magic as armor. "Got you covered, brother."

Joshua didn't answer. He drew a blade from a waist sheath and ran right at the demon, driving it up and under the red scales and twisting hard. The blade had been smelted with silver and iron. It had to hurt like hell.

Andras closed scaled forelegs around Joshua, raking sharp, curved talons down his back, but Joshua held fast and drove the knife deeper, rotating it savagely.

"Hold him down," Sam screamed.

"Got him," Joshua yelled back. "Aim your mage fire to follow my knife blade and finish this."

Fire from the other four enforcers flashed and flared around him, but didn't burn him. Enforcers were immune to its effects—unless they'd been turned to evil. He held a conduit open into the demon's chest, fanning mage fire into it. Andras thrashed and writhed, screeching in demonspeak, while he ripped the shit out of Joshua's back.

He willed his blood to flow, cleaning Black Magick's taint from his body.

The demon's form began to vibrate. Joshua pushed mage fire into the abomination just as fast as the other enforcers sent it his way. Vibrations shook him like a rag doll where he clung to the demon just before the thing burst, spewing him with vile, noxious smelling black ichor, bits of bone, and other things that didn't bear thinking about.

"Don't stop," he exhorted the other enforcers. "Not until there's nothing of him left. We don't want this bastard regenerating on us."

"Roll out of the way," Sam said tersely.

"Yeah, gives us a cleaner line of fire," Chris said.

Joshua did a backward somersault and joined the line of enforcers. At first he didn't think he'd have a shred of magic left to lend to their final effort, but he found some somewhere, augmented by his stone. It felt good to have mage fire flow at his command. Cleansing.

Breana's arms closed around him from behind. "You killed him," she crowed. "The bastard's finally met his end."

"Hester?" He turned to meet Breana's direct gaze, girding himself to hear the worst.

"I'm harder to kill than ye might think." The other witch limped over. "And I smell a damn sight fresher than you."

"Ain't that the truth. Breana, sweetheart, I love your arms around me, but you're getting gore all over you."

"Small price." She smiled at him, and his heart took flight.

The last flares of mage fire flickered and died out. "A good day's work, boys," Sam said before turning to face Cory. "I want a full explanation now. Before we go inside. Before we clean up."

"Hell, before we do anything," Joshua muttered and sent

power skittering around the barn to put out the places hay and wood still smoldered.

"Yeah, I want to know too," Breana chimed in. "I overheard you and Andras in the springhouse."

Cory narrowed his dark eyes. "I knew you were out there. Enforcers are attuned to witch energy. It's a subtle thing, and Andras didn't have a clue. I wasn't kidding when I said he was stupid and arrogant. It never occurred to him I wasn't under his complete control—"

"Back up," Sam barked, looking as foreboding as an avenging angel. "You said this was an undercover operation, yet I wasn't informed. Start at the beginning. Who assigned you to infiltrate Andras' circle?"

Cory straightened his shoulders and dragged his hands down his face, smearing soot and ichor in their wake. "Drop a truth spell," he invited. "That way you won't be forever wondering about what I say next."

"I'll do those honors." Chris drew magic, and Joshua felt the *thunk* as it settled around Cory, glowing softly.

He nodded and began to speak. "Our Founder, whose name we never give voice to in case evil is listening, held grave concerns about Don Giraud. My original assignment was tracking him and coming up with evidence he consorted with dark sorcery."

Cory ground his teeth together and set his mouth in a harsh line. "Don was one wily son of a bitch. He stymied me time and time again—and then the two of you—" he jerked his chin at Breana "—left. Made it impossible to keep an eye on him. It wasn't that I didn't know he'd been turned, but I lacked evidence to prove it."

"What's the link with Andras?" Sam pressed. "So far what

you've relayed is old news. I knew you were assigned to shadow Don."

Cory spread his hands in front of him. "Simple enough. When it became clear we needed an edge, our Founder narrowed the circle of who knew what I was doing to him and me. Feel free to check in with him the next time you see him. We also decided we were wasting time—and manpower—chasing down minions when we could gain access to the whole operation by me cozying up to Andras."

"How the hell did you get him to trust you?" Chris asked, his question lined with suspicion.

Cory grinned wryly. "Wasn't easy. I had to learn demonspeak and drink my share of demons' blood. Then there were the absolutely disgusting spirits I had to fuck." He shrugged. "Once I'd debased myself sufficiently, Andras bought my defection hook, line, and sinker. After that, things grew much easier."

"How'd I end up the bait in today's scheme?" Breana asked, tightlipped.

"Because he wanted to possess you," Cory said. "I was never far away. If Joshua and the others hadn't had a rescue effort in the offing, I'd have stepped in."

"When?" she demanded. "Things were heading for disaster."

Cory planted himself so he faced her. "You're not thinking. If I'd burst back into the barn immediately, I'd have blown my carefully-constructed charade, months and months of work. Andras would've realized I'd played him for a sucker, and he'd have grabbed you and whisked you away immediately. By me remaining hidden, it allowed you time to engage him in a sparring match, which gave everyone else ample opportunity to ride to your rescue."

Cory inclined his head. "I'm most humbly sorry for any discomfort you suffered. I'm sworn to protect all witches, but our battle with Black Magick isn't a game. It's real, and it's not a war without casualties. I'll feel used and dirty from my time with Andras for a very long time."

He spun slowly, matching gazes with everyone in turn. "The stones accepted me. They'd never have done that if I'd truly joined up with our enemy. They rejected Tom, and he was only a passive recipient of dark power."

"I didn't need a reminder," the other enforcer snarled.

"I bet if you tried again, you'd have different results." Cory smiled encouragingly.

"You told the truth," Joshua said. "And by God, I'm relieved. I don't want to lose another man, woman, child, or animal to darkness."

Sam clapped Cory on the back and pushed him toward the barn door. "I'm more than relieved. Hell, son, I raised you. To have you turned by evil would be the worst slap in the face imaginable. Let's rinse off in the creek and then we'll go inside and settle in with a bottle of something. And maybe leftovers, if we can scrounge something up."

"We'll come too," Chris tugged on Tom's arm. "I'd welcome cold, clean water to wash off the demon stench." They followed Sam and Cory out the open barn door.

Joshua brushed his lips over Breana's. "I'll join the guys," he said. "I'm dirtier than any of them."

"I could run you a bath," she offered.

"Nah. You and Hester can heat water for yourselves. I'm tough. I actually developed a fondness for creek water these last few years on the road."

"Well, head on in once you're done," Hester said with her trademark astringency. "Your back's a fright, and I want to make certain 'tis good and clean, doctored with herbs and magic."

"You couldn't keep me away if you tried." Joshua loped after the other enforcers. He wanted Breana's arms around him something fierce, but she'd be there for him after he'd cleaned up. Faith in her caring warmed him, even after he'd stripped off his clothes and cannonballed into the icy waters of the creek running behind the barn.

BREANA WALKED SLOWLY across the muddy yard toward the house with Hester by her side. "I almost can't believe we made it through today without any casualties," she murmured as they made their way up the front steps.

Hester snorted ruefully. "Doona ye think Arawn will come gunning for me once he realizes what I did? Not all those shades will return to the paths of the dead. Sooner or later, he's bound to notice."

"In truth? No. It's rare the gods have anything to do with us. My experience with Danu was exceptional, a once-in-a-lifetime event. Somehow, we came through unscathed. Not that we're done battling the dark, but losing someone as important as Andras should at least slow them down."

"We hope." Hester pulled the curtain at the back of the kitchen and began filling the tub from the pump mounted on the ledge. "Who gets the first bath?"

"You. I'll go upstairs and clean myself up with the basin and ewer. And change my clothes. When I come down, we can figure out what we're going to feed everyone."

Hester caught her up before she'd cleared the kitchen and folded her arms around her. "I never did thank you properly. Ye saved my life, and I'm most grateful."

Breana hugged her back. "I've never been so sorry healing wasn't one of my natural strengths. But the stones seemed to sense your need. Mine kindled against yours, and the two of them together worked a miracle, knitting the broken places in your lungs."

"Aye, but ye forced me to cling to life long enough for them to do their work. Left to my own devices, I might've followed the light and joined my kin in the beyond. The pain after that monster struck was beyond dreadful."

Letting go, Breana stepped back. "I know, and I felt like the worst kind of selfish bitch, but I couldn't let you go. Not without a fight."

The harsh planes of Hester's face softened. "Go find something to wear that doesna reek of demons, and I'll do the same."

Breana walked down the hall and mounted the stairs. She untied the lacings holding her clothing together in the hallway outside her room, so she wouldn't drag their stench into her bedroom. Dropping everything into an untidy heap, she walked through her door in her chemise and stood over the basin. A thin stream of magic heated the water to a tolerable temperature, and she sponged herself off.

A quick glance in the glass over her dresser showed streaks and smudges she'd missed. Her hair hung in gore-streaked tangles. When Andras' body had exploded, the bits and pieces traveled a long way. Dampening sections, she combed the worst of the particles out of her tresses. She'd wash it properly tomorrow. For tonight, it was good enough. She kept it down, rather than re-braiding it, so it could dry.

She looked longingly at her robe, but she had to get dressed before she went downstairs. Not wanting to face her stays, she settled for draping a soft, black woolen shift over herself, belting it with a length of leather. Barefoot, she padded back to the kitchen using the front staircase.

Everyone had gathered in the kitchen around the stove. The men stood when she came into the room, but she waved them back into their seats and joined Hester where she worked at the sideboard. "What'd we decide?" she asked, glancing into a mixing bowl that looked suspiciously like the beginnings of chocolate cake while she tied an apron around her waist.

Hester rolled her eyes. "The men wanted cake, so I'm making one. Oven's hot, and I'm about to pour my batter out."

"We might have enough sugar left for frosting." Breana stood on her tiptoes and pulled open one of the cupboards.

Joshua covered the distance to her in two long strides and wrapped his arms around her from behind. He didn't say a word, just held her so close she felt the beat of his heart.

"Hey!" Sam called out. "None of that until after the cake's done."

"Yeah," Cory seconded. "Don't disturb the women while they're cooking. I can boil beans with the best of 'em, but I haven't the first inkling how to make frosting. Or cake."

Breana leaned against Joshua's chest, reveling in the heat of his body. It seared her, rich with promise. What a treat it would be to actually get naked together so she could look at all of him, not just parts they uncovered as they grappled with each other.

He nuzzled her neck before letting go. "I'm looking forward to the same thing," he informed her with a roguish wink.

She swatted him. "Stay out of my mind."

"You'll have the devil's own time enforcing that one." He made his way back to the table and pried a dark brown glass bottle out of Chris' hand, drinking deep.

Breana eyed the group of enforcers. "You found the brandy. Damn good batch if I say so myself, but it could do with a tad more aging."

"Not going to last that long," Tom said and laughed.

Hester had popped her cake pans in the oven a few minutes before, so Breana snapped up a bowl, cocoa powder, sugar, and the butter she churned from goat's milk and got busy mixing frosting.

"I almost hate to bring this up, but what's next for everyone?" Sam asked. "Now that the current disaster's been dealt with."

"Might be a different answer for each of us," Hester replied. "My plan is to wait here until Abigail shows up."

"I'll hang around for a few days," Tom said. "Long enough to see if I can link to a stone. Whether that happens or not, though, everyone else needs to practice with them. Not much point in having something that powerful if we're not more proficient using them."

"We need to see if we can duplicate Hester's gear-driven gadget." Cory looked thoughtful. "If those power stones are as useful as I think they're going to be, we'll want a way to create them that doesn't involve a side trip back here to Hester's witchy workshop."

"At least then I'd get to see everyone," she pointed out. Opening the oven, she peered inside and grabbed her cake pans, using a towel so they wouldn't burn her.

Breana poured frosting over the warm confections and carted one of the three pans to the table where the men dug into it. She watched them make short work of the cake and smiled. It might be nice to slice a piece for herself, but what she really wanted to do was drag Joshua upstairs and not surface for days. Maybe even weeks.

He raised his eyes from the almost empty cake pan and shot a meaningful look her way.

Damn the man! He was living inside her mind, but she couldn't chide him for it. She wanted him just as close to her as a man could get. To cover her discomfiture, she snatched the pan up and shook her finger at the men. "I swear, you're worse than a passel of puppies."

"Mighty good cake." Sam pushed to his feet and captured another pan, plopping it onto the table.

"If ye want any of this—" Hester jabbed Breana in the side "—best cut yourself a slice before there's naught left to be had."

Joshua's gaze never left her as she ferried cake onto a plate for herself. Hot, feral, untamed, it set her body alight with possibilities, and her throat constricted with wanting him. Hunger curled her toes with pure, unslaked lust and set every cell alight with craving. She put her cake in the pie safe, untied her apron, and walked slowly and meaningfully out the kitchen door.

He'd follow her. She was as sure of it as she'd ever been of anything. And she couldn't wait.

# CHAPTER 18

*J*oshua sprang to his feet. "Night, everyone," he mumbled, and followed Breana's retreating form as she left the kitchen.

Catcalls and ribald suggestions followed him, and he spun and stalked back to the table. "Lay off, all of you. She'll be my wife soon."

"Maybe so." Sam grinned in the engaging way only he could pull off. "But she's still Breana too."

Joshua felt the corners of his mouth twitch. "True enough. At least have the decency to not come pounding on our bedroom door."

Chris snorted. "Build a ward, brother. You just never know about the rest of us. We might think of a really creative suggestion and—"

Joshua mock-slugged him, and everyone burst into raucous laughter.

"Why are ye still here?" Hester asked, raising an eyebrow. "Breana's upstairs."

"As if I need a reminder." Joshua sprinted from the kitchen and took the stairs three at a time. He smiled broadly when he saw the pile of clothes outside her door. Meant she was just as hungry for him as he was for her.

He reached for the knob, but then stopped and raised his fist to knock gently. Just because they'd soon be locked in a tight embrace wasn't a reason to abandon all his manners. A small jolt of her unique magic buffeted him just before the door popped open. He cleared the doorway and held out his arms, nudging the door shut behind him with a booted foot.

Breana melted into his arms, grinning up at him. "When I heard the ruckus from down below, I wondered how long it would take you to break free."

"Not long at all. You still have your clothes on. When I saw the heap outside the door, I thought… I mean, I hoped—"

"Ssht." She laid a hand over his mouth before twining her arms around him. "Those were what I had on out in the barn. I was rather hoping you'd want to undress me. And I want to do the same. To you." She licked her full lower lip, her eyes gleaming with eagerness. "I can't wait to see what all of you looks like without those leathers on."

His heart hammered into triple time, and desire spilled through him, hot and urgent. He crushed his mouth down on hers, claiming it. She opened to him and teased his tongue with her own as she bit, nipped, and sucked. Her hands tightened across his shoulders, and she pulled him more tightly against her, so close he felt her nipples peak against his chest.

It was hard not to ruck up her skirts, free his cock, and lift her atop him, but they had time. All they needed to let desire build to a fever pitch. She thrust her tongue deeper into his mouth, and her body turned to quicksilver in his arms, all liquid craving. He loved the way she tasted, sweet like the cake with sharp undernotes from the brandy, and he explored every corner of her mouth and lips in a kiss that developed a life of its own.

He didn't need words to tell her how much she meant to him, how long he'd waited, and the wonder and awe he felt at his longstanding dream finally coming true. He told her those things with his mouth and his fingertips trailing down her back, caressing her.

He could've stood there with his mouth glued to hers forever, the moment so sweet and poignant and fraught with promise of loving her, he didn't want it to end. His cock strained against the laces of his breeches, and she pressed a hand between them to curve around it. He leaned into her touch, loving that she wanted to explore his body.

Breana broke their kiss and smiled at him, her lips swollen with passion, as she tightened her hold on his ridged flesh. "What do you suppose the odds are of getting rid of some of these clothes?"

"Damn good."

His voice was harsher than he meant it to be, raspy with need. He untangled her hand from him and untied the length of leather she'd strung around her waist. Next he lifted her dress over her head in one fluid movement. He'd known she wasn't wearing stays, but the sight of her, barefoot and clad only in a white, silk chemise stole his breath and any further words.

Her breasts were clearly outlined behind the thin fabric, their nipples pebbled into points. He wanted to tell her how beautiful she was with her golden hair, the color of summer wheat sheaves, falling to her waist in curls. Broad-shouldered for a woman, her collarbones made hollows above her high, generous breasts.

She tilted her chin and gazed right at him, her forthright nature shining through. "Don't stop there." She reached for the sides of her chemise, but he batted her hands away.

"I'm admiring the view. You're gorgeous. No goddess could be more beautiful."

Breana shook a warning finger his way. "Best not say that. You might annoy the hell out of Danu or one of the others."

He grinned crookedly. "They'd be lenient with a man in love." He sucked in a tight breath. "I still can't believe you want me too."

"Believe it." She laughed, the sound like crystal bells. "But I could change my mind if you don't get moving."

He ran his hands down her silk clad sides until he reached lace edging the bottom of her chemise. Ever so slowly, he raised it and pulled it over her head, letting it slide through his fingers. The parts of her he'd only imagined were laid before him. Her slender waist, flat stomach, and flared hips atop long legs shapely with muscle snared him. He couldn't have torn his gaze from her if the world shattered around them.

His inner nature, usually firmly leashed, exploded with wonder and a sexual hunger so intense, it tightened his muscles and narrowed his throat.

"Your turn." Her voice resonated with urgency, and she reached for the laces holding his shirt to his body. Once they were loose, she pulled upward, and the snug-fitting garment cleared his head. She tossed it aside and ran her fingertips over his chest, teasing his nipples with her nails. "Sometime I want to know where each and every one of these scars came from."

"Sometime, but not now." He cupped the side of her face in his hand. "The only thing right now is you and me."

He reached for her breasts, filling his hands with them, and rolled the nipples between his fingers. She made soft, mewling noises as she pressed into his touch and leaned in to swipe her tongue over one of his nipples. Electric heat shot though him. He made a grab for her head to hold her against his chest, but she sidestepped him neatly and moved to the laces of his trousers. He'd taken off his boots when he came into the house after his bath in the creek. When she pushed his pants down his legs, he stepped out of them.

Her gaze raked from the tip of his head to his toes. "You're one beautiful man," she said, her words thick with desire. "Your hair reminds me of what I always believed dragon's fire would look like. Brilliant, living red. Promise me you'll never, ever cut it."

He would've promised her the moon on a platter if she'd requested it. Scooping her into his arms, he carried her to the bed and laid her atop it. She turned onto her side and patted the space next to her, but he wasn't ready to lay there. Not yet. Once he felt all of her next to him, skin to skin, he wouldn't be able to restrain himself, and he wasn't done looking at her.

Circling, he took in the perfect curves of her ass and the long, straight march of her spine. Her hair cascaded around her, and her blue eyes had darkened with lust. "Are you going to lie down?" she demanded.

"Impatient wench. I'm getting there."

"If you don't, I'm going to back you up against a wall and crawl up your body with my tongue."

"Sounds intriguing. Maybe we can start with that next time."

He came around to where he faced her and sat on the edge of the bed. His cock jutted in front of him, rigid with need, but he ignored it and ran his hands up her legs, taking his time as her body twisted and writhed beneath his touch. Muscle rippled beneath his fingertips, and he stroked her calves and the sensitive inside of her knees. By the time he got to her inner thighs, her legs trembled and she was moaning in Gaelic, telling him to hurry.

He settled his palm over the center of her sensation. She bucked against him, so he pressed harder. Extending two fingers, he slipped them inside her, delighted by her hot slickness and the way she tightened around him.

She closed a hand over his cock, holding him snugly and rubbing the head with his own fluids that were dribbling out. Her touch upped desire that had already been at flood stage. With a savage growl, he pushed her thighs wide and knelt between them, seating himself at the entrance to her body.

Breana still held onto his cock. She positioned him and thrust her hips upward to capture him inside her. He tried to take things slow, but his body didn't cooperate and buried itself in one desperate plunge. The heat of her body engulfed him, igniting desire so intense it shut out the rest of the world. The controlled lovemaking he'd imagined where he brought her to peak after peak, while holding back his own climax turned into a fantasy, and he drove hard into her.

She met him thrust for thrust, holding onto his hips and digging her nails into his sides. Her intense gaze never left his face, and color splotched across her cheeks and chest. Already hard, her nipples turned into tight buds, and their rich, coppery color intensified. She clutched him harder, and her sex dissolved around him in a rush of contractions and heat. Magic streamed from her, snaring him in an irresistible tide.

Riding it through was impossible. His balls tightened, snugging hard against his crotch, and his cock juddered inside her, shooting white-hot jolts of ecstasy. Gaelic spilled from him as he chanted the incantation to bind the woman bucking beneath him to his side as his soul's own mate.

Joy burned bright when she answered his refrain, accepting the bond. Back in olden time, those words had been the same as marriage vows for those with magic, even if they chose to have another solemnize their joining.

He supported himself on his arms, gazing down at her. When he could coax his tongue into cooperating, he asked, "Are you sure?"

"Sure as I've been of anything, Joshua Kingman." She snugged her body around his still hard cock, moving suggestively. "There'll be time for talk later. Roll us over. We've scarcely begun."

He flexed his shaft inside her and was rewarded by her hot slickness teasing him back.

"Over." She bucked her hips.

He grinned. "Randy wench."

She winked lazily. "You've worked with witches forever. Surely it doesn't come as a surprise."

"I wouldn't have it any other way."

Her deep, lush sensuality thrilled him. Holding her in place with his arms and legs, he flipped onto his back. He opened his mouth to tease her about what happened next, but she covered his lips with her own, kissing him deeply. Gripping her close, he opened his mouth to her questing tongue. Deep inside her, his cock twitched, clearly more than ready to keep right on making love. He'd never remained with a woman once the tip of his lust was satisfied, but he'd never fucked a woman he was in love with before, either.

She bit his lower lip, then planted her hands on his chest and pushed herself upright until she sat astride him, knees tucked beneath her. He closed one hand around a breast, loving the puckery feel of her nipple as he rolled it between his fingers. His other hand found its way between her legs where he rubbed her swollen nub, feeling an instant tightening around his shaft.

She moved upward until only the head of him was encased in her, teasing him until he pushed himself back inside. He needed an extra hand to hang onto her hips, so he deployed magic, instructing it to circle her breasts, pinching and tweaking her nipples. He curved his newly free hand around her waist and plumbed her.

Her back arched and her breasts danced up and down her ribcage. He rubbed her harder, and she placed a hand atop his, showing him the motion she needed. Heat scalded him as he fucked her, and sensation coursed through him, radiating outward from his achingly hard erection. The way his body was reacting, he couldn't believe he'd just come.

He was beginning to know her responses, and he recognized the hitch in her breath and the increased tension in her muscles as she gripped him harder. Sure enough, the rhythmic contractions of her orgasm began. They rippled around him, filling him with need so pure and lust so vibrant, it made every other sexual experience of his life pale by comparison. Semen flowed from him in hard, little bursts that shattered his world.

Breana lowered herself until she lay atop him, her body still quivering from his touch. Cupping his face in a hand, she murmured love words in Gaelic, followed by, "You're an amazing man."

"You're pretty spectacular yourself." He snugged her into his arms, every cell still alight from their lovemaking. "Sleep a little, sweetheart. I'll watch over you."

She had to be exhausted, so he followed his words with a spell to draw her eyes closed. He meant what he said. He'd make certain nothing harmed her. She had traumas to heal from, and he'd ensure she had everything she needed to become whole again.

~

BREANA WAKENED to midday light streaming through her bedroom windows. Joshua held her against him, and the rhythm of his breathing told her he was resting, but not asleep. She leaned into him, enjoying the solid planes of his muscled body pressed close to her.

"You're awake." His voice rumbled against her hair. "Did you get some decent rest?"

She nodded. "I did. Thank you. It's the first time I've felt safe enough to truly sleep for a very long time."

Joshua stroked her hair back from her face. "I aim to make certain you feel secure and cared for. This was the barest beginning."

She kissed his cheek and rolled to a cross-legged sit. "I'm amazed no one bothered us."

He grinned engagingly. "They have shown amazing restraint, now that you mention it."

"On a more serious note—" Breana chewed her lower lip thoughtfully "—I haven't heard that particular Gaelic incantation for a couple hundred years." She looked away, feeling suddenly shy. "It surprised me, but pleased me too."

"The mages' hand fasting blessing?"

Breana nodded solemnly. "Haven't heard it since I left the Old Country. You must really love me, since there're no exits from that binding. You'll never love another."

His eyes shaded to golden, warm and compelling. "I never have, Breana. Not since I first laid eyes on you, and not before that, either. Why would things change now?" He drew his brows together. "What about you? You answered me, joined your life to mine, soul to soul. You'll never love another, either."

"That I did. It wasn't a thinking moment, but a heart-driven one. I'm falling in love with you, and it's the most amazing thing. I may have been married before, but I've never been in love."

Joshua's face wreathed in smiles. "I don't have words for how happy that makes me."

"You don't need any. Your joy is so intense it's turned the air around you multicolored. You're glowing."

He glanced around him. "So I am. I told the others downstairs that you were going to be my wife, but I never asked you formally." He pushed himself upright and sat facing her, placing his hands on her knees. "Will you marry me, darling Breana?"

"I thought I already did."

"Yes, but we want things to be legal in the eyes of the world. The non-magical one. I waited a long time for you, and by God, I'm going to do things right."

"Well we can't very well disappoint Hester. I drew her back from the paths of the dead with promises she could officiate at our wedding."

"Many reasons then." His smile faded. "You still haven't exactly answered me. If you'd rather wait until we have a few miles under our belts, I'll understand."

"You're not listening." She stroked his hands where they rested on her thighs. "When I sang the response to the Gaelic wedding prayer, I bound myself to you, and just as permanently as anything Hester might do. There's no out clause to either contract, so I fear you're stuck with me."

He pulled his hands from beneath hers and traced the lines of her body, coming to rest them on either side of her face. "No, darling. We'll be stuck with each other, and it's a place I've longed to be for so long, I still can't quite believe it's real."

Breana felt a soft smile form. So long as he was baring his soul's secrets, she would too. "Before I met Don, I used to imagine a wonderful prince. A man who'd love and cherish me forever. When Don came along, I tried to stuff him into that role, except he never quite fit."

"Why'd you marry him?" Joshua raised a quizzical brow.

"It was time. I was almost a hundred years old, and he was the first man who'd appealed to me at all. I figured there wasn't much percentage to waiting any longer and that I'd come to love him over time." She rolled her eyes. "You know how well that turned out."

"It pains me to say it, but yours wasn't a bad marriage." Joshua frowned. "I know. I spent enough time watching it for signs of cracks."

"Not bad, but nothing like a grand passion, either. Yet if Don hadn't succumbed to evil, we'd still be together, raising Carolyn."

Joshua snorted, and continued to cradle her face between his hands. "First time I've ever been grateful Black Magick claimed one of our own."

Breana thought about his words. Her next ones came slowly. "Even though it was hell to live through, I'm glad things unfolded as they did. If they hadn't, I'd never have discovered you—or your love."

Bending forward, he angled his head and brushed his mouth over hers. "Want to get dressed and find Hester?"

"Sure, but first I want to run myself a bath and wash my hair. It still has dried demon bits in it from the battle."

"What can I do to help? Bring water? Heat it for you? Join you?"

Heat flared between her legs, desire so intense it was hard to believe they'd just spent hours making love. She cast a come-hither look his way. "How about all three?"

Untamed fire blazed in his eyes, shading them to golden. "You're on. There's a tub up here, isn't there?"

"Yup. Next room over. I don't use it much because I have to haul the buckets of water upstairs, but at least it drains into the garden."

He got to his feet and wrapped a towel around his midsection, casting a randy look over one shoulder as he strode toward the door. "Don't even think about leaving."

"No worries on that front."

Just watching him move, all fluid muscles and long-legged grace made her want him with a sweet, urgent ache. The room was saturated with the musk of their arousal, and she got to her feet, unabashedly sucking in the rich, sexual scents from their lovemaking.

By the time she tucked a robe around herself and moved into the slate tiled room next door, the claw foot tub was almost half full. Settling into it, she made the water a touch warmer, dipped water over her hair, and worked on scrubbing it clean.

Joshua's energy drew near, shining brighter than any sun, and her heart cracked wide open.

"Good timing, I see. If you tilt your head back, I can rinse it for you."

"But that water's cold," she protested.

He put the bucket next to the tub. She felt a jolt, and he said. "Oh ye of little faith. I just warmed it with magic. Tilt that gorgeous head back, wench. The sooner we get all that soap out, the sooner we can move on to other things."

"Other things is it?" She sent a coquettish smile skittering across the air between them.

"Unless you're already tired of me, and that would be a damned shame because—"

Using the sides of the tub to lever herself upright, she yanked the towel off him and pulled him into her arms, cutting off the rest of his words with a kiss. Soapy water ran down her sides from her hair, but rinsing it could wait.

# CHAPTER 19

*Five Weeks Later*

Joshua rolled his shoulders and straightened his legs in their stirrups. He slowed his stallion to a walk as he waited for the others to catch up with him. He and Breana, along with Hester and Chris, had decided to ride cross country to meet up with the Coven's wagon train on the Mormon Pioneer Trail. Tom, Sam, and Cory had planned to come along, but a last minute crisis communication from a splinter group of witches in the San Francisco area changed all that.

The witches were part of a group Hester had formed. While not officially Coven-linked, they needed help. A cadre of Black Magick practitioners from the Far East had shown up on the docks. They'd no sooner left their ship, when they began killing witches outright. Consequences be damned. Hester's friends had gone into deep hiding, swathed in layers of invisibility spells, but they couldn't remain there forever.

Sam had alerted every enforcer within range, and they would put out the call to others as they traveled. By the time they got to San Francisco, they might have as many as twenty enforcers—

three of whom had power stones—to deal with the newly arrived dark mages. If they still required help, Joshua's plan was to cull Luke and a few other enforcers out of the wagon train and ride hard for the western coast, unencumbered by wagons.

Time had healed the stones' ambivalence toward Tom, and he'd laid claim to a gold-veined chunk of turquoise that turned a lovely teal when magic kindled its potential. Even better, Joshua had worked with the other enforcers to create a duplicate of Hester's steam and gear driven machine. Sam and the others took it with them. That way they could bring other witches and mages abreast of what was proving to be an incredibly powerful method to focus and intensify their magic.

Hester's horse trotted to his side before she slowed it to a walk. "I sensed ye thinking about my friends. I do hope they're all right."

"So do I," he replied. "I considered all of us going. Sam and I kicked it around, but this made more sense."

"I agree." Breana said from his other side. "Putting all your eggs in a single basket never was a sound strategy. This way, we can use the stones to check in with Sam, Tom, and Cory. They'll let us know if they need us."

Joshua eyed the gradient of the setting sun. He glanced at Chris, angling toward them from off the main wagon route. "Where were you, brother?"

"Just checking our flanks. I didn't sense anything, but thought I'd swing a little farther out—in case anyone was warding themselves and we were too far away to sense anything."

"And?" Joshua inclined his head.

"Nothing. In some ways that's excellent news."

"Makes me a little nervous," Hester cut in.

"Me too," Breana said. "We've been a week on the road, and it's like evil doesn't exist in this part of the country. Yet it was here in force when Luke and Abigail came through with my Carolyn."

"Could be Andras' death took a toll," Chris ventured.

"Or they're saving themselves and waiting for the wagon train where they can do maximum damage," Joshua muttered.

"How would they even know the Coven is moving?" Breana asked.

"Those bastards have spies everywhere," Chris replied. "They know. I bet they even had the exact day our wagons left Council Bluffs circled on a calendar."

"Not much we can do about that," Joshua cut in. "This day's nearly gone. We've ridden until past dark every other night. How about if we knock off early today? There're groves of trees a quarter mile away. They're so thick, they have to be growing next to water."

Breana tossed her head. "Maybe I'll get that honeymoon you've been promising me after all. We should have at least an hour to ourselves before it's time to cook supper—after we've washed the dust and dirt off."

"We could've gone to San Francisco and worked in a night or three at the fanciest hotel in town after the fighting was over," he pointed out archly, following it with, "I wanted to take you into Salt Lake and book us into a luxurious hotel there, but—"

"—I wanted to stay home." She laughed merrily. "And I did— want to stay home, that is. That way, I could scream my head off without worrying about complaints from neighboring rooms."

Hester broke into laughter too. Soon, Chris and Joshua joined in. When Hester stopped snorting and cawing, she said, "No complaints. We loved listening to you squeal and Joshua making those manly grunts. Ye have no idea how many bets we placed on exactly what spurred those noises. I learned buckets about all the wonderful, perverted new things your generation's come up with. Sex was much more humdrum three or four centuries ago."

"That does it." Breana was still chortling. "I'm out of here." She spurred her horse toward the line of trees Joshua had pointed at.

He kneed his horse after hers. Aspens and scrub oaks growing thickly by a rushing creek provided a choice of many excellent campsites. Once they'd settled on a spot, he led Breana a hundred yards downstream to a deep pool that he warmed with magic.

"Oooh, a bath," she purred. "We could both use one. Between riding all day and making love all night, we're getting a tad bit ripe."

He patted a flat rock illuminated by the rays of the setting sun. When she sat, he unlaced her boots and stripped off her stockings, rubbing her feet between his hands.

"That feels heavenly. I'm not used to riding all day, and the stirrups hurt after a while."

"How's your butt?"

"Yeah, that's sore too, but it's getting better."

He slid his hands up her legs, reveling in the feel of her bare skin beneath his fingers. When he got to her knees, she slapped his hands away and stood. "Bath first." She shook a finger at him in mock severity. "Do you suppose we'd be lucky enough to find soap root around here?"

Joshua worked his boots off, followed by his socks as he glanced around. "That patch over there might be some. Get into the water, and I'll join you as soon as I've checked it out."

She unbuttoned her skirt and draped it across the rock she'd been sitting on. Next came her jacket and her blouse. "Soap root," she urged, extending an arm. "Over there. It's not going to dig itself out of the ground."

Joshua muffled a snort. He'd been rooted in place gazing at her body as it emerged from her dust-caked clothing. "You should be glad you have that effect on me. I'll never, never tire of the view. Your body is perfection. It's—"

"So's yours, and it's still all covered up. Soap root and naked. Maybe naked first." Tossing a come-hither look over one shoulder, she whipped her chemise over her head and sauntered slowly to the bank and into the water, swinging her hips suggestively.

His cock vaulted to attention, and he hurriedly undid the laces holding his leathers in place. First his shirt, then his pants, fell atop her clothing on the flat rock. He made his way to what he thought might be soap root and drilled two feet into the ground with magic. When the familiar brown globes came into view, he snagged enough of the bulbous roots to fill both hands. That done, he hurried back to the pool and set his bounty down, except for two roots.

Breana floated on her back, the tips of her breasts visible above the waterline. "Hey! Success." She flipped over so she stood upright and waded toward him, hands held out for the plant.

He walked into the water, making it a little warmer. "Dip your head back and wet your hair," he instructed. Breaking one of the roots open, he rubbed the cleansing herb into her wet hair, working it into her scalp. She made little purring sounds, and arched her back as she bent backward to rinse it out.

Taking the other root from him, she said, "Now you."

He untied the bits of leather from the bottoms of his braids and quickly undid them. Kneeling on the sandy bottom, he bent forward to dampen his hair. She came around in front of him, breasts almost at mouth level, as she washed his hair. Surging forward, he captured a nipple in his mouth and sucked hard, feeling it lengthen in appreciation of his efforts. Wrapping his hands around her ribcage from both sides, he held her in place and switched to the other breast.

"Ummm. Not fair," she murmured. The words may have been a protest, but she pushed into him and cupped her hands to sluice water through his hair, getting the soap root out of it.

He shook wet hair back from his face, and water streamed down both of them. "Do you suppose we're clean enough for now, darling?" he asked.

"We can make love here in the water." She crinkled her nose, teasing. "That way we'll stay clean."

"My practical wife." The most amazing feelings filled him whenever he said that word. "I love calling you that. Even more, I love that you are my wife."

She silenced him with her mouth, kissing him deeply as she twined her arms around him and pressed her wet breasts and belly against him. His cock jerked against her body, enjoying the hell out of the wanton nymph plastered against it.

He placed his hands under her ass and lifted her. She locked her legs around his waist and held on while he thrust into her, never breaking their kiss. The water helped support them, and he surged deeper, withdrew, drove back inside. The heat of her seared him, a welcome counterpart to the water he'd warmed from icy cold to tepid.

She raked her nails down his back and cried out as he loved her. Telling him to move faster, harder, and a phalanx of other lascivious suggestions, all in Gaelic.

Making love to Breana was never the same twice, but it was always so amazing, he could never get enough of her. They'd become endlessly inventive, and while he had favorites, everything they did together heated his blood to a fever pitch. She grew hotter and tighter as he took her, or maybe he got harder. Sensation intensified until their bodies were everything, the only thing.

He gave a little push with magic, and her muscles clenched around him as orgasm took her. Repositioning a hand, he tickled her anal opening to push her into a string of climaxes. Somewhere after her third release, he couldn't hold back any longer, and semen juddered from him. His passion pushed her over the edge once more. They clung to one another in water that was growing cold since he'd been too caught up in lovemaking to feed magic into warming it.

"Ready to get out?" he asked.

"Um-hum." She kissed him lazily. "Have I told you how much I love you?"

"Not since our midday break." He kissed her back and carried her to the bank where he lifted her off his still-hard cock. Bending, he rinsed himself and directed a stream of magic to dry his body before getting back into his dusty clothes.

Her body was beautifully flushed from their lovemaking.

"It's such a shame to cover all that up," he said.

"It'd be a bigger shame to walk through poison oak getting back to the others," she retorted. "I've seen both it and poison ivy around here."

"Touché." He picked up the soap root. "Do you know a way of preserving this?"

She shook her head. "Too bad. It comes in handy." She fell into step next to him as they made their way back to Hester, Chris, and the horses. "When do you expect we'll meet up with the wagons?"

"Could be as soon as tomorrow. They've made good time."

"Not that I won't be happy to see everybody—or I will be once they reassure me they don't want to try me for my sins— but I've really enjoyed this time that's just been you and me."

He draped an arm around her shoulders and pulled her close. "Maybe we'll have to take a long trip—just the two of us. I've seen a whole lot of this country the past few years. Beautiful places I'd love to share with you."

She stopped and turned to look at him. "Do you suppose we'll ever have that kind of freedom? Where we won't have to be available in case evil comes calling?"

"I hope so. Come on. I smell wood smoke. They started supper and we should help."

"There ye are," Hester cried as they walked into the clearing. She straightened from where she'd been hunkered next to a cook fire. "Hey, Chris! I won this time."

"Aw, Jesus. Are you still placing bets?" Joshua rolled his eyes.

Chris strolled over from where he'd been settling the horses. "Put it on my tab, Hester."

"You need to fall in love," Joshua told him. "You'd be more tolerant."

"I've been in lust plenty," Chris retorted.

"No more sex talk. I need greens to go with these rabbits." Hester made shooing motions with both hands.

"Slave driver," Chris groused and motioned to Joshua. "Come on. I saw bunches of wild onions down on the riverbank."

Joshua followed him. Once they got some distance from the women, he said, "It doesn't take two men to gather a few bunches of onions. What'd you want to talk about?"

"Am I that transparent?"

"Maybe only to me, but then I know you. Spill it."

Chris turned to face him. "Nothing bad. Not really. Just a feeling. I even used my stone to search for Black Magick and came up dry. We'll meet up with the wagons tomorrow morning, though."

"Did you talk with Luke?"

"Yeah. Just a little bit ago." Chris blew out a breath. "I suspect we'll be in the thick of things once we join them, but I could be wrong. Maybe we should split up the train, divert the women—"

"They're better off with us watching over them. You're not thinking."

"Nah. Problem is I think too much. Let's get those onions so we can have dinner."

"In a minute. First, you get the Dutch uncle talk," Joshua said, as understanding dawned, and he recognized Chris' mindset because he'd lived it himself. "Agents of the dark will always be there. If there's a final battle to be fought, we're years away from it. In the meantime, we keep on slugging, fighting battles as they present themselves. It's the life we signed on for. You're young, more or less. All of us go through a phase when that reality sinks in—and it's one tough nut to wrap your mind around."

"Don't be absurd. What reality?" Chris turned away, discomfort stamped in the tight line of his shoulders.

"The one where you come face-to-face with the fact that that this is a dirty war with no finish line in sight, only endless skirmishes where we do our damnedest to come out on top."

"Can I go now, Dad?"

"Sure. I'll get those onions. Let what I said percolate for a bit. There's no shame in what you're feeling."

"I'm not feeling anything." Chris bit off the words. "I'm a Coven enforcer."

"Does that mean you can't ever be scared or lost or hurt or worried?"

Chris narrowed his eyes. "Yeah. That's exactly what it means."

Joshua closed the distance between them. "No. It's not. We're human too. Well, sort of. Being an enforcer means you're sworn to uphold a certain creed. It doesn't make you immune from wanting to chuck it all and live out your days somewhere evil can't ever touch you, or those you care about, again."

Chris' shoulders sagged. "Jesus. Have you ever got my number. How? I don't get it." He moved past Joshua and bent to pluck clusters of wild onions from the marshy area next to the water.

Joshua went to help him, and the sharp fragrance made his eyes water. "Only reason I know is because I've felt the same goddamned way—and more than once. Eat a good supper. I'll take first watch."

Chis met his gaze, an unspoken question dancing behind his eyes.

"Don't worry. I know how to hold confidences," Joshua reassured him. "I won't say anything about this—to anyone. Besides, things will look better come morning. They always do."

Chris grabbed Joshua's onions and stalked past him, heading for camp. After rinsing his hands in the creek, Joshua followed him, but not too fast. Establishing détente with the part of himself that wasn't all tough and infused with bravado hadn't been easy. He still struggled with it from time to time.

Enforcers who only embraced the soldier-of-fortune motif—and stifled their softer side—grew into hard, embittered men. He'd seen it happen time and time again. They were excellent warriors, but not good for anything else.

Breana made her way to him when he returned to camp. "Everything all right?" she asked.

"Yes, love. Everything's fine. How could it be anything else now that we're together?"

She twined an arm around his waist. "Hokey words, but sweet. Keep 'em coming."

"I fully intend to. Anything I can do to help with supper or anything else?"

"Dinner's in about ten minutes," Hester called.

"We'll be ready," Breana assured her. "That's not enough time to drag him off into the forest."

"Want to bet?" He shot her a look pregnant with challenge.

"You're on!" She dashed between two trees, laughing like a banshee, with him in hot pursuit.

# CHAPTER 20

Just before noon the next day, dust rose in thick clouds coating the horizon. Breana sucked in a tense breath and sent her magic spinning outward. Even though she'd expected the wagon train, she was still relieved when witch magic greeted her seeking spell.

"I'm going to run ahead. I want to see my Abigail," Hester shouted and urged her horse into a lope.

Breana followed at a more sedate pace. They'd meet the wagons soon enough, and it was possible the Coven's leaders would tell her to have a nice life and kick her out for not turning Don in to Coven justice. She wasn't totally certain why she cared, but she did.

"It'll go better than you think," Joshua said as he brought his horse abreast of hers.

She glanced sidelong at him. "Unless that moonstone doubles as a crystal ball, you'd have no way of knowing that."

"No magic involved." He smiled crookedly. "The Coven elders are fair. I wouldn't have worked for them all this time if they weren't."

Breana nodded. "My take too. They are fair, but I did wrong. I can't claim ignorance. Hell, I even learned demonspeak—and Black Magick. I don't have any good excuses for my actions beyond loving my daughter and hoping I could save her, given enough time."

He cut his horse in front of hers, forcing her to stop. "No matter what happens, I'll stand by you."

"But if they banish me, it'll mean none of the others can have anything to do with me. That would include you since you work for Coven government."

"I'll quit." He looped the reins around the saddle horn and dusted his hands together. "You and I will go on a long trip and decide where we want to live. It would actually be a relief to be free from the responsibility of always sleeping with one eye open."

"Evil is everywhere," she reminded him. "If we were on our own, we'd have to be twice as vigilant because we wouldn't have any backup."

"Doesn't matter. I'd still look forward to anything—so long as you rode next to me."

Despite her worries, joy washed through her like a warm tide. The man by her side had put her first, and he hadn't even stopped to mull it over. Enforcers ate, lived, and breathed their get-the-bad-guys-no-matter-what lifestyle. That he'd lay it aside for her meant the world. She searched for words to tell him his sacrifice touched her to her bones, but he shook his head.

"You're worth a hundred enforcer jobs. A million. A man like me can always get work. Finding a woman I want to grow old with was much harder. You're her, and we have a long, intriguing life to look forward to."

"I like the sound of that. Let's go meet the wagon train. I want to see Luke and Abigail, and the others too. Even if they don't feel the same about me anymore."

"Luke and Abigail haven't changed."

"I meant the others. Not them. Come on." She kneed her horse, wheeling it toward the wagon train's dust that had all but blotted out the sun. Now that the inevitable confrontation with Coven leadership was upon her, she wanted to get it over with. See which way the rest of her life would unfold. She may have skirted around revealing what Don turned into, but she'd never been a coward.

Breana set a purposeful course for the front of the wagon train, not sure quite who she'd find there, but certain it would be someone who had definite ideas about her future as part of the Coven. She caught up with a tall, broad-shouldered man cloaked in black, sitting razor straight astride a coal-black stallion. Because she came at him from behind, she had no idea who it was until she was even with him, and then her jaw dropped and she looked away.

"Sir." She kept her head down and her eyes averted. "Goddess's blessings on you. I had no idea you were part of the wagon train."

Their Founder turned the full force of his dark eyes on her and slowed his horse to a walk. "And if you'd known, Breana Giraud, what would you have done differently?"

"Nothing, sir. I was just surprised."

"I created this Coven. Why would I send them off across America without me?" He arched a bushy brow.

It was a reasonable question, and it made her feel stupid. "I wasn't thinking. Of course you wouldn't remain by yourself in New York." She tried out several other phrases, wanting to hurry his verdict regarding her along, but none sounded quite right.

"Not thinking, eh?" He kept right on staring at her. "Appears to be a bit of a theme for you here of late."

Breana squared her shoulders. "With all due respect, that's not exactly true."

"What is? I'm waiting." He let the hood of his cloak drop onto his shoulders, displaying a silvery head of hair braided tight against his skull.

"In truth, I did nothing but think once I knew what Don had done. Trouble is, my mind raced in endless circles, and I never did come up with a solution."

The Founder narrowed his eyes to slits. "Evil has no *solution*. Surely you would've realized that. You're scarcely a young witch, and you've had dealings with sorcerers for a very long time."

"I was trying to save my daughter. It's not much of a reason, and I failed on that front too, but it wasn't for lack of effort."

"Ah but Luke and the other enforcers did save Carolyn." He softened his tone. "A death in mage fire to purify her soul redeemed her through eternity. After what happened, it's as good an end as she was likely to come by."

"I am grateful for that." Breana closed her teeth over her lower lip until she tasted blood. "But I still miss her."

"I have one question for you." The Founder reined his horse to a stop and turned to face her. The rest of the wagon train moved past them.

Breana felt a truth spell drop over her and girded herself for his next words. She had a feeling they'd determine his final judgment, and she couldn't lie—or even hedge a little. She lifted her chin, waiting.

"If you were in the same situation again, what would you do?"

A rush of images clawed at her. Don binding her with Black Magick until she was half-dead and dragging her to hideous rituals. The unnatural gleam in Carolyn's blue eyes when Don read to her from Black Magick tomes. The way her own child spied on her, reporting her every move to Don. Truth rushed in from all sides, and she felt the quick, hot bite of tears, but the answer to the Founder's question flared brightly, impossible to evade.

"I'd turn both of them in to Coven justice. My loyalty to my daughter was misplaced because once Don seduced her with dark power, I no longer had a daughter. I only thought I did." Tears welled, but she didn't brush them away.

The Founder's magic probed deep. She felt it rake through her, but held herself open to his scrutiny. He didn't speak for long enough, she believed the worst. Maybe simply banishing her wouldn't be enough. Perhaps her life would be forfeit. Regardless, she'd abide by whatever he decreed. He was old beyond reckoning—and unerringly wise.

Her heart ached for Joshua, but she hoped he'd be sensible enough not to challenge the Founder's decision.

"You're quiet," the Founder observed.

"I have nothing else to say. What I did was wrong, and I see that now, but if I'd looked harder then, I'd have seen it too." She stared at her hands clutched around the reins and waited.

"You learned a hard lesson, Breana. I'm confident you wouldn't stand by while wickedness flourished a second time."

She swallowed hard and forced herself to meet his gaze. "D-does that mean you're not going to order my execution?"

"That's exactly what it means, my dear. It's not my way to kill off loyal Coven members. Or ones married to my enforcers." He actually smiled at her, and she fought to keep her mouth from gaping open. The Founder never smiled—at anyone.

"Thank you, sir. I promise you won't be sorry. I won't let you down again."

"We need every single witch and mage in our organization to

move our war against Black Magick forward. I'm impressed Andras is dead. That bastard's been a thorn in my side for centuries."

"I wasn't liking him much, either, and I didn't know him for nearly that long." She pursed her lips together, still not quite believing her reprieve.

Joshua trotted to where they stood. "Is this a good time to intrude?"

"Even if it weren't, you already have," the Founder commented dryly.

Joshua leaned close enough to thread an arm around Breana. "She's my wife. You have no idea what it cost me to hang back until it appeared the thorny part of your conversation was over."

He focused his next words at Breana. "See. I told you it would come out all right."

"Indeed you did," she replied. "But even you made backup plans—just in case."

The Founder cleared his throat and skewered Joshua with his dark eyes. "You'd have left right along with her."

It wasn't a question, and Joshua met his gaze head on. "I've loved her since the moment I first saw her, and she's finally mine. Of course I'd have left if you cast her out of the Coven. We all make mistakes. The question is whether we learn from them, not whether we're perfect to begin with. She's suffered enough."

The Founder smiled—again. "Then it appears I made the proper decision. No point chewing over dead bones. Let's get moving. We'll never get to Salt Lake standing still." He dropped into an archaic form of Gaelic and ordered his horse to catch up with the rest of the wagon train.

Joshua swung down from his horse and pulled her out of her saddle and into his arms. He closed his mouth over hers before her feet were even on the ground, kissing her until she was breathless.

"There." He tore his mouth away. "Now we can follow the others. We move faster than the wagons, so it won't take long to fall in with them."

Breana smiled softly. "For a while there, I thought he was going to order me doused in mage fire."

"I'd never have stood by and let that happen."

"Which is exactly what I was afraid of. That you'd get yourself into trouble defending me."

"It's all part of a day's work, sweetheart. I'll defend you to my dying day, and from beyond the veil too, if it comes to that." He cupped his hands and boosted her onto her horse. Vaulting atop his own mount, he kneed it into an easy lope.

Breana cast a fond smile his way, her body still alight from his touch. "During the time you were exercising admirable restraint and not storming the fortress while the Founder and I sorted things out, did you visit with anyone in the wagon train?"

"Yeah, I did. Chris and Hester joined up with Luke, Abigail, and Aethelred—a really powerful mage, who was Luke's teacher when he was young. They tied their horses behind the wagon and were figuring out who'd sit where for the journey. At the point I left, Hester, Abigail, and the mage were in the back, with Luke and Chris on the box directing the team." He hesitated before adding, "Almost forgot. There's this amazing raven too. Her name's Mollie."

"Maybe you should start at the beginning. Witches haven't used familiars in the last hundred years. And why do you think the mage is all that strong?"

"The bird belongs to Aethelred, and he's not a witch." Joshua inhaled sharply. "Wait till you meet him. Magic fairly bleeds from him. It's not conscious, but he's so formidable, the air around him actually shimmers."

"Like I said, start at the beginning, so I'll have it all sorted out when we camp for tonight."

"I don't really know all that much, but here's what little I managed to glean." Joshua gifted her with one of his special smiles—the ones that made her tingle all the way down to her toes—and began to talk.

THE DAY PASSED QUICKLY. Though Joshua hadn't given voice to it, he was almost as relieved as Breana by the Founder's decision. Not that he'd had serious doubts, but it was better this way. He and Breana could begin their life together without a cloud hanging over their heads.

The wagons formed a tight circle, and Joshua went to see if he could help the men who were securing the stock for the night.

Luke led two oxen to the line of animals. When he caught sight of Joshua, he trotted over and clapped him on the back. "I didn't get to this before, but congratulations, brother! Breana is one fine woman, and I wish you every happiness."

"Why, thank you. We'd have postponed the wedding until everyone was here, but neither of us wanted to wait."

Luke made a chopping motion with one hand. "Never mind that. I knew you were sweet on her. I've known it for a long time. I'm just gladder than hell you got past whatever was holding you back."

"You mean the small, niggling detail that she was married—to someone else?"

"Eh." Luke tossed both hands in a dismissive gesture. "That's why we're Coven enforcers. We live to tackle the tough problems. Come on. I've still got the rest of the team to bring over here, and I could use some help."

Joshua fell in next to Luke as they made their way back to the wagons. "Tell me about Aethelred."

Luke shrugged his shoulders. "Words won't do him justice. He was the strongest mage I ever knew, and the years have augmented that power. He can spell circles around me. I'm stronger now than ever, but my power still doesn't stack up to his. And Mollie—that's his raven—is in a class by herself. Almost makes me want to pair up with my own familiar—if I could find one."

"I heard that, son." Gruff words floated from the back of Luke and Abigail's wagon. "Idle flattery won't buy my goodwill."

"Only good deeds can do that," Luke chanted a refrain the two of them obviously had down pat because both men laughed heartily.

Hester walked around the wagon, dusting her hands off on her skirts. "Hey there, Aethelred." She poked her head in the back of the wagon. "Our supper will be done soon. Time to wash off some of the dust afore we eat."

"Time to wash. Time to wash." A large, black raven flew out of the wagon, circling it as she cawed.

"Goddesses' tits, I can't fight the both of you," Aethelred grumbled and jumped down from the wagon's interior. A tall, spare man swathed in robes, he focused his midnight dark eyes on Hester. Long, white hair fell to his waist.

"More like it." Hester looped a hand around his arm and tugged him toward a nearby creek. The raven flew after them, still squawking.

Breana and Abigail waltzed up. The women leaned toward one another, looking thick as a pack of thieves. "Did you see that?" Abigail asked in a very low whisper.

"Yup." Breana grinned broadly.

Joshua felt confused. "See what?" He draped an arm around Breana, enjoying the way she fit against him.

She nuzzled his ear. "Hester. And Aethelred."

He nuzzled her back. "What about them? They went to wash up."

"They've been talking about anything and everything—for hours," Abigail informed him archly. "Especially Hester's gear-driven magic concentrator. Apparently, Aethelred's had a power stone for years. I vote with Breana. And it makes my heart glad. I've gotten to know Aethelred, and he's been alone for far too long." She lowered her voice still further. "His power scared the bejesus out of his wife, so she left him fifty something years ago."

"Witches! You're nothing if not a bunch of gossips." Luke rolled his eyes.

"Gossips and matchmakers, one and all," Joshua agreed.

"It's why you love us," Breana said and hugged him tight. "Dinner's almost ready, so do whatever you need to before we eat."

Abigail elbowed Luke. "Same message from me."

Joshua glanced around. "The other two oxen need to go to where we've corralled the stock. Anything else?"

"My horse, but then we'll be done," Luke replied.

Breana let go of him and swatted him on the butt. "Sooner you get cracking, the sooner we can eat. And the sooner supper's over, the sooner—"

"Randy wench." He silenced her with a kiss before breaking free and heading after Luke with a horse in tow.

"Another witch trait," she called after him, and she and Abigail broke into gales of laughter.

Happiness crashed over him, blotting out everything else. The emotion was so foreign, he understood he'd given up on anything beyond existing after his family joined forces with dark sorcery. He led the horse to a lush patch of grass where it could graze and hobbled it. Whistling a jaunty Gaelic folksong, he turned back the way he'd come and hurried toward Breana.

His love.

His life.

His everything.


This is the end of *Blood and Sorcery*. Please leave a review. Doesn't have to be fancy. A couple of lines would be great. The next book in the Coven Enforcer series, *Blood and Illusion*, features Sam, who deserves his own shot at love. Keep reading for a sample.

# ABOUT THE AUTHOR

Ann Gimpel is a USA Today bestselling author. A lifelong aficionado of the unusual, she began writing speculative fiction a few years ago. Since then her short fiction has appeared in a number of webzines and anthologies. Her longer books run the gamut from urban fantasy to paranormal romance. Once upon a time, she nurtured clients, now she nurtures dark, gritty fantasy stories that push hard against reality. When she's not writing, she's in the backcountry getting down and dirty with her camera. She's published over 70 books to date, with several more planned for 2019 and beyond. A husband, grown children, grandchildren and wolf hybrids round out her family.

Keep up with her at www.anngimpel.com or http://anngimpel.blogspot.com

If you enjoyed what you read, get in line for special offers and pre-release special reads. Sign up for Ann's newsletter on her website or her blog.

BLOOD AND ILLUSION, CHAPTER ONE

Sam Jennings made his way to San Francisco's docks through muddy streets teeming with people, horses, and every variety of wagon and carriage imaginable. The odors of food and sewage mingled in an unpleasant brew, with the food smells predominant near saloons, hotels, and restaurants, and the raw, acrid stench of human waste nearly overpowering from every alleyway. Smoke billowing from wood and coal fires thickened the air, making it difficult to see very far ahead in some places.

Despite all that, a sense of excitement permeated everything. San Francisco was a young city, boisterous and bustling. Everybody seemed to be in a rush, and Sam pulled magic about himself hoping it would speed his journey. His horse, unused to crowds and traffic, shied whenever anyone or anything got too close, so he wound his power around the animal as well to create a buffer zone.

Tom and Cory, two other Coven enforcers just like him, were also headed for the docks. They'd split up on the outskirts of town so they wouldn't draw undue attention to themselves. They had a job to do, and being waylaid by the local sheriff, who was sure to recognize them as trained killers, wouldn't help matters. Humans maintained a healthy distrust of nearly anything that smacked of magic. While the Coven had established a fragile détente with law enforcement back east, Sam suspected tolerance for his kind hadn't made it too far west of the Mississippi.

"And now's not the time to test it," he muttered to the accompaniment of nickering from his horse, who seemed to agree.

Sam glanced around. He'd been to the city when it was still called Yerba Buena, but it had grown by leaps and bounds since those days with many new streets. Still, if he followed the scent of water, he was bound to find the bay. A group of threatened witches had gone to ground beneath one of the many warehouses lining the docks. As a Coven enforcer, part of his sworn duty was to protect witches. This group weren't officially affiliated with the Coven, but they were close friends with Hester Thorne, a witch who'd been one of the original founding members of the Coven hundreds of years ago.

Hester had intercepted the witches' distress call back in Salt Lake, and Sam and the others hastened to offer aid. They'd been on the road for many days, riding hard, only resting when their horses went into full rebellion.

Every enforcer had a telepathic connection to every other enforcer, and Sam had reached out to others in their brotherhood who were close enough to San Francisco to help the witches. Fifteen men were presumably on their way. He kicked himself for not checking in with them on the edge of town. To do so now wasn't wise. Sending power spiraling outward would surely alert any dark sorcerers in the area, and he wanted to maintain the element of surprise as long as he could.

He, Tom, and Cory had agreed to avoid mind speech until they met on the docks for just that reason—unless one of them ran into unexpected problems. The other enforcers could find them through the link they all shared. Because each of them went through the same training regimen, even enforcers who'd never met before meshed well in battle situations. The only problem was they wouldn't have an opportunity to craft a coordinated attack plan. It wasn't ideal, but it couldn't be helped.

His bay stallion crested a hill, its hooves clanking loudly on cobblestone streets that took a definite downward slant on the far side. He swept the horizon, taking in waves crashing on the shore. The brisk salt tang of the sea, mixed with rotting fish, stung his nose.

Almost there.

He tightened the shrouding around himself and hunted for the particular taint all Black Magick held. Better to rid the area of dark sorcerers before they drew the witches out of hiding. The women would be weak from their enforced seclusion. They could sink into a kind of stasis where their needs for food and water diminished greatly. Not surprisingly, that particular casting carried a hefty price. Witches had good recuperative skills, but it would take at least a day or two for them to bring their power back to a full charge. They'd need him and the other enforcers to protect them until they were up to snuff again.

His horse shied violently, snapping his head upward and yanking him out of his thoughts. At first he didn't see anything, but then a pervasive chill moved in from all sides, surrounding him. An opaque, gray cloud rose from nowhere, cutting him off from the surrounding city.

*Shit!*

What would come at him out of the mist? Wraiths? Mad wolves? Other turned animals? Dark sorcerers?

While he still could, he raised his mind voice and called for Tom and Cory.

Amid whinnies and shrill neighs, the stallion crab-walked, stumbling on the uneven surface. Sam slid from his back, hands raised as he summoned power, focusing it with the opal that was his power stone. Multihued fire streamed through the gem, slicing through the gray and illuminating two men wearing badly tanned leathers. Both stank of Black Magick and its peculiar combination of sulfur, ozone, and brimstone.

"You killed our leader," one growled in thickly accented English.

"Your turn to die," the other grunted in the same guttural dialect.

Were these some of the crew from the Far East who'd cut a swath through San Francisco's witch population?

Sam narrowed his eyes. It didn't matter a good goddamn who they were. Or where they'd come from. He was sworn to eradicate evil, and these two qualified. Kill first, ask questions later had always been his creed.

Before he killed them, though, maybe he could glean information. "I'm sure I have no idea what you mean," he said smoothly as he balanced power, ready to loose it at a moment's notice. "Who was your leader?" He grinned viciously. "If I'm getting credit, I like to know what it's for."

Instead of answering, black-tinged fire flew from the taller man's hands. It bounced off Sam's warding. With a furious cry, the dark sorcerer rushed him in tandem with his companion.

Annoyance bubbled from Sam's guts, thick and viscous. Fine. Too much trouble to interrogate these bastards, and it wasn't as if he'd ever planned to let them live. Grim determination straightened his spine, and he focused his power. Two fewer sorcerers was always a desirable outcome. Drawing the opal's nascent ability into himself, he let mage fire fly from his fingers.

Pure, white light surrounded the sorcerers' fire, snuffing it out. Before shock stamped itself too deeply into the men's stark features, Sam sent power auguring into their chests, stopping their hearts. They dropped to the street like stones, and the gray bubble enclosing all of them shattered to nothingness. Sam dusted his hands together. That had been almost too easy. He whistled for his horse about the same time Cory galloped up from one direction and Tom from the other.

Both men leapt from their horses, adding mage fire to the two smoking pyres. "What the fuck?" Cory turned his dark-eyed gaze on Sam and raked a hand through his close shorn black hair. Skin tight leathers encased his tall, hard-muscled form.

"Who knows?" Sam shrugged. "They must've sensed my magic. They did say they were out for blood because I'd murdered their leader."

"Which leader?" Tom asked tight-lipped. Wrath burned hotly behind his blue eyes, and thick brown hair fell to his broad shoulders in an unruly mass. Like the others, he wore buckskin leathers, but his shaded to almost black, probably from the time he'd spent in front of a forge crafting shoes for horses.

"I tried to get information, but they weren't very forthcoming," Sam replied. "The leader they were grousing about pretty much has to be either Alistair MacDuff or Andras, the Dark Angel. Did either of you sense anything?"

Cory shook his head. "No. Thought it odd too since I was only about a block from the wharf when I heard your distress call."

"And I was on the docks," Tom said and wrinkled his nose. "They should clean up the fish guts, not just let them rot."

"Yeah, well town didn't smell too swift, either," Sam countered.

"It's because we're used to living on the road," Cory said.

"Sooner we finish up and get back there, the better I'll like it," Tom replied. "City living never was for me."

"Someone apparently knows we're here," Sam said. "I'm going to see if I can't locate the rest of us. Maybe we can attack as a unit and be done with things so Tom gets his wish."

He raised his mind voice and was rewarded with replies from other enforcers. After a hurried cacophony of *where are yous*, he instructed them to meet up on the docks as soon as they could get there.

"Well?" Cory quirked a brow. "I'd have listened in, but I didn't want to paint a sign that screams we're here."

"Six of us are close enough to arrive soon," Sam replied. "The rest will come when they can, but I suspect it'll be all over but the crying by then." He nudged the burning bodies with a booted foot and sent more mage fire to finish them off. Sparks exploded with a loud, hissing *whoop*. The bodies cracked open, but nothing spilled out. No organs. No entrails.

"What the hell?" Sam stared at the corpses who were looking like they'd never been alive to begin with. He squeezed his eyes shut and opened them wondering if they were playing tricks on him. Surely the sorcerers had been more than empty husks.

"Jesus!" Tom stared at the pyres.

"No point worrying about it now," Cory muttered. "Besides, it's probably nothing. Let's get our asses moving. Whatever those two were, they won't bother us—or anyone else—again."

Sam vaulted atop his horse. The others followed suit, and all of them made their way down the steep street to docks that lined San Francisco's waterfront. Cobblestones gave way to wooden planking at the bottom of the hill. Ships of all sizes were either tied up to quays or moored out in the bay. Men hurried this way and that, shouldering loads as they went. Tom had been right about the fish stench. It grew worse as they got close to the boats. It was late afternoon, and ships were returning with the day's catch, dumping their bounty on the beach and the docks.

Sam reined in his horse and dismounted, scanning for further signs of dark enchantment. Flipping the reins over the animal's head, he secured it to a hitching post. Cory and Tom did likewise. The horses stamped and laid their ears flat, not liking the noise, stench, or crowds any better than their owners did.

"I don't get it," Sam glanced from Tom to Cory. "I just looked for more evidence of Black Magick and came up dry. Surely those two I made short work of weren't the only ones."

"I don't sense dark corruption." Cory spoke slowly. "But it'd be easy enough to hide damn near anything behind all the activity down here."

"Do you think we should smoke out the witches?" Tom asked. "Sooner we rescue them, the sooner we can be gone from here."

"Not yet. It's what our enemy is expecting us to do," Sam replied. "Assuming they're here, it's why they're shrouding themselves. If it was only two dark sorcerers, the witches could've handled them."

Cory frowned. "So the absence of evil is a trap? Something to lure us into complacency?"

"That's my thought," Sam replied.

"Well, that's a bitch. They can wait us out," Tom chimed in.

"Let's settle in and postpone doing anything until the rest of us show up," Sam suggested. "We're daunting when there's an army of us, and it might make whoever's here think twice."

"Ha!" Cory chortled. "While they're *thinking twice*, maybe they'll make a mistake and we can figure out where the hell they are."

Sam gazed up and down the uneven planked street lining the waterfront. At least five hundred men were engaged in some aspect of boat maintenance or fishing. Any kind of pitched battle here would kill some of them. Collateral damage was inevitable when warfare occurred in crowded places. Far better to move the party on down the beach, well past where docks jutted into the bay.

"I agree," Cory said.

Sam glanced askance at him. "You might've waited for me to say something, rather than mining through my thoughts."

"Why? Faster this way."

"Agree with what?" Tom snapped, sounding out of sorts. "I didn't tap into your mind, so I missed whatever it was."

"Come on." Sam gestured. "Let's put some distance between us and all these people. It'd be a shame to kill some of them by mistake."

"Black Magick is more likely to do that than us," Tom countered, "but I'm on board with it. Besides, there's a dude in a shack down that away selling fishcakes."

Sam laughed. "You don't like how it smells, but you'll eat it."

"Damn straight, brother!" Tom laughed too.

The unmistakable feel of enforcer power pummeled him as four men rode up and jumped from their horses. "Where's the fight?" Kane asked, scratching his bearded chin. Dark red hair was braided tight against his head, and his green eyes missed very little.

"Yeah, we found the pyres up yonder." Another man jerked his chin uphill. Blond hair was chopped off unevenly, and his gray eyes twinkled with mischief. "Don't tell me we missed all the fun." He stuck out a hand. "I'm Roland. Haven't met you before, Sam, but I've heard a lot about you."

"Where are the others who were supposed to be with you?"

Sam asked, sidestepping the comment about fun as he shook Roland's hand.

Pounding hooves almost drowned out his words as two more enforcers threaded through the crowded wharf, heading their way.

"Six more plus us makes nine." Cory clamped his jaws in a tight line. "Ought to be enough to give almost anyone pause."

"Yes, but where are those anyones?" Kane persisted. "None of us felt a thing."

"Now that we're all here, let's move on down the beach," Sam suggested. "Away from all these humans. We can talk more then."

"Have you sensed any more Black Magicians?" Roland pressed.

"No, but that doesn't mean they're not here," Sam replied. The other enforcers tied their horses to the hitching post, and Sam herded all of them down the beach, his senses tuned to the slightest disturbance. Nothing met his antennae but an eerie vacuum, almost as if someone had sucked everything magical out of the world. His stomach tightened, and the small hairs on the back of his neck twitched in protest.

Tom ran to catch up to them with grease-stained paper sacks that he handed around. "Something in the air doesn't feel right," he muttered around a mouthful of fried fish.

"My point exactly, brother." Sam extracted a piece of fish coated in cornmeal. "Until we know more, we wait."

Isla huddled with six other witches in a sub-basement beneath one of the warehouses lining San Francisco's docks. Her hair hung in filthy strands. Grime caked beneath her nails, and she stank, but at least she was alive. Russian sorcerers—or at least sorcerers who spoke Russian—had killed four of her sisters before she'd dragged the rest of their small band to a defensible position and swathed them in layers and layers of magic.

It had been a short term solution, but they hadn't had any choice. Not really. Only problem was they had no easy way out. If they dismantled their spell, the sorcerers would find them in a trice. If they remained where they were, eventually they'd starve to death. She was far weaker than she'd been a week ago when they'd barricaded themselves into the underground room with its dirt floor and dirt walls. Small cutouts high on two walls coincided with ground level, and provided their only source of light.

In desperation, she'd used her power stone to call Hester Thorne, a witch who'd been instrumental drawing their group into a cohesive unit. Hester promised help, but it had yet to materialize. Breath steamed through Isla's teeth as she bent forward and stirred the shallow pool she'd created from a broken pot made of crockery and water dripping down the walls. It took a while, but the water had finally grown deep enough to become a scrying instrument.

Weariness dogged her, and her vision blurred. She squeezed her eyes shut, willing them to focus next time she dragged her lids open. Thinking it might help, she pushed herself upright and walked around the six- by ten-foot room.

"What are you doing?" Kat eyed her balefully out of bloodshot blue eyes. "I was asleep." Dirty blonde hair had been braided to keep it out of the way.

"Aye, and ye'll be asleep permanently if ye're not careful," Isla shot back, the brogue from her native Scotland thicker than usual. It was one of the reasons she and Hester had bonded so tightly. Shared roots from the Isle of Skye.

"Isla! Come look at your pool!" Rowan cried. Gray hair fell

about her, dragging in the dirt, but her brown eyes were lit with hope.

Isla skidded to her knees and stared at the water's surface. Nine men strutted down the rock-strewn sand fronting the ocean. Tall, rangy, hard-bodied and clad in leathers, it was obvious they were used to ruling the world. At first she thought they were a new passel of sorcerers, but she forced herself to look closer.

Not trusting her first take, she took a ragged breath. Maybe she wished for salvation from the room that was likely to become their crypt so desperately, she was imagining things, "What does it look like to you?" she asked Rowan.

The other woman turned to face her. "Help. That's what it looks like. Those men are bleeding power, and it's the good kind."

The other women skittered across the floor, jostling one another to get close to the pool so they could see.

"Be careful!" Isla cautioned. "Else ye'll tip the dish and we might not live long enough for me to refill it."

Her heart hammered against her ribs as she took in the men. One of them in particular caught her attention and held it. Long, blond hair spilled across his shoulders, and his eyes were a bright, turquoise blue. Strong bones carved his cheekbones into bas relief, and his jaw was square, determined. Buff colored leathers covered him, and they were skin tight, leaving virtually nothing to her imagination. Broad shoulders led to deeply muscled arms and narrow hips with a high, tight ass. Long legs disappeared into boots that laced to his knees.

Her throat grew dry. Many a year had passed since she'd experienced such an immediate reaction to a man, and it confused her.

*Must be because I'm half-staved.*

*Och aye, and ye know better,* the other half of her brain inserted dryly. Whoever he was, he was one gorgeous man.

Understanding slammed into her, and she was ashamed she hadn't put two and two together immediately. "They must be the help Hester promised us." She glanced at the other women.

Rowan lurched upright. "If that's true, then we need to go outside and help them."

Isla licked her chapped lips. "They're not looking as if they need any help, but at least that way they won't have to hunt for us, and mayhap we can leave this accursed place."

"You're the one with the strongest magic," Kat pointed out. "And the only one who can project telepathy beyond the enchantment hiding us. See if they answer."

Isla exhaled sharply. It was a reasonable suggestion, but not without risk. If she was wrong, and those men were actually allied with the dark, she'd have given away their position. Opened them to a certain death. Or worse, imprisonment at the hands of evil.

"I was in your mind," Rowan said, her voice surprisingly gentle. "We're as good as dead now. I say we chance it."

"I was coming around to the same conclusion." Isla breathed deeply to center herself and drew out her pink moonstone. Before she could think things to death, and her courage failed utterly, she linked to the stone and sent her magic thrumming outward. No need to make things fancy, so she settled on the shortest phrase imaginable.

*"Are ye who Hester sent?"*

Depending on the answer, she'd ask for proof and take things from there.

www.ingramcontent.com/pod-product-compliance
Lightning Source LLC
Chambersburg PA
CBHW071243190726

48292CB00007B/2387